THE CARVER AFFAIR

PAM LECKY

Storm
PUBLISHING

Ebook ISBN: 978-1-83700-181-1
Paperback ISBN: 978-1-83700-182-8

Cover design: Ghost
Cover images: Adobe Stock, Adobe Firefly, Shutterstock

Published by Storm Publishing.
For further information, visit:
www.stormpublishing.co

ALSO BY PAM LECKY

The Lucy Lawrence Mysteries

No Stone Unturned

Footprints in the Sand

The Art of Deception

A Pocketful of Diamonds

The Wild Atlantic Murders

The Clew Bay Detectives

To Sinead, Dave & Hannah

PROLOGUE

A Dublin Brothel, Thursday, 19th July 1894

Peggy O'Reilly climbed the last flight of stairs as slowly as she dared, then shut the door of her boudoir. At least that was what that hideous woman, Mrs Burton, told her she was to call it when clients were present. It was more like a prison cell to Peggy's young mind.

She slumped against the door and closed her eyes. Peggy wished she were dead. She might as well be. The shame of what she had become. Not willingly, but still. It made her face burn. The family would never forgive her. She could never go home again. And the thought of that tiny two-room cottage down in Wexford, and its occupants so dear to her heart, almost undid her.

The young girl shivered even though the room was warm. Not that the flimsy night attire she was forced to wear held any heat. No, it was fear that made her quake. For two weeks now, she had been subjected to the most disgusting violations at the hands of the flash-house clients. Yes, violation was the only word for it. And now her soul was as black as night. No priest would give her absolution. Hell was the only place she was bound when that happy release finally came.

Like an automaton, she took a seat at the dressing table, picked up the brush and with slow, deliberate movements dragged it through her hair. The face staring back in the mirror was ghost-like and rigid with panic. She eyed the clock, her stomach twisting. A few more minutes alone before the next one...

She drew a breath and prayed, *dear God, release me from this.* But she could go no further with her plea to the Almighty. The brush slipped from her hand and hit the dressing table with a thump. She clasped her hands together to stop them from shaking. Was escape possible? But even if she managed it, where would she go? She was a stranger in Dublin. As much so as her sister, Bridget. *Oh no, poor wee Bridget.* Where had that awful man taken her? Peggy had cried and screamed and pleaded as they had separated them, but that brute on the door, Mulcahy, had just dragged her upstairs and into this room. Then he had locked the door. They had left her alone for two whole days. Breaking her spirit.

Peggy snapped to attention upon hearing voices out in the hallway. Her stomach lurched, and her fists clenched. But she was powerless. No escape.

The door opened. Peggy's heart rate soared. She couldn't bear to look.

'Claudine, is that any way to greet a friend?' Mrs Burton spoke from the doorway, her voice scoldingly playful, but Peggy heard the steel beneath. The light-hearted tone did not fool her. She'd seen with her own eyes what the punishment was for disobedience. Peggy rose and faced her. Taking a deep breath, she lifted her eyes to look at the man who had pushed past the madam and she almost wept. It was the person who had taken her sister away. Was he here for her now?

Even from across the room, she could smell his vile odour. Sweat, whiskey and tobacco. He was a hulk of a man, with a shock of white hair, and he leaned on a walking stick. Peggy reckoned he was old enough to be her grandfather.

'A shy one, eh, Celine?' he joked, winking at Peggy. 'Don't you worry. We'll soon be acquainted.'

'I'm sure youse will get along just fine,' Mrs Burton said, staring hard at Peggy. Then she addressed the man, placing a hand on his arm. 'Come see me after.'

'Will do,' he said, his mouth twisting in what Peggy considered a demonic manner, which petrified her.

The madam left. Peggy remained frozen in fear as the man's eyes sized her up. Her mind was blank. In desperation, she tried to summon a prayer, but her brain would not obey.

He stepped closer. She backed up against the dressing table.

He laughed, but his eyes were flint-like and cold.

A primaeval instinct to survive gave her a sudden rush of courage. With desperate fingers, Peggy sought a weapon. Anything to stop him. Her fingers curled around the brush handle.

'Well, now, my pretty one. Won't you come closer?' he asked. 'I'm not in the mood for games.'

They were inches apart now. She could smell his foul breath and see his pock-marked cheeks.

What did she have to lose?

With a burst of strength, Peggy swung her arm from behind her back. The head of the brush glanced off the man's ear. To no immediate effect. Horrified, Peggy gasped as he lunged and grasped her wrist. The brush fell to the floor. Useless.

'Why, you little bitch,' he snarled, pulling her towards the bed. As she resisted, the sleeve of her wrap ripped.

Peggy twisted and fought to release herself. She wanted to scream, but her throat was tight, closed off in sheer terror.

'Stop wriggling,' he shouted, tearing at the strap of her negligee. Then she felt a blow to the back of her head before he pushed her down on the bed. Lying helpless, all Peggy could do was stare up at him, realising too late she had unleashed a monster. His face was blood-red, his eyes now slits of pure venom. 'No one refuses me,' he growled as he brought the head of his cane crashing down on her temple. 'No one.'

A searing pain shot through her head, and her eyes lost focus as she slid off the bed down onto the floor. Her last conscious thought was of her sister.

ONE

Lucy Stone gazed at the opulent surroundings of the Gaiety Theatre as she and Phineas took their seats. It was a pleasant surprise to see that the Dublin theatre was as fine as any she had ever visited in London. It was altogether charming, with a profusion of red velvet and damask, green velvet-covered seating, and golden accents on the columns and decorative panels above the stage. Their host was quick to point out that the enormous chandelier, which hung from the recessed ceiling, was the finest Waterford crystal.

It was Lucy's first visit to Dublin and such an auspicious beginning, for someone had just informed her that the magnificent couple in the royal box opposite was none other than the viceroy—the lord lieutenant—who represented her majesty in Ireland, and his good lady wife. After the lights dimmed, Lucy examined the couple through her opera glasses and concluded they were a very self-satisfied pair. The vicereine was resplendent in a purple dress with silver beading, a large ostrich feather dressing her coiffure, whilst her husband appeared to be in full court dress. It was a little ostentatious for a night out at the theatre. Would they even acknowledge a lowly private investigator and his wife if someone introduced them? she wondered. It was possible they would be, as they were here as guests of one of the viceroy's many acolytes, Sir Valentine DeWinter.

On their way to the theatre in their hired cab, Phin had explained that Sir Valentine was the Ulster King of Arms, based in Dublin Castle, the seat of British power in Ireland. DeWinter's office granted coats of arms, maintained family trees and arbitrated on the rights of inheritance. Most importantly, DeWinter was the keeper of the Irish Crown Jewels. A fact that struck Lucy with some force.

Phineas had only met Sir Valentine for the first time that morning at Dublin Castle. Despite some very unsubtle probing by Lucy, Phin would not divulge the nature of his secret mission— their reason for this visit to Dublin. Much peeved, Lucy had resorted to silence during the rest of their journey through the streets of Dublin. However, Phin, as ever, was impervious to this stratagem.

But upon arrival on South King Street, Lucy forgot her grievance. Even if Phin hadn't told her a little about their host, that the man and his wife were important figures in Irish high society was plain to see. Heads had turned and conversations had stilled when the couple had arrived. On spotting Phin, DeWinter had come forward and made a fuss of greeting him, much to Lucy's amusement. Formalities dealt with, Lucy and Phin followed the couple up the steps, the crowd parting as they went. Lucy and Phin were treated to curious glances, and Lucy spotted more than one woman, their eyes on Phin's tall figure, making a remark to a companion. No doubt the onlookers wondered who they were and why they were receiving such preferential treatment.

Later, as they settled down for the next act of the play, *Diplomacy*, Lucy reflected on the whirlwind that had been the last few weeks. Out of the blue, Phin had been summoned to Downing Street. However, his refusal to repeat his conversation with the

Prime Minister, the Earl of Rosebery, was a fatal error of judgement on his part. Lucy brooded for days. Phin's secrecy both intrigued and frustrated her, and the more he fobbed her off, citing confidentiality, the more determined she was to find out the reason for this urgent trip to Dublin. So, one evening at dinner, she suggested the entire family should accompany him to Dublin as it would be a very pleasant way to spend the summer. Phineas was suspicious but eventually agreed. That had been a week ago. It hadn't been easy to uproot the entire family in such a short period, but Lucy was thoroughly enjoying herself and the children considered it to be a grand adventure.

Life for Lucy since the birth of her twins, Harold and Eleanor, had been full of novelty and she was enjoying motherhood to the fullest. But when Phin would tell her about a fascinating case, the old tingle of excitement returned. She missed being involved. Lucy had been delighted when Phin made his brother Sebastian a partner in the business, but a small part of her feared she would be pushed out. Now the twins were older and more independent, she longed to dip her toe into the Stone Agency's cases again. Phin's initial reaction when she had broached the subject had been encouraging, and for the last few months, he had discussed his caseload with her.

Except, of course, the current one. And that rankled. For some reason, it was the only one that interested her.

After a tedious crossing of the Irish Sea, during which Mary, her maid, and Jenny, the nursery maid, had been violently ill, they had settled at last into a rented house on Dublin's most prestigious of locales, Merrion Square. The twins, now five, were in their element and had enjoyed the upheaval and exploring their new world. Their sense of adventure was fast becoming a source of amusement. Both children were high-spirited, something their mother applauded, but Phin worried about them all the time. Lucy suspected he was concerned they took after her more than him.

As the curtain rose and the lights went down, Lucy stole a glance at Phin, thinking how attractive he looked in his evening clothes. His expression, however, told her something was off. His focus was on DeWinter, not the stage. Perhaps their initial meeting that morning hadn't gone very well. She would love to probe, but it was neither the time nor the place to do so. Lucy had to hold her tongue, something that never came easy. She'd have to bide her time until they were alone at home later.

And soon, Lucy's thoughts drifted. The play, with a ridiculous espionage plot, was nothing compared to whatever Phin had undertaken. She had no doubt about it. But what might his mission be? Why Dublin? Once the second city of the empire, since the Act of Union, Dublin's decline had been rapid. She concluded the case had something to do with Dublin Castle, the seat of Victoria's power. As the queen's image came to her, she suddenly realised what must be going on. Phin specialised in insurance fraud, often relating to the theft of valuables...

'The Irish Crown Jewels. Good heavens, Phin. Is that why we're here?' Lucy exclaimed, albeit in a whisper.

Phin reached out and grasped her hand, nodding his head towards their hosts seated in front of them in the box, before brushing his lips against her ear. 'Not here, my dear. I'll explain when we get home.' His proximity made her shiver, but with delight. Even after six years of marriage, he still had that effect on her.

'Are you cold?' he asked with a wicked gleam in his eye.

Her answer was a smile, which promised a scold when they were once more alone. In front of her, Sir Valentine DeWinter shared a glance with his wife. They must have overheard her outburst. As their guests, she and Phin ought to behave with more decorum. Well, *she* ought to behave, but she had taken an instant dislike to Caroline DeWinter and was sure it was mutual. During the interval, the woman had spoken about her acquaintances, dropping titles like confetti, as if she wished to impress Lucy. However, as most of the illustrious personages Lady DeWinter mentioned were unknown to her, Lucy remained unimpressed. Unfortunately, her boredom must have been obvious. After that, the conversation had become a little stilted.

Lucy tried to concentrate once more on the performance on the stage below, but it wasn't easy while her pulse was pounding and her mind was conjuring up all kinds of fascinating scenarios. She knew nothing about the Irish Crown Jewels, and she would have to remedy that immediately. That old familiar tingle coursed down her spine, as welcome as the first day of spring. Perhaps the weeks to come would prove far more exciting than she had first envisaged. And the first step would be to drag the truth from her unusually reticent husband.

Later that evening, Merrion Square, Dublin

'Good evening, sir, ma'am, I hope you had a pleasant time?' George, Phin's valet and their butler, asked as he stood back to admit them to No. 81 Merrion Square.

'Very enjoyable, George,' Phin said, handing over his hat and cape.

'Ma'am?' George said with a raised brow. 'As you may recall, Mary is out this evening visiting her mother. May I take your cloak?'

'Thank you, George.' Lucy smiled as she handed over the heavy velvet and brocade opera cloak.

Meanwhile, Phin was heading for the library. If he holed up in there for the evening, she'd never find out about the situation at Dublin Castle.

'May I join you for a nightcap?' she asked.

Phin shot her a sidelong glance. He knew what she was up to, but that didn't deter her. Without waiting for a reply, she sailed past her husband into the study.

'And what did you think of Sir Valentine and his good lady wife, Lucy?' Phin asked as he handed her a brandy.

'He is top-lofty and slightly ridiculous,' she said, taking a sip. 'She's a snob.'

Phin guffawed. 'Precise and to the point, as ever, my dear.'

'And you have to work with him?' she asked.

'Yes, unfortunately, I do.' Phin cleared his throat. 'Well... possibly.'

'Hmm. As I am here and might be of assistance, perhaps you'd like to tell me what is going on.' He wouldn't meet her gaze. Could she goad him into a disclosure? 'Did someone steal the jewels?'

Silence greeted this. Phin was scrambling for an answer. 'My dear,' Phin said at last. 'I have been asked to keep my... assignment here, confidential. By the highest authority.'

'The PM?'

'Yes.'

'Even from me?' Phin spread his hands and shrugged. 'So, they *have* been stolen.'

'No,' Phin sighed. 'Information obtained—'

'—Phin!'

'Oh, very well, I suppose you're halfway there. There's no point in prevaricating.' He threw her a wry look. 'And I know if I want a quiet life, I'd best tell you.'

Lucy didn't bother to hide her triumph. 'You said something about information?'

'How much of Ireland's recent history are you familiar with?' he asked.

'Not a great deal, I have to admit.'

'Well, people have been calling for Home Rule here for many years and the House of Lords defeated an attempt to get it over the line last year. This has led to a resurgence of republican ideology and unrest. An informant of the Dublin Metropolitan Police claims to know of a conspiracy involving the Fenians to steal the jewels. Their motivation appears to be maximum embarrassment to the Crown, the PM and Sir Valentine. The Order of St Patrick owns the jewels, which are worn by the viceroy, and the queen when she visits. They are stored in a safe at Dublin Castle.'

'But is not Dublin Castle well-guarded?'

'Yes. It's home to the Dublin Metropolitan Police and the lord lieutenant's offices, and several army units as well.'

'Then this sounds like an outrageous joke. I'd have considered it to be a foolish enterprise even to contemplate breaking in and stealing the regalia.'

'Perhaps, but if these men are desperate, they might attempt it. And if they pulled it off, it would create an uproar both here and in London,' Phin said. 'You see, it's a thoroughly dull assignment. I'm here to advise on security matters only. So, no, I'm not here to hunt down jewel thieves, if that is what you were hoping. I'm sorry.' He chuckled. 'You look disappointed, Lucy.'

She finished her drink and stood. 'Yes, I am. That all sounds unexciting, my dear, to be honest, and I was hoping for an adventure.'

Her husband smiled as he pulled her into an embrace. 'I wouldn't expect anything less of you, my dear.'

TWO

Merrion Square, Thursday, 19th July

When Lucy woke late the next morning, it didn't surprise her to find Phin was already up, dressed and gone from their suite. Hearing voices outside, Lucy jumped up and made her way to the window to pull back the wooden shutters. Below, she caught sight of Phin getting into a cab. He must be off to Dublin Castle again, she mused. And without her.

The door opened. 'Morning, ma'am,' Mary, her maid, greeted her as she entered the room.

'Good morning, Mary,' Lucy said, turning from the window. 'It looks as though it will be a fine day.' She sat at the dressing table, watching Mary head for the bathroom through her mirror.

'Yes, ma'am. I'll run your bath.'

'Thank you. I plan to take the children to the zoological gardens in the Phoenix Park. Bash spotted an advertisement for it yesterday and is keen to go. Perhaps you will come with us, Mary? I'm sure Jenny and I would be glad of the help. You know how energetic the children can be when they are excited.'

There was silence. From the bathroom, Lucy heard the water running. 'Mary?'

A moment later, Mary appeared at the door. 'Yes, ma'am?'

'Would you like to visit the zoo with us today?' A subdued smile followed by a nod was the maid's answer before she returned to the bathroom.

Concerned that her normally bubbly maid was out of sorts, Lucy followed. 'Is something the matter? How was your mother last night? Is she well?'

'Yes, ma'am, thank you. And she expressly asked me to pass on her best to you. She's in fine fettle... but for...' Mary was kneeling beside the bath, testing the temperature of the water with her hand. She looked up. 'It's probably nothing at all, ma'am.'

So, there *was* something up. Lucy sat on the edge of the bath. 'Whatever it is, it's best you tell me. I'll get it out of you in the end, you know.'

Mary tried to smile as she got to her feet. 'I don't want to trouble you, ma'am. Sure, you have enough to be worrying about with the twins and all and setting up home here for the summer.'

'Nonsense, Mary. I may be able to help you or your mother, but I can't if you don't tell me what the problem is.'

'Ma... well, not just her. We all think something terrible is after happening to me young cousins, ma'am.'

'Good gracious,' Lucy exclaimed. 'Tell me more.'

'Well, me mother was in a dreadful state about it last night when I was there. About a week ago, she got a letter from her sister down in Wexford. That's where they are from, see.'

'Oh dear. Some bad news then?'

'Aye, Peggy and Bridget, they've disappeared and not a word from either of them these last few weeks.'

'Disappeared? Oh my, how dreadful, Mary.'

The maid wrung her hands. 'Aye. Vanished. They travelled up here to Dublin to find work. Jobs are scarce down there, you see. But me aunt hasn't heard a word from them since she waved them off at the station. That's like almost three weeks ago.'

'Perhaps in the excitement of coming to Dublin, they've forgotten to write,' Lucy suggested. 'If they are a little flighty...'

'Ah no, ma'am, sure, they are both good girls. A bit young in some ways and sure they didn't want to come at all, but things weren't great since their father died last Christmas. Anyways, me ma thinks it's odd they haven't even visited her.' Mary's chin trembled. 'Ma thinks something bad has happened. She's heard such stories about what can befall young women—with barely a brain cell between them, like our Peggy and our Bridget—arriving here and knowing nothin'. Silly young things, the pair of them, when they're together, and that's as often as not. They're fierce close.'

'How old are they?'

'Peggy's sixteen, her sister a year younger, ma'am.'

'That is worrying. They are little more than children.' Mary nodded. 'What sort of work were they looking for?'

'To go into service. 'Tis the only respectable way to go.' Mary smiled. 'They heard how well I was doing with you, ma'am, and sure it gave them the gumption to have a go themselves. Now, when me mother heard their plans, she wrote to tell them the Jacobs factory was taking on biscuit packers... But they were not keen on that, the silly widgeons. Now, I'm fierce worried about 'em, ma'am. What if something awful has happened?'

'We can't assume the worst, Mary. Hopefully, there is a benign reason for their silence.' But even as she said it, Lucy didn't believe it.

'What would your advice be?' Mary asked. 'How do I go about finding 'em? Should I go to the polis?' Mary's voice cracked on the last, and she hurriedly bent over the bath to turn off the taps. When she looked back at Lucy, her eyes were bright with tears.

'Why, Mary, it is perfectly simple. I will help you find them,' Lucy said. 'And we shall make a start when we get back from the zoological gardens.'

Later that afternoon

By the time the twins had been put down for their much-needed nap after the morning excursion, it was almost three o'clock. Lucy summoned Mary to the charming breakfast room she had commandeered for herself. It was a sunny room with views out towards the stables at the end of the long, narrow rear garden. As she waited, Lucy mulled over the morning visit to the zoo. Harry and Eleanor had loved it, and it had been a full-time job to keep them from running ahead to each new exciting animal enclosure. But although both Jenny and Mary had kept the two under control, it was plain to Lucy that Mary was brooding over her cousins' disappearance. Mary was usually full of mischief, and the children loved being with her, but today there had been few smiles, and the twins' entreaties to marvel at the animals went over the maid's head. Not that she blamed her. The disappearance of the young women was a concern. Lucy didn't know Dublin, but she knew that, like every other large city in the empire, it was bound to have its dark side. For both girls to disappear suggested something awful had befallen them.

Mary entered the breakfast room and greeted her, unsmiling.

'Any news from your mother?' Lucy asked.

'No, ma'am. Not a peep.'

'That's disappointing, but I have been giving your problem some thought,' Lucy said. 'Please sit down and we can have a chat.'

Mary hesitated but then dropped into the seat opposite, her shoulders slumped. 'I'm sure I haven't a clue what to do for the best, ma'am. It's mithered I am about it.'

'I can see that, Mary, and I'm sorry for your family's trouble. Now, we must be logical, and that means we must retrace their steps and find out if anyone remembers seeing them. We need to prove they arrived in Dublin at all. It's possible they got off the train somewhere along the line. I'm sure there are several stations along the way.'

'There are, but I doubt it, ma'am. Why would they? Their best chance of getting work was to come here to the city. Me aunt paid for their tickets and, God knows, she could ill afford it being a widow with so many mouths to feed, but it's desperate times for the family.'

'I understand, and she must be frantic. Still, I believe we need to check if they showed up in Dublin. You don't have a photograph of them by any chance?'

Mary's face brightened. 'I do, ma'am. Aunty May sent one to Ma last Christmas. I have it in my room.'

Lucy smothered a smile. The only reason Mary would have the photograph was that she had always intended to rope Lucy into finding them. She rose quickly. 'Then fetch it, along with your coat. If your aunt waved them off, we know they caught the train from Wexford. Where is the terminus? That would be the place to start.'

'Oh, that would be Westland Row Station, ma'am. 'Tis just a short walk from here.'

'Excellent. Let us not delay.'

As Mary had indicated, it didn't take long to reach the station on foot. Below the railway bridge, hansom cabs lined each side of the street, and there was a constant flow of people in and out of the station entrance. Horse-drawn trams trundled past, adding to the noise and bustle. On entering the station at ground level, Lucy joined the queue at the ticket kiosk, and when her turn came, she asked to speak to the stationmaster. Mary stood biting her lip, scanning the busy area. A short while later, a dapper man in uniform, with a heavily waxed moustache and sideburns the most ginger Lucy had ever beheld, approached them.

'Ladies,' he said. 'How may I help you?'

Seeing how uneasy Mary was, Lucy performed the introductions and then said, 'I wonder if we might speak to you in private? We won't take up too much of your time, but we would appreciate your help in a certain matter.'

'It would be my pleasure.' He nodded to Mary, who bobbed a curtsey, which betrayed her state of mind. 'Please come to my office where we can talk in private. It's not far, madam. Just up the stairs to the southbound platform.'

They followed the stationmaster into a small office before taking the seats he offered.

'Thank you so much, Mr...?'

'Hegarty, madam. Simon Hegarty at your service,' he said as he took his seat. He smiled at them both in turn. 'Now, what appears to be the problem?'

'We are concerned about the welfare of two young women.' Lucy glanced at Mary, who was sitting staring down at her clenched hands in her lap. 'Miss O'Reilly's young cousins travelled by train from Wexford to this very station, we believe. It would have been about three weeks ago. They were coming to Dublin to find employment. For some reason, both young girls have disappeared. Their family has heard nothing from either girl since they left Wexford. We are trying to confirm they arrived here. And if possible, trace their onward journey. We wondered if perhaps a member of your staff might recall seeing them.'

Hegarty quirked his mouth, and Lucy rushed on. 'I know there is only the slightest possibility as this is such a busy station, but we have brought along a photograph. It might trigger a memory.' She turned to her maid. 'Mary?'

Mary opened her bag, drew out the picture and passed it to the stationmaster.

He studied it, then grunted.

Lucy continued: 'They are striking girls, and the fact they were travelling together... well, they may have been noticed.'

Hegarty cleared his throat. 'This is a sad situation but, unfortunately, not an uncommon one. And not just here but at the other major stations in the city.' He shook his head as he placed the photograph down on the desk. 'There are scoundrels who hang around outside the station, and they can pick out a naïve country girl at thirty paces.' He threw Mary a sympathetic glance. 'These men promise the women they will find them work. And they do, but not the kind of work that respectable young ladies want.' He paused, his face tinged with colour. 'It is difficult... I do not wish to offend your sensibilities, ladies, but these women often end up in houses of ill-repute.'

'Mother of God,' Mary exclaimed, her hand flying to her mouth. 'That's what I feared most.'

Lucy leaned over and grabbed her hand. 'It's not certain, Mary, only a possibility.'

'We do our best to get rid of these men, and indeed the DMP also moves them on if they spot them, but it is impossible to eradicate the problem completely,' Hegarty said. 'We have tried. But these girls, they are often so innocent that they don't sense the danger. They are far too trusting, and once they get into the clutches of these gangs…'

Lucy was losing hope but was determined to try. 'I understand… but would you mind asking your staff? At least then we might know if they made it as far as Dublin. Though I am not sure how we will proceed even if that is confirmed.'

With a sympathetic look, Hegarty scooped up the photograph. 'Give me a few minutes and I will see what we can do. Please, you're welcome to stay here. I'll be as quick as I can.'

'Thank you, Mr Hegarty.' Lucy's gaze followed him out onto the busy platform. 'At least he's willing to try,' she said to Mary.

'Thank you, ma'am,' the maid said. 'I knew I could rely on you.'

'Oh, Mary, it's not such a great beginning, and if he's right and one of those awful men lured your cousins away, I don't know how we will find them. But don't fall into despair. I'll talk to Phineas this evening. He may have contacts within the local police. At the very least, he'll have some ideas on how to proceed.'

'Ma'am, no. I couldn't ask that of you or him. You've already done this much.'

'Nonsense, Mary. You're part of the family, you and George. We look after our own.'

Mary sniffled and dug in her bag for a handkerchief.

Several minutes later, Hegarty reappeared in the doorway. He took in Mary's distressed state and gave Lucy a look full of understanding. Then he sat and slid the photograph back across the desk towards Mary. 'I'm very sorry, but none of my staff recall seeing these young women.'

For Mary's sake, Lucy tried to remain cheerful. 'Thank you for trying. Come, Mary, we cannot take up any more of this kind gentleman's time.' Lucy stood and held out her hand to Hegarty, who leapt to his feet once more. He shook her hand, then Mary's.

Out on the platform, Lucy spotted a cigar and cigarette stall, the sign above proclaiming that Delany & Co sold only the most exclusive brands. 'I have an idea, Mary. Give me the photograph, please, and come with me.'

Lucy waited for the gentleman ahead of her to finish his transaction, then she stepped up and smiled at the young woman behind the stall.

'Good afternoon,' Lucy said. 'I wonder if you might help us, please?'

The woman raised an eyebrow but smiled. 'I will if it's possible. Are you looking for a recommendation?' she asked, glancing down at the array of products on the stall.

Thinking it might soften her up, Lucy pointed to a variety of cigars she knew Phin liked. 'Is this a popular brand?'

'Oh yes, madam, one of our bestselling lines.'

'Excellent. I'll take a box, please,' Lucy said.

Lucy handed over the requested amount in payment and, as the woman put the box of cigars into a paper bag, Lucy winked at Mary, who was giving her strange looks. 'Was there anything else, madam?'

'As it happens, yes. Are you here most days?'

'Generally, yes. On the days I'm not here, one of my sisters takes over.' She waved her hand. 'This is a family business. Might I ask why you wish to know?'

Lucy produced the photograph and showed it to her. 'Forgive me... Miss Delany?' The woman nodded. 'But we are trying to find the whereabouts of these two young girls. They came here about three weeks ago and have since disappeared. I wondered if perhaps you might recall seeing them?'

The woman took the photograph and peered at it. Then she tilted it to get a better view, a crease forming between her brows. 'You know, I think I do recall them. This young girl bought some peppermint creams.' She looked up. 'We stock them as some gentlemen like them, so their breath doesn't offend the ladies. Yes, I'm certain of it. Shy young thing.' She shook her head. 'It was difficult to hear her; she spoke so quietly. Then she asked me how to get to Irishtown, so I told her what tram to get. Told her it was easy enough as the No. 4 stops right outside the station here.' She paused and frowned. 'They couldn't have missed it as it's one of the few single-decker tram routes in the city.'

'Oh, thank you so much. That is very helpful,' Lucy said.

'I do hope you find them, madam.'

Lucy thanked her again and fell into step with Mary, who tugged her sleeve, halting her. Mary's face was ashen. 'Ma'am, did you hear? Irishtown. That's where Ma lives. Oh, what has happened? They never got there.'

Lucy comforted her as best she was able, but a hard knot of anxiety had formed in her stomach. The fate of Mary's cousins looked bleak indeed.

THREE

The Monto, Dublin, Thursday, 19th July

Myles Carver, Esq., the chairman of the Royal Ireland Bank, stared in horror at the body of the young prostitute at his feet. The bloody, metallic smell and the sight of her broken body made him gag. Swallowing hard, he clutched the footboard of the bed for support. A voice in his head urged him to flee the brothel as quickly as possible. He grabbed his coat and pulled it back on and was almost at the door when he remembered his walking stick. Cursing, he turned around. What had he done with it?

As panic rose in his throat, he spotted the carved wolfhound head of the cane on the floor near the bed. He couldn't recall dropping it. It must have been the fright. He couldn't leave it behind, not because it had been an anniversary present from Edith, but because everyone who knew him was familiar with its unique design. To his dismay, it was lying close to the girl's body. As he stooped down to retrieve it, he hesitated, hand outstretched. The shaft was covered with blood. He couldn't leave with it in that state. Someone might see. Trembling and sweating profusely, he wiped it, and then his hands, on the bedsheet and made for the exit once more.

After a couple of deep breaths, he opened the door a sliver and chanced a peep out on to the landing. The sound of raucous male laughter came from another room, but there was no one in view. Taking the steps two at a time, he flew down the flights of stairs from the top floor until he saw the entrance hallway below him. He stalled, uncertain, on the return. Mulcahy, the porter, was sitting inside the front door, browsing through a newspaper. Could the bowsie read? Who'd have thought it? Still shaking, Carver took a moment to catch his breath. He needed a clear head to extract himself from this mess.

From Celine Burton's sitting room came raised voices. No doubt the bitch was trying to fleece some unfortunate. Her booze prices were notoriously high. He'd locked horns with her about it the previous week. The witch had laughed at him, holding out her hand for payment, and all the while Mulcahy had lurked in the background. Always a threatening presence.

The doorbell jangled and Mulcahy grunted, tossed the paper to the floor, and rose to answer the summons. This was Carver's best chance to get away.

He slipped down the last few steps, and on the balls of his feet rushed to the door he hoped would lead to the rear of the property. Thankfully, the kitchens were empty, and he exited through the back door, into a none too fragrant yard. Once he gained the safety of the laneway, he raced down past the fetid mews buildings. Within minutes he was out of breath and needed to stop to lean against a wall, hoping he was far enough away from the brothel. How was he to leave the area without being seen? If only he knew where the entrance to those damned tunnels was located. But only the lucky few knew about those, and if rumour was to be believed, the Prince of Wales was among the select few.

Struggling to regain his breath, Carver scanned the laneway. He knew it wasn't safe to stay here. The locals would rob you as soon as look at you. Besides, speed was of the essence; he had to escape before that young girl was discovered. If he were implicated in any way, it would mean ruin, not just for him but for the entire family. Edith would never understand.

Breathing hard, he cut through the archway that led out to the street just as a cab approached. He waved it down and sprang up into it.

'No. 83 Merrion Square,' he barked to the cabbie. Overcome with relief, he leaned back and wiped the sweat from his brow with an unsteady hand. He might be on his way out of The Monto, but he knew the trouble had only begun.

Merrion Square, Dublin

It was common knowledge in the close environs of Merrion Square that Edith Carver, at No. 83, wasn't long for this world. But it was Olivia, her daughter-in-law, who tended the dying woman, an onerous duty she fulfilled without complaint. Edith had shown her nothing but kindness from the day Olivia arrived at the Carver residence as James Carver's bride, five years previously.

Olivia glanced down at Edith's pinched cheeks. The woman was having a wretched time of it. Not only was her heart weak, but her digestive system was also in turmoil. Of late, she often complained of blurred vision as well. Olivia was convinced Edith would join her son James in Mount Jerome Cemetery soon, a thought which caused a shiver to dance down the young woman's spine. The speed of her mother-in-law's deteriorating condition had shocked everyone in the household. And once the doctor had diagnosed heart failure, Edith appeared to give up. Sometimes in the evenings, she would perk up, but by mid-morning the next day she would struggle once more, a circumstance which baffled the doctor.

Olivia turned away, her gaze sweeping over the medicines the so-called medic had quacked Edith with. All the Ipecacuanha Wine and Gregory's Powder had done was make the poor woman suffer even more. Olivia's protests to both the doctor and Myles had gone unheeded. The little blue bottle of tincture of digitalis, which Olivia dispensed twice a day, helped when first prescribed, but in the last few weeks, even its restorative properties appeared to have waned. The doctor could not explain that either.

A sudden downdraft ejected smoke from the dying fire into the room, and Olivia's eyes stung. Even though it was the warmest July in many years, her father-in-law insisted on keeping a fire lit in the room. He was such a strange man for he fussed over such little details yet appeared oblivious to the broader situation; that his wife was dying. In frustration, she peered at the smoking wood in the grate. Wearily, she went to the fireplace and poked at the log, which refused to ignite. Damp timber again. But it was not surprising when the servants were so poorly paid and overworked. Thankfully, the bellows performed their magic, and the tip of the log caught at last. Lost in thought, Olivia stood before the fire. How she hated being stuck in this sickroom, day after day. If it weren't for Edith, she'd have left long ago. That and penury, but she would have to decide soon. Once Edith was gone, living here would be intolerable and, hopefully, unnecessary. A sudden squall of rain hit the windowpane with a violence that unnerved her. She hated thunderstorms.

With a groan, Edith's eyes flew open, and Olivia returned to her side, but her mother-in-law's eyes were glassy with fever. Olivia felt her forehead; it was still on fire. Olivia dipped a piece of linen into the bowl of tepid water on the nightstand, squeezed it out and applied it to Edith's forehead. With a glance at her watch, she was surprised to see it was already past seven. Myles had not appeared for dinner, and she was very relieved. Hopefully, he was dining at his club and would not bother her this evening. Time enough to face his sour features over the breakfast table.

Olivia stretched her arms above her head and yawned. Why did James have to die and leave her in this intolerable situation? It was almost as if he had done it on purpose.

. . .

Thirty minutes later, Olivia eased the door closed to her mother-in-law's sickroom. Edith was sleeping at last. As she walked along the landing, Olivia heard the front door open. He was home. Would he even bother to check on Edith? He rarely did in the evening, keeping his visits to the early morning when he would sit with Edith, all others banished. Olivia often wondered if Edith was even aware of his presence. No more than herself, she imagined the woman derived little solace from that dour countenance looming over her.

She hurried along the landing to her room, reluctant to have any dealings with him. Sitting down, she took up her book, but she had only read a few pages when Sally, her maid, entered the room.

'Himself is looking for ye,' the maid said, from the doorway. Then she stepped inside and shut it, lowering her voice. 'And he's in one of *those* moods. Bit the nose off me for sayin' you'd retired for the night.'

'Thanks for trying, Sal,' Olivia said, her heart sinking. The older woman shrugged, but her grey eyes conveyed sympathy.

When Olivia entered the library, her father-in-law was standing before the empty grate with a glass of amber spirits in his hand. She took in his tall and gaunt figure as a shiver of revulsion went through her. Her gaze darted to the portrait of Myles Carver as a young man, which graced the wall behind his desk. Sometimes, she wondered if James would have aged to look like Myles did now. Certainly, she could see James clearly in his father's picture. But whereas Myles was cold, even calculating, James had been warm and charming. Too late, however, she had discovered he was also persuadable, parting with money at the racetrack as if there was a bottomless supply of it. And therein had been their downfall.

Myles swung around and glared at her. 'You took your time. Sit down.'

She did as she was told, fuming inside. Ever since James had died, Myles had treated her like a servant. There was little she could do, however, as James had gambled away every penny and left her financially dependent on his father. Her only living family was a married brother in Shropshire. He had been against the marriage and warned her of her probable fate, but she had been desperate to escape the ignominy of being a spinster aunt to Christopher's growing family and had defied him. Consequently, he had washed his hands of her upon her marriage. How she regretted daily not heeding his advice. After James's death, Christopher had sent back her pleading letters, unopened. Her only friend and ally was her maid, who had stuck by her all these years. Olivia had soon realised she would have to rely on her wits to extract herself and Sally from their current predicament. As a result, she dedicated a considerable amount of time every day on cementing her escape plan.

'How was Edith today?' he asked, glaring down at her.

'No change, sir.'

'Not much of a nurse, are you?' he said with a sneer as he took a sip of his drink. 'I should have sent you packing to that brother of yours when James died, but I'm too soft-hearted.' Olivia had to bite her tongue. 'I don't believe I need to remind you how precarious your position is,' he continued, his eyes flint-like. 'Well, for once you can be of use. You must and you *will* help me.'

Olivia noticed his hand was shaking and wondered what on earth was going on. He wasn't easily rattled, in her experience. 'I will if it is in my power,' she said, keeping her eyes downcast.

'You will do as you are told,' he shouted at her. He slammed the glass down on the mantel, the liquid tipping out and running down the marble. Carver ignored it and loomed over her. 'I had to flee the scene of a nasty crime this evening. There are people—dangerous scoundrels—who will try to lay the blame on me. Any breath of scandal would ruin me, and that will not augur well for you, either. So, this is what you will tell anyone who asks. Make sure that precious maid of yours toes the line, too, or I'll kick her out. Is that clear?'

Olivia kept her gaze fixed on her hands, her blood running cold, not with fear but with fury. 'Yes,' she said, for she knew it was no idle threat.

FOUR

Dublin City, Thursday, 19th July

There were two constants in the world of Detective Inspector Fergus Ryan: the determination of the city's criminals to practise their nefarious dark arts, and his resolution to force them into early retirement. His zealous pursuit of duty had earned him a formidable reputation with both his colleagues in 'G' Detective Division in Dublin Castle, and those who inhabited the underbelly of the city. His ambition to become chief inspector was well known, much to the annoyance of the present incumbent.

The air was still heavy after the storm that had battered Dublin for the previous two hours. It was half-past eight, but the lamplighter would not begin his work for at least another hour. Fergus paused at the railing of Grattan Bridge and looked up the Liffey to the west, as a troop of cavalry crossed the bridge behind him. He knew most of them by sight but kept his eyes on the river. A coil of tension was forming in the pit of his stomach, as it always did starting a new case. He needed to clear his mind of all the humdrum distractions, not to mention the interview he'd had with Chief Inspector Malone, earlier that evening.

Malone had done it out of spite, the old bastard. Volunteering him to liaise with this English private investigator, Phineas Stone, who had just arrived in Dublin. Fergus gripped the bridge handrail. As if he didn't have a full workload already. And now he had a murder to solve. God only knew what he would face tonight in The Monto, Dublin's notorious red-light district. The prostitutes were often beaten, usually by the bully boys engaged by the madams, but murder was rare.

A Guinness barge chugged up and passed beneath him, destined to quench a foreign thirst, perhaps. He lit a cigarette and inhaled deeply, watching the moody black clouds painting the sky above the dome of The Four Courts. A jarvey coming down Ormond Quay hailed him, and he returned the salute with a curt nod. Billy Murphy was one of his many informants. Much as he liked to stand here and observe city life, he had to get on. He pulled his hat down a little further and proceeded towards Dublin's most squalid parish.

Fergus kept his eyes cast down as he hurried along the pavements of the lower end of The Monto. Policemen were not welcome here. The once pristine Georgian houses of the wealthy were now greasy terraces, and home to some of the worst brothels in the city, where the old and sick ladies of the night worked out their remaining days in the kip-houses. Washing flapped from the poles stuck out of the upper storey windows or clung immodestly to the railings for all the world to see. The working women lurked in the doorways or down the darkened laneways. Their invitations carried on the air, and those who recognised him sent him on his way to the tune of a curse.

No. 29 Mecklenburgh Street, at the furthest end of the district, was a flash-house that catered to more affluent clients. Fergus paused for a moment at the foot of the steps. The three-storey Georgian house was a blaze of light that spilled out onto the wet pavement, creating shimmering reflections at his feet.

A burly young DMP constable stood to attention at the door. 'Good evening, sir,' he said as Fergus mounted the steps and showed him his warrant card.

Fergus entered the hallway. Expensive velvets lined the walls, and antiques and crystal chandeliers jostled for his attention. With a shudder of distaste and a deep breath, he advanced towards the raised voices coming from the front room.

'And I'm tellin' ya, I knows who done it,' a female shouted as he entered the room.

Two pairs of eyes swivelled towards him, one angry, the other bearing a harried expression.

'You!' the woman exclaimed, throwing up her hands. 'Bloody hell.'

'Evening, Celine,' he answered. Something very serious had rattled her, for her usual cultivated tones were absent. In appearance, she could be mistaken for a lady of quality. A buxom, round-faced woman in her early forties, with blonde hair that owed more to a clever hairdresser than Mother Nature, she was always lavishly dressed. One of the most notorious madams in the city, she owned at least five brothels in the district and was a friend to judges, politicians and men of wealth and influence. With her fine clothes and the luxurious carriage she travelled about in, the local Monto wags had christened her Lady Muck. In his many dealings with her over the years, Fergus had always found her shrewd, devious and as slippery as an eel.

Beside her, Detective Sergeant Tim Hughes was looking relieved to see him.

'You better sort out this bloody mess, Ryan,' she growled. She cocked her head at his sergeant. 'This fella's no good.'

'Now, now, Celine, be nice,' he said, then turned to Hughes. 'Has a doctor arrived yet?'

'No, sir, but he should be here any minute. It's Doc Peters, sir.'

'Excellent. Now be a good fellow and wait outside for him while I have a quick word with Mrs Burton.'

The door closed with a snap. Celine grimaced at Fergus and sat down before gesturing towards the sideboard heaving with bottles of spirits. 'Be a love and pour me one. I'm in desperate need.'

Fergus walked over and poured out a brandy. Already, he had a bad feeling about this case. He was sorely tempted to join her.

'Ta, love,' she said and downed the lot in one go. 'I needed that bad, I did.'

'What's happened here tonight, Celine?' he asked, sitting on the arm of the plush sofa.

'Murder, Ryan. That's what. One of me tenants... I won't be the better of this for a long time.'

'I can't help until you explain what occurred,' he repeated, wondering just how genuine her distress was. She had, according to one of his narks, slashed the face of one of her girls she'd caught withholding money from her only the week before. That this house was a brothel was undisputed, however, a pretence was maintained by Burton that the girls who happened to live in the house were lodgers and their clients merely visitors. In one sense, this was true. Their 'rent' was deducted from their earnings, leaving them almost penniless and trapped in a vicious cycle which nearly always ended tragically.

'Yes, yes, all right. It's the new girl. Only here a few weeks. Peggy's her name, but her working name was Claudine... nice and classy, that, isn't it?'

'Lovely. What's her surname?' he asked.

Celine glared at him. 'How the hell would I know? Hardly worth my while getting to know them. Little beggars run off given half a chance, usually with a wad of me hard-earned money.'

So much for the girls' welfare. 'So, Celine... what took place tonight?'

'Well, she entertained a *guest* about five. Then a regular called about seven. He always wants to visit the youngest and newest girls. Very particular, is Mr Carver.'

'He gave you his real name?' Fergus asked in disbelief.

'Well, no, but I make it me business to know the names of the regular... visitors. You never know when it will come in useful,' she said with a shrewd smile.

Fergus suppressed a stinging retort. In other words, the girls were told to go through the visitor's clothes, not only to find out their clients' identities but also to rob them. But Fergus needed to keep Celine in a cooperative frame of mind. Her ruthless business methods were no surprise, but he had little sympathy for anyone who fell into her clutches. 'So did he ask to see her specifically?'

'No, but I know he always likes them fresh up from the bog. And she was, and not the brightest either. Anyway, Mulcahy and I were busy, so I sent Carver up to her room. About an hour ago, another gentleman arrived, and as he was new, I took him up meself.' She stopped and blew out her cheeks. 'Lord, Ryan, I've never seen the like. Sprawled on the floor, she was. And the blood. So much blood. The carpet's ruined. Pure wool it is, too.'

'What did you do?' he asked, digging his fingers into his palm.

'I screamed for Mulcahy to fetch a constable.'

'Not a doctor?'

'No doctor could have helped her—dead, she was—it was obvious, and I checked so I did. I shall never forget the sight of it, even if I live to be a hundred.' With a dramatic shiver, her eyes flew to the bottle of brandy.

He ignored the hint. 'So, this Mr Carver was the last visitor she had?'

'Yes.'

'What time did he leave?'

'No idea. He scarpered, the rotten bastard. But ask Mulcahy. He was on the door and might know when he left.'

'All right. We'll be taking statements, Celine, and not just from who you want us to talk to. Is that clear?'

Her reply was a quirk of her mouth.

'When was Peggy last seen alive?'

'I saw her at about six o'clock. She came down for a cuppa.'

'And Carver arrived at?'

'Must have been close to seven, as I said.'

'Right. I'd better take a look.' As he passed, he paused, looking down at her. 'Any idea where the man lives? This Carver chap.'

'No, but he is Dublin and well-to-do. Posh accent and a right arrogant bastard.'

That narrows it down, he thought. 'If the name's right, we'll find him.'

'And be quick about it, Ryan. It's not good for me business,' she said, staring up at him, her face etched with worry. 'When can I reopen?'

Gritting his teeth, Fergus closed the door behind him without responding.

FIVE

Burton's Flash-house, The Monto

Celine's description of the scene had Fergus on edge. Crime scenes were never pretty, and this one sounded as bad as any he might have witnessed before. When he reached the landing on the top floor, several young women stood huddled together, all of them scantily dressed. Their hushed conversation ended abruptly as he approached. Fergus knew one of them well, Virginia O'Mara, who had grown up only a few streets away from him. They had played together in the back alleys as children. He nodded to her, and she acknowledged him with a sad smile.

'Ginny, might I have a word?' he asked.

Virginia dismissed her companions with a jerk of her head. 'Sure, Fergus.'

He glanced down the corridor to where he saw his sergeant and the doctor waiting for him. 'Did you know her?' he asked as she stepped towards him.

A flash of weariness ignited on her face before it closed down once more. She turned away and leaned on the handrail of the stairs, staring down into the hallway below. 'Not really. Poor little cow only started a few weeks ago.'

'Did you see or hear anything this evening? Say, between seven and eight?'

'Besides Lady Muck screaming the house down? No.' She gave him a sideways glance. 'Sorry. That doesn't help much, does it? Violence is as much a part of this world as it is in yours, *Inspector*. We expect it, live with it, most days.'

Fergus leaned against the handrail. 'I'm aware of that, Ginny. I've seen the beatings you girls have to endure, but murder is taking it to another level. So, you didn't see who the girl's clients were tonight?'

She straightened up. 'No. I was otherwise engaged.' This was said with a shrug of her thin shoulders. Then she leaned towards him and said so quietly he barely heard her, 'Look, I don't want no trouble. I nearly have enough saved to get out of this shithole. I ain't doing nothing to jeopardise that.'

'Sure, I understand.' He directed a searching look at her. 'Good luck to you, Ginny. If I can help...'

Up on her tippy toes, she planted a kiss on his cheek. 'Ta, but I won't involve you, cos if herself found out, she'd make no end of trouble for you. And you're one of the few good 'uns left in this cursed city.'

'Sorry to drag you out on such a filthy night, Dr Peters,' Fergus said as he joined the men outside the victim's room. Peters was a local GP and past sixty, but he was a first-rate doctor, and they had worked together before. Peters was unique by Dublin GP standards in that the science of death fascinated him, and he could read a crime scene as well as any policeman. In fact, it was an obsession that had helped Fergus on more than one occasion. It was a stroke of good fortune that Peters had been available tonight. Fergus knew he could trust his judgement.

A grunt, albeit a good-humoured one, was the doctor's only response to his greeting.

'Right, Sergeant,' Fergus said. 'Open it up.'

Hughes unlocked the door, and Fergus scanned the scene from the threshold. A large double bed, draped in burgundy and gold damask, dominated the room. A wardrobe, chest of drawers and a dressing table and chair were the only other items of furniture. Dark burgundy wallpaper and drapes gave the room an oppressive ambience as opposed to the romantic one Celine was aiming for. The room was stuffy, and the distinctive metallic odour of blood was all too obvious, almost drowning out the pungent sweetness of cheap perfume.

Fergus entered the room and stopped at the foot of the bed. The victim was lying on her back on the far side. Blood matted her dark hair, and a pool of it stained the carpet beneath her. Clutching the bedsheet in one hand, the purple satin negligée barely hid her thin and pale body. Shreds of what he assumed was a wrap was bunched up behind her. Her attacker had wrenched off one lace strap of her negligee as well, but the expression of terror, etched onto her features, made him shiver. He closed his eyes briefly. She didn't look old enough to be out of school, and it was all too clear that her death had been a violent one. He only hoped it had been quick. He dragged his gaze away and noted the few pathetic personal items on the dressing table. There was a hairbrush lying on the floor, more evidence of a struggle.

Dr Peters, now on his knees examining the body, suddenly grunted.

'Well?' Fergus asked.

'No rigor mortis... so she died within the last four to five hours.'

'That ties in with what Lady Muck said.'

Peters lifted one of the young girl's arms. 'There are some defensive wounds and bruising to her arms, see?'

'So, she tried to fend him off?'

'Aye, but the blows to her head killed her; probably cracked the skull at the temple. There is a large gash at the back of her head, too, so the first blow was likely from behind. I'll have to take her away and do the postmortem to tell you any more than that.'

'What kind of weapon was used?'

Peters peered at the wounds on the girl's head before answering. 'Probably something heavy and rounded.'

Fergus looked around the room for an object that might match the description. 'What about that poker?' he asked. He stepped round the body to the fireplace and, using his handkerchief, he picked up the poker. The handle was rectangular, not rounded, and there was no trace of blood on it. He showed it to Peters.

'Wrong shape and would be something with a larger diameter than that.'

Fergus replaced it. While Hughes searched through the chest of drawers, Fergus tackled the wardrobe. He flicked through the few items of clothing, all of which reeked of the same awful scent. The victim's cheap clothes stood out against the brothel's satin and lacy negligées and stylish dresses that Celine made them wear.

He turned to Sergeant Hughes. 'When you arrived, was there anyone in here with the body?'

'Mrs Burton and Mulcahy; the ladies of the house were out on the landing, cackling like hens. We shooed them all away and locked the room to preserve the scene.'

'They had plenty of time to change or remove things if they needed, though,' Fergus said, more to himself than the room. 'Is the photographer coming?'

'Yes, sir.'

'All right, Dr Peters, you can have her once he is finished.'

'Very well,' the doctor answered, getting stiffly to his feet. 'I'll wait downstairs.'

SIX

The wall fell towards Fergus, then hung suspended in mid-air. Wasn't it strange that the individual bricks stood out? And the roses, too, on the wallpaper that Ma was so proud of. Then he saw the Bovril advertisement stuck over the hole where his sister had put her fist through during one of her many tantrums. What was happening?

The room was deconstructing before his eyes.

He struggled to breathe through the dust as panic rose to a crescendo. The roaring in his ears was unbearable. Almost like thunder but far more deadly. He heard his sister cry out, his mother moan in pain.

Abruptly, there was silence and choking blindness. This was the point he always woke up.

Fergus dragged himself into a sitting position and gulped air. His nightshirt was stuck to his body. He kicked away the bedclothes with impatience, swung his legs over the edge of the bed, and stared out the window. As he concentrated on the blackened brickwork of the house that was almost touching distance behind their lodgings, his heart rate slowed. Nine months and it was all still so vivid. The night their tenement collapsed. He never drew the curtains at night, hoping it would keep the dreams at bay. At thirty-two years of age, he was terrified of the dark. How his colleagues at Dublin Castle would laugh if they knew.

Da's snore brought his focus back into the room. Lying on his back with his mouth open, his father was in a deep sleep. His silver hair fell across his forehead, hiding the livid scar that ran down the side of his face. The bedclothes showed the outline of his left leg and the gap where the other one should have been. Fergus squeezed his eyes shut and took a lungful of air. The gaps between the nightmares were gradually increasing, but they still left him shaken.

The image of the dead prostitute flashed into his mind. Now that was his reality. Cursing quietly, he checked his watch on the bedside table. Soon he would have to leave for work. But not before he would have to tend to Da's needs for the day. With a new case on his hands, God only knew what time he would get home tonight. He would have to sweet-talk Mrs Walsh, his landlady, again. One of these days, she would call in those favours. It was lucky she had a soft spot for Da.

He washed with haste in the tepid water from the pitcher on the chest of drawers, then pulled out the ancient, speckled mirror he used for shaving from the top drawer. He flinched at his own image. His face was grey beneath the stubble and his eyes red-rimmed. As he looked closer, he noticed the silvery threads amongst the black at his temples. His years were not sitting easy. Fergus took a deep breath, but his hands were still shaking. This was the ultimate test of his self-control he faced every morning. He took up his cutthroat and set to work.

DMP Detective Headquarters, Exchange Court, Dublin Castle

Much to Inspector Ryan's chagrin, his chief inspector was waiting for him in his office, but Fergus didn't utter the expletives which came to mind; instead, he greeted him with civility, congratulating himself on his forbearance.

A portly man with ridiculous mutton chops and an effeminate manner, most of 'G' Division jokingly referred to Malone as Molly, a reference to the famous bearer of that name from the song. Fergus didn't hold him in high esteem either. His pedantic ways and love of the Standing Orders and Regulations Handbook meant they were often at loggerheads. Fergus was a keen advocate of the scientific method, but he also placed reliance on his own instinct and that of his men.

After some rudimentary questions about the murder in The Monto the night before, Malone threw Fergus off-guard when he went off on a tangent. 'No need to sit down,' he said as Fergus went to do so. 'Come with me, Ryan. That damned English investigator is here about that other matter. I've given him an office upstairs for the duration of his stay. Seeing as it was your nark that caused all this... furore, you had better give him the details and any help he requires.'

'Sir, with respect, this murder case—'

'Can wait, Ryan,' Malone thundered. 'This is far more important than some silly chit's death. I have DeWinter and the lord lieutenant breathing down my bloody neck.'

Not trusting himself to reply, Fergus nodded and followed his superior to a room on the third floor, in which a tall, well-dressed and distinguished-looking gentleman awaited them.

Malone introduced Phineas Stone, who greeted him cheerily.

'I'll leave you gentlemen to get acquainted. Inspector Ryan is *wholly* at your disposal, Mr Stone,' Malone said with a significant glare at Fergus as he edged towards the door. 'I'll bid you good day.'

'Thank you, Chief Inspector,' Phineas Stone said.

Never mind that I have a murderer to catch, Ryan thought as he watched his superior leave.

Something of his feelings must have shown, for Phineas Stone stepped forward with a knowing smile. 'I won't detain you long, Inspector, for I suspect you are a busy man.'

This left Fergus feeling churlish. 'I am, sir; however, I am happy to help if I can.'

'Excellent,' Phineas Stone said. 'Won't you take a seat? I only have a few questions. As you are aware, I have been engaged by... well, that isn't really relevant. This threat to steal the emblems of the Order of St Patrick—is it a serious one?'

'To be honest, sir, I think it is unfounded gossip,' Fergus said. 'I cannot believe that anyone would contemplate a robbery here in the castle grounds, not with several regiments and us DMP stationed within the confines.'

'And the source?' Mr Stone enquired.

'A nark. One of mine, as it happens. She's usually reliable; however, in this instance I'm not sure.'

'A female informer, Inspector. I'm impressed. I assume you have a network across the city?' Mr Stone asked.

'I do. I couldn't do my job without 'em.'

'And in this instance, you have doubts about the information she gave you?'

'Yes, because the source... where she claims to have heard this threat, was in her father's public house.'

'Which would get her father into trouble,' Stone said, folding his arms.

'Yes, exactly. Her father, Ignatius Byrne, is no saint, and has something of a reputation. He is involved in moneylending, charging exorbitant rates, and possibly the smuggling of alcohol from the continent. We have yet to catch him in the act, unfortunately. His public house, or I should say, one of his pubs, was a known Fenian meeting place in the past. We have tried to infiltrate The Sleepy Druid on several occasions, but they can smell a police constable within minutes. Also, strapping lads over six feet tend to stand out.' Mr Stone chuckled as Fergus continued, 'Frankly, I don't think this is a credible threat. Unfortunately, Chief Inspector Malone was panicked by it and went straight to Sir Valentine, and there was complete pandemonium after that.'

'Why do you suppose that is, Inspector? Did your superior already have concerns?'

Fergus didn't know this man but felt he had a right to know the truth if he wished to tighten security. 'Perhaps... But you didn't hear this from me.'

Mr Stone nodded, rapt with attention.

'Sir Valentine isn't as security conscious as he should be,' Fergus said.

'Could you be more specific, Inspector?' Stone asked.

'There have been several incidents involving the jewels.' Fergus stalled. This was a gamble that might backfire, but as the incidents in question had led to Sir Valentine being dubbed 'Butter Fingers', making DeWinter a laughingstock in DMP circles, he felt Mr Stone ought to know the details.

'Sir Valentine likes to entertain here at the castle. He enjoys showing his guests the jewels. Even lets them try them on, I've been told.' Mr Stone's brows rose. Fergus couldn't blame him for being horrified, but DeWinter was a buffoon. 'On one occasion, Sir Valentine was the worse for wear and fell asleep, leaving the safe open. A guest removed the regalia, then posted it back to Sir Valentine some days later. There was uproar in the interim. Sir Valentine almost lost his position over that particular prank.'

Mr Stone whistled silently. 'Hmm, it sounds as if I have my work cut out for me. A diplomatic nightmare, too. It would not be appropriate for me to reprimand the man.'

'But perhaps someone should,' Fergus said. 'I'm not in a position to do so,' he continued, 'not if I wish to keep my job, but you, as an outsider with the backing of... whoever... may do so with impunity.'

'I understand, Inspector; however, my focus is to advise on security. Any Fenian threat is more your department. Perhaps if you have a spare minute or two, you might speak to your informer again. Any update on that situation would be something I could use to my advantage if I need to *persuade* any of the parties involved to implement my recommendations in due course.'

'Understood.' Fergus chuckled. 'I'll keep you informed.'

'Thank you, Inspector.'

Fergus regarded him steadily. 'You know, your name is familiar, Mr Stone. You wouldn't be the man who solved that art theft case a few years ago? What was his name? Ah, yes, Hardwicke, wasn't it? Menzies Hardwicke.'

Mr Stone bowed. 'Indeed. And I'm guilty as charged.'

'I say, that was a fascinating case. You almost died, did you not?'

'But for the actions of my good lady wife and my valet, I would be at the bottom of the North Sea. My wife is highly intelligent, headstrong and intrepid, Inspector. If she had been a man, she would have made an excellent detective,' Mr Stone said, his voice full of pride. 'Why don't you come to dinner this evening and see for yourself? It will give us an opportunity to discuss our task in a more congenial atmosphere, too.'

'Won't your wife mind?' Fergus asked, thinking Mrs Stone sounded fairly terrifying.

Mr Stone's lips twitched with amusement. 'Not at all, Inspector, Lucy would love to meet you.'

An hour later, Fergus was again at his desk reading through the statements from Mecklenburgh Street.

Detective Sergeant Hughes hailed him from the doorway. 'Morning, sir. You won't believe it. We have found Myles Carver,' he said with a grin.

'Good heavens, that was quick work, Sergeant,' Fergus said, sitting back in his chair. 'Well done.'

'Thank you, sir, but I can't take the credit. Luckily, Constable Rafferty from Store Street recognised the name and wired us. He cautioned him only last month.'

'Did he indeed? So, who is this Carver fellow?'

Hughes handed him a sheet of paper. 'A banker well-known in financial circles. Chairman of the Royal Ireland Bank, no less. He was caught in a raid on Maggie Mitchell's place. Not *in flagrante delicto* as such but drinking on the premises and she not having a licence, he was facing a charge. Was keen to cooperate and hush it all up. Paid a fine and promised to be a good boy from now on.'

'But he could not stay away from The Monto, eh? Our quarry must have a propensity for seeking pleasure in the kip-houses,' Fergus remarked, looking down the sheet. 'He *has* been a naughty boy.' He looked up at Hughes. 'What say you to a morning call on the gentleman?'

Hughes twizzled his moustache. 'I think I'd enjoy that very much, sir. I'll call us a cab.'

SEVEN

Merrion Square

Merrion Square, the bastion of upper-class respectability, was almost deserted as their cab drew up outside Carver's townhouse. The red-brick facades of the Georgian buildings looked out upon a private square in which a solitary gardener was tending the paths, his sweeping brush moving back and forth with an easy rhythm. A coal merchant's cart went by, the carter's clothes as black as his produce. Fergus knew him only too well; his heart was fairly black, too.

They climbed the granite steps to the door, and Fergus tugged the iron ring. They heard the echo of the bell through the house from where they stood. Eventually, a maid with a beleaguered expression and a high colour answered the door. Fergus introduced himself and Sergeant Hughes and asked to see the master of the house.

'Please wait in here,' the maid said, opening the door to a bookshelf-lined room off the hallway, 'I'll see if Mr Carver is available.'

Fergus and Hughes exchanged looks. 'Should I go around the back in case he makes a run for it?' Hughes whispered as the door shut.

Fergus grinned. 'I don't think that will be necessary, Sergeant. This isn't a farce at the Theatre Royal.'

Hughes smirked and shrugged.

Fergus surveyed the room. It was a typical library cum study, and he would lay good money down that the owner hadn't read ninety-nine per cent of the pristine books with their perfect spines that graced the shelves. All for show, he reckoned, and strolled over to the mahogany desk that stood close to the window. A newspaper, folded and ironed, was the only item of note. Even the blotter was clean. He gazed out the window into the square. For all its beauty, mere feet away lay some of the worst tenements of the city. On a warm day you could smell them, but they were as much a part of what made his beloved Dublin as the fancy squares of Pembroke ward.

The door swung open, and a tall, thin man walked into the room. Soberly dressed, he was middle-aged with grey hair and a full beard. He was in appearance a gentleman, judging by his clothes and how he held himself. Pity he doesn't act like one, Fergus thought. He didn't look particularly vicious, but Fergus knew killers came in many guises.

'I'm Myles Carver,' the man said, his voice a surprisingly rich baritone for so slight a man. 'What can I do for you?'

Fergus stepped forward and presented his credentials. 'I'm Detective Inspector Ryan and this is Detective Sergeant Hughes of 'G' Division.' He watched for Carver's reaction.

Carver gave a helpless gesture with upturned hands. 'I assume you are here on some serious matter, but I'm at a loss as to how I can be of assistance.' Then he froze and took a sharp breath. 'Has something occurred at the bank? I can leave straight away if that is the case. My keys are in the desk.'

'No, sir. We are here because of an incident at 29 Mecklenburgh Street last night.'

Carver's brow puckered. 'That is on the north side of the city, is it not? I understand it is a less than salubrious area. Naturally, I don't have any business there.' Carver gave a nervous little laugh.

'That is odd, sir, as we have witnesses who say that you were present at that address last night, around seven o'clock,' Fergus said.

'Well, they must be mistaken, Inspector. I was at home all evening.'

Fergus caught a glance from Hughes, which echoed his own thoughts. 'Can anyone corroborate that, sir?' he asked.

'Indeed, yes,' Carver said. 'My family and servants can vouch for me.'

'Then we will have to take statements from everyone in the house, sir. I assume you have no objection?'

Carver shrugged. 'Why should I object? This is some kind of scurrilous nonsense, Inspector, and the sooner it is cleared up the better. I can assure you that I have not been involved in any crime. Would you care to tell me what happened at this address?'

'It is a brothel in The Monto, and a young prostitute was bludgeoned to death in her room. We believe the perpetrator was one of her clients,' Fergus said.

Carver's eyebrows rose. 'Good Lord, how terrible, but it doesn't surprise me. The city should raze these dens of iniquity to the ground. I hope you catch whoever did it.'

'I fully intend to, sir,' Fergus answered, and Carver's lips twitched. Fergus's mind raced. Celine had been so sure of the identity of the killer. Either Carver was a very nonchalant individual, or he was as innocent as he claimed.

'Shall I have the maid fetch my daughter-in-law? She dined with me last night and can verify what I have said. Then you can be on your way, Inspector.'

'That would be most helpful, sir,' Fergus said. 'Perhaps we could conduct our interviews in this room?'

Carver nodded, then walked to the fireplace to press the bell. The maid appeared in the doorway within seconds. Fergus suspected she had eavesdropped at the door.

'Ask Mrs Carver to join us, please,' Carver said. The maid frowned. 'My daughter-in-law, woman, not my wife,' he snapped.

The maid bobbed her head and quit the room. Carver turned to him. 'Useless woman,' he said. 'I should explain... my dear wife is bedridden, Inspector.'

Fergus's dislike was increasing: the way a man treated his servants was a good indication of his character.

'I'm sorry to hear that, sir. Did she see or speak to you last night, by any chance?'

Carver sat down behind his desk with a proprietary air, running his hand along the smooth surface. 'I would prefer that she wasn't disturbed, besides the fact that it is unnecessary. However, yes, I went to her room to say goodnight, but she was sleeping. She takes laudanum. She is in considerable pain, you understand. Unfortunately, she is often confused.'

That is convenient, Fergus thought. 'It won't be necessary to disturb her if the other members of the household can vouch for you,' he said.

'I find all this most inconvenient, Inspector, and a waste of my time... and yours. Is a gentleman's word not enough?'

Hughes shuffled his feet and coughed.

'The law is the same for everyone, sir,' Fergus said, flicking a quelling glance at Hughes.

Carver snorted and drummed his fingers on the desk. Fergus felt uneasy. This was all too pat—perhaps rehearsed? The silence stretched; the tension grew. A tram passed the window, full of workers on their way into the city centre, and yet, it was the image of that unfortunate dead girl that filled Fergus's mind.

EIGHT

The library door clicked open, and a young woman glided into the room. Simply dressed hair offset her delicate features and slender figure, and her only jewellery was a gold wedding band. The deep lavender of her dress proclaimed her half-mourning state. He reckoned she was no more than five and twenty, and something about her strawberry-blonde hair and pale skin reminded him of Millais's painting of Ophelia which he had seen in a book. An air of melancholy clung to her. He had a powerful urge to see her smile. Surely it would transform her pretty face into a beautiful one?

Carver stood and made the introductions. Her cool green eyes met Fergus's with a nervous look.

'The inspector wishes to ask you some questions, Olivia, my dear,' Carver said to her as she sat down. She intertwined her fingers, her knuckles showing white. 'Though perhaps you should take my statement first, Inspector?'

'As Mrs Carver is here, sir, I'd like to start with her,' Fergus said.

'Very well,' Carver said, sitting back down.

'I wish to speak to Mrs Carver alone, sir,' Fergus said.

Carver looked like he wanted to object. 'If you must,' he said, giving his daughter-in-law a hard look. 'Please remember that you are interviewing a lady. I strongly suggest that you refrain from mentioning anything of an *unsavoury* nature.'

Mrs Carver appeared to find the pattern of the carpet of considerable interest. She did not raise her eyes or react. In fact, she was holding herself rigidly. Was she just uncomfortable or afraid? Fergus's curiosity was piqued: something was bothering her.

'I'm sure we won't be long,' Fergus said. Hughes made a great show of taking out his notebook.

Carver cast the sergeant a filthy look. 'Good. I must leave soon for the bank. Can't dillydally over this foolishness, you know. I have important meetings this morning.'

'It would be no trouble to arrange for you to come to Dublin Castle to take your statement... if you prefer?' Fergus asked, full sure that was the last thing Carver would want. Carver scowled and pulled at his beard, but whatever he was going to say, he thought better of it.

'That won't be necessary, thank you,' he snapped. With a grunt and a severe glance, this time aimed at his daughter-in-law's bowed head, he quit the room.

Olivia Carver raised her chin. The tension in her shoulders appeared to ease somewhat, but her expression was wary. Fergus placed a chair so that they were opposite each other. Upon sitting down, he caught the subtle scent of roses. Such a sharp contrast to the cheap perfume in the brothel the night before.

'Thank you for taking the time to talk to us, Mrs Carver. My sergeant will take notes and draw up a statement, which we will need you to sign.'

'I understand,' she said. A ghost of a smile flickered across her face, and he regretted what he would put her through. He had a hunch she had enough troubles in her life living in Carver's household.

'We are investigating a serious crime and need to confirm the whereabouts of certain individuals,' Fergus said.

'And my father-in-law is one of them?' she asked, her voice gentle.

'Yes.'

'Why do you believe he is involved?'

'A witness has claimed he was present at the scene,' he said.

Her eyes widened. 'And the crime?'

'Murder, Mrs Carver.'

For a few moments she sat in silence. 'I see. Who was the victim?' she asked, her brows drawing together.

'A young girl newly arrived in Dublin.'

'How dreadful, Inspector. Her family must be distraught. What do you need to ask?' Her voice was unsteady, but he was relieved that his first impression was incorrect. She was no shrinking violet, only cautious.

'Can you confirm your name and address and your relationship to Mr Carver?'

'I am Olivia Carver, widow of James Carver. I have lived in this house for about five years.'

'Mr Carver's son?' Fergus asked.

'Yes, James died almost two years ago.'

'I am sorry for your loss, Mrs Carver,' he said. She acknowledged this with a slight dip of her chin but regarded him with a steady gaze. If she were still grieving, she was hiding it well. 'Can you tell me who else resides here?' he asked.

'There are only the three of us and the servants: my lady's maid, a cook and a parlour maid. A gardener comes once a month. Mr Carver's valet left some weeks ago.'

'Why did he leave?'

'Like all the others, I imagine he found his job somewhat difficult,' she said with pinched lips.

He nodded, surprised at the candid comment. Carver appeared to be a regular charmer, and he wondered why the young woman stayed, but perhaps she had no choice.

'And who was present yesterday evening from five o'clock onwards?' he asked.

She hesitated for a fraction of a second. 'The servants, naturally, and I was with Edith—Mrs Carver—most of the afternoon and early evening. She is unwell, and I help to nurse her.'

'What time did Mr Carver arrive home?' he asked.

'About six, but I did not see him until half past seven when dinner was served.'

'So how can you be certain that he came in at that time?'

She faltered, and her hand went to her throat, where her fingers fiddled with the lace on her collar. 'I heard him come into the house.'

'Are you sure it was Mr Carver?'

'Yes. I heard him speak to Sally as she let him in. I was upstairs on the landing, on my way to my room.'

'Did he visit his wife's room?'

'No,' she said. Her hands clenched. 'He enquired about her at dinner. He may have visited her room before going to bed, but he does not usually do so in case she is resting.'

'So, you did not see him before dinner?'

'No.'

'Is there any possibility that you are mistaken as to the time he came home? Could you be confusing last night with a previous evening?'

Again, a split-second of hesitation. 'No, I'm sure.' Her eyes dropped to her lap.

'Can you tell me what he was doing after he arrived, up to the time that dinner was served?'

'I imagine he was in here,' she answered, looking about the room.

'Did he leave the house later in the evening?'

'I don't believe so. I retired to my room after dinner. About twenty past eight,' she said.

'Does Mr Carver normally dine at home?'

'He sometimes dines at his club. The Kildare Street Club. Since James died and Edith became ill, he tends to work longer hours. He...'

'Yes?'

'He doesn't like being near illness.' A hint of derision under-lined her words.

'How would you describe your father-in-law's temperament?'

She looked startled. 'You put me in a very difficult position, Inspector.' She lowered her voice. 'Maybe I shouldn't answer that.'

'I would be grateful if you did,' he said gently.

She gazed out the window. 'He is not an easy man to live with, Inspector, but if you are asking me if he is capable of murder, I would have to say no. Words are generally his weapon of choice.'

Fergus stood. 'Thank you for being so forthright. If you should think of anything you'd like to add to your statement, please contact me,' he said. He held her gaze, hoping to communicate his understanding. She was definitely in a compromised position. He would not push her now.

'Thank you, Inspector. If that is all, I'd like to get back to Mrs Carver.'

She rose and extended her hand, an apologetic hint in her eyes.

'Well, I'll be damned!' exclaimed Hughes when the door closed behind her.

'That is highly likely, Hughes,' Fergus muttered under his breath.

'What now, sir? If she maintains this stance, we are without a suspect.'

'Sergeant, I have no doubt Carver has put her under pressure to provide that alibi. I will try my hand at him while you go down to the kitchens and find out from the servants what is really going on in this damned house.'

An hour and a half later, Fergus and Hughes hailed a cab to return to Dublin Castle. In frustration, Fergus banged his fist against the armrest and exhaled as he settled back in his seat. 'What a damned waste of our time.'

'Agreed, sir, but we had to try,' his sergeant said, flicking through his notes.

'They were all lying. Every single one of them. What is he holding over them?'

'That is indeed an excellent question, sir. I would imagine in the case of the servants the threat of dismissal without a reference. Few will risk that at the present time.'

'True. And the young Mrs Carver?'

Hughes pursed his lips and looked up. 'Financial, I'd guess. Why else would she be living there?'

'I suspect you're correct,' Fergus said. 'Somehow, I will have to get her alone to learn the truth.'

'That won't be easy, sir. Carver, if he's our man, will ensure she doesn't stray into our clutches.'

'Hmm, we'll see about that, Sergeant.' Fergus drummed his fingers on his thigh. 'In the meantime, we need to find out who Peggy was. Find her family.'

The sergeant grunted his agreement. 'None of Burton's girls know.'

'So they claim, but you and I know the hold Burton has over them.' He glanced out the window. 'Let's hope our luck changes and someone talks.'

NINE

The small family group had spent the morning at the Botanical Gardens in Glasnevin and were returning home. Lucy gazed across the carriage at her son Harry, or as he was lovingly referred to by most of the family, Bash. He was explaining to Ellie why trees lose their leaves in autumn. Ellie rolled her eyes with impatience and told him in no uncertain terms that she had been listening to the man, too, and didn't need him prosing on. It was often the way with the twins, both exhibiting robust personalities and strong competitive streaks.

Any hope that the outing would tire Bash and Ellie out had been in vain. If anything, they had gained energy. Lucy checked a smile, trying to catch Mary's eye, but her maid was looking down at her lap and Lucy's heart sank. She'd hoped the little outing might distract Mary, even for an hour or two, but the confirmation of her cousins' arrival in Dublin, and that they had intended to go to Mary's mother's house but never arrived, was a huge blow. Lucy could well imagine the fears rattling around in the young maid's head.

It hadn't been possible to discuss the case with Phineas the previous evening as Phin had been a guest at DeWinter's club. Phineas had promised at breakfast that he would be home tonight and that they might discuss it then.

Lucy hated to confess, but she was stumped and had lain awake half the previous night pondering their options. Besides going to the police and reporting the disappearance, there didn't seem to be much else they could do. It was so exasperating. How would they find the girls in such a large city, a city Lucy didn't know, and Mary hadn't lived in for at least ten years?

When they reached Merrion Square, the carriage stopped at No. 81, and before Jenny the nursery maid could catch hold of him, Bash had swung the door open and jumped down onto the pavement. He took off at a run. Ellie, never one to be outdone, followed suit.

The two maids sprang down, and Lucy only had one foot on the pavement when she heard someone exclaim in fright. To Lucy's horror, she turned to see that Bash had collided with a young woman approaching them, with the result that she had dropped her parcels on the ground.

'I'm most dreadfully sorry,' Lucy exclaimed, hurrying up to the young lady. 'Bash, you must apologise at once.'

'Really,' the young lady said, 'I'm fine. More of a fright than anything else. No harm done.'

Lucy pressed Bash's shoulder and walked him closer to the lady. 'What do you say, young man?'

'I'm... I'm very sorry, miss,' he squeaked, looking up at the woman under his lashes. 'But it was very important that I ring the bell before my sister.'

The young woman's lips twitched as she looked down at him. 'I understand, young man. Nothing could be more important than that. And I accept your very gracious apology.'

Lucy was relieved that the woman was taking it so well. Bash blushed scarlet, then pulled out of Lucy's grasp and sprinted off to join Ellie and the maids at the front door.

'Truly—' Lucy said as she helped to pick up the parcels from the pavement.

'No, no. High spirits and no harm done. I see you are the new tenants in No. 81,' the lady said, before holding out her hand. 'My name is Olivia Carver, and I live at No. 83. I thought I heard children's laughter the other day in the back garden. It's lovely to have youngsters about the place.'

'Lucy Stone, how do you do?' Lucy said, returning the handshake. 'Yes, we're only here a few days and already creating chaos. Actually, you're the first of our neighbours that I've met.'

'Are you here for the summer, Mrs Stone?'

'We're not entirely sure at present. My husband's work will dictate how long we stay.' Lucy smiled. 'I don't suppose you'd like to take tea with me this afternoon, if nothing else as a way for me to apologise for Bash assaulting you like that.'

Olivia's eyes widened. 'Why, that would be lovely. I'd enjoy the company. My mother-in-law, unfortunately, is ill and bedridden. She's not able for much in the way of conversation.'

'I am saddened to hear that, but please do join me if you can. Say three o'clock? And I guarantee the children will be corralled so as not to cause you bodily harm.' Lucy glanced at the twins, who were hanging onto the railing at the front steps, watching and listening. Ellie gave Bash a dig in the ribs with her elbow. 'Mama means you.'

Lucy resisted rolling her eyes, gave Olivia a nod and hurried to get the children inside before they disgraced her any further.

At precisely three o'clock, the door to Lucy's drawing room opened, and George stepped in. 'Mrs James Carver to see you, ma'am.'

Lucy rose to greet Olivia. 'I'm delighted you could be spared. You are very welcome.' Then she turned to George. 'Tea, please, George.'

He nodded and withdrew.

The ladies shook hands, and Lucy waved Olivia to the sofa, but not before noting the dark smudges under the young woman's eyes. 'I'm delighted you didn't change your mind. I'm sure I wouldn't blame you,' Lucy said. 'Again, I must apologise for earlier. The twins tend to get overexcited on outings, I'm afraid.'

'Please don't apologise,' Olivia said. 'There was no harm done and nothing broken. In fact, I'm delighted to have made your acquaintance. My life here since my husband's death has been so quiet.' With a sad smile she continued, 'Between my state of mourning and my mother-in-law's state of health, I don't have a social life as such.'

'Let me guess,' Lucy said. 'The ladies of your acquaintance, with whom you and your husband used to dine, suddenly stopped acknowledging you? It's always the way. People often view young widows with suspicion, particularly pretty ones like you. I experienced much the same when my first husband died. And I sympathise with you about your husband, though I had inferred from your half-mourning that you had lost someone close.'

'Thank you. Yes, James passed two years ago.'

'And your mother-in-law lives with you?' Lucy asked.

'No, the other way around. I live with my husband's parents due to... well, necessity, to be honest.'

'Ah. I fully understand,' Lucy said. 'Upon the sudden death of my first husband, I was left in very straitened circumstances. You're lucky, though. My parents-in-law wanted nothing to do with me.' A flash of sorrow passed over Olivia's features, and Lucy guessed she had hit a nerve. Much as her curiosity flared, she could not probe on such a brief acquaintance.

At that moment, Mary broke the strained silence, entering with the tea tray.

'Thanks, Mary. I'll manage,' Lucy said, waving her hand towards a side table. Mary deposited the tray, gave a little curtsy and left. Lucy poured the tea and handed Olivia a cup. 'Milk and sugar, Mrs Carver?'

'Call me Olivia, please. Just milk, thank you,' she said.

Lucy flashed her a smile. 'And you must call me Lucy, I insist. This is lovely. To have a lady neighbour to take tea with and hear all the latest gossip is such a relief. My husband, Phineas, is out most of the day, and in the evenings, he is often invited out to dine with...' She waved her hand and smiled. 'Would it shock you if I said with dead bores? The few interactions I have had with them left me cold. The Dublin Castle set are all horse and hunting mad.'

'And you are not?'

'Definitely not. So, I've been making excuses and dear Phin has braved them alone. Mind you, I don't see much of him during the day either. He is engrossed in his work, which would be fine if I were involved...' Olivia raised a brow. 'I should explain. My husband is an investigator and, in the past, before the children came along, I used to help him.'

'How wonderful,' Olivia said. 'And how modern.'

Lucy chuckled. 'He had little choice in the matter. In fact, it was during one of his cases that we first met.'

'So romantic, too,' her guest said.

'We had our moments. Oh, enough about us. You must tell me all about our neighbours, for I am always curious. It's my besetting sin, so Phineas says.'

'I'm afraid I only know some of them by sight. As my mother-in-law is so ill, I daren't leave her alone for long. At best, I have a walk around the park to get some fresh air. The sickroom can be so terribly stuffy.'

'I understand. How good you are,' Lucy exclaimed. 'Do the doctors not hold out any hope for her recovery?'

Olivia took a sip of tea, her eyes glistening with unshed tears. 'It is only a question of time.'

'That is so sad, my dear. And your father-in-law must be devastated,' Lucy said. To her surprise, a flash of revulsion crossed Olivia's features, so fast Lucy almost missed it. She felt a powerful pull of friendship towards this demure young woman and hoped that with time, they would become better acquainted. Then perhaps Olivia might share her worries. Was her father-in-law a difficult man, perhaps?

'He... that is, Mr Carver, is a very busy man. I believe it is how he copes with what life has thrown at him. He took James's death very hard and now Edith is so ill...'

'Was your husband their only child?' Lucy asked.

Olivia nodded. 'Only living child, yes. There was a little girl, but she died aged two of diphtheria, I understand. Edith sometimes calls for her when her fever is high.' Olivia shuddered. 'I'm sorry. I'm sure you have no wish to hear about any of this.'

'On the contrary, if it helps you in any way...'

Lucy hoped Olivia would feel able to open up to her. She sensed the young woman was under some strain, whether because of her mother-in-law's imminent death or for some other reason. To her utter astonishment, however, Olivia's lips trembled as she searched for a handkerchief. Lucy moved closer to her and put an arm around her shoulder. 'My dear, please don't cry. Can I offer any assistance? Are you in trouble of some kind?'

But Olivia buried her face in the handkerchief, her shoulders heaving. 'I'm... so so-rry,' she mumbled. 'I must go.'

Olivia rose and rushed for the door, leaving Lucy flabbergasted. What on earth had she said to cause such a reaction?

TEN

'Well, my dear, it sounds to me like you had a somewhat eventful day,' Phineas said as he raised his chin so that George could fix his bowtie in place.

Lucy glanced over as she secured her pearl earrings. 'Yes, indeed. That poor woman. There she was walking along, minding her own business when Bash ran straight into her, the little scamp. He is so careless, Phin, never looks where he is charging off to. However, Mrs Carver was very good about it, though I'm sure she must have thought him terribly wild and me a dreadful mother.'

'He has a lot of... energy,' Phin said with a wink at George, who disappeared into the dressing room with a chuckle. 'I'll have a word with him in the morning about it, though invariably it is Ellie who eggs him on.'

'Certainly. She enjoys goading him into mischief.' Lucy laughed. 'They are miniature versions of us, I fear, my love.'

'You may be right. So, then you invited the young lady to tea.' Phin sat down on the edge of the bed.

'Yes, partly because I felt guilty and partly because I thought it would be pleasant to have some female company... over five years of age.' Phin grinned as she continued. 'But there was something about her that caught my attention even in those brief moments on the pavement. A certain sadness in her demeanour. I was delighted when she accepted, but then, I upset her with something I said, and she dissolved into tears, and fled. She must be in an unfortunate position at home. The way she spoke about her parents-in-law, it was clear it's not a happy house... not that she said anything she ought not to, as I'm a stranger, but it was more her tone and expression. Edith Carver is dying, and the task of nursing her appears to be solely hers.'

'I'm sure she realises you didn't deliberately upset her. You could not have known her circumstances, Lucy.'

At that moment, George reappeared. 'Will that be all, sir?'

'Yes, indeed. Thank you,' Phin said. 'Oh, and George?'

'Yes, sir.' George turned at the door.

'We will have an extra person for dinner. Detective Inspector Ryan of the DMP will join us.'

'Very good, sir. I'll inform cook.' George exited, his usual unflappable self.

'You don't mind my inviting him, Lucy, do you? I've rather taken to the chap. He is my liaison with the DMP regarding the Fenian threat. Mind you, I do not intend to get involved in that aspect of things.'

'Why not?'

'Too dangerous, my dear, with you and the children here. I've no wish to make us a target for their mischief. So, I've clarified that aspect of this security scare is his business, and he was happy enough about that. He's a busy chap, from what I overheard at the castle. He has a nasty murder case to solve, and yet his superior has foisted me onto him. Despite that, he was friendly and, more importantly, forthcoming about what's really been going on. I think you will like him.'

Lucy motioned for Phin to close the clasp on her necklace. 'I'm sure I shall. I wonder if he would help me with Mary's problem.

Though if what you say is true, he may not have the time. Should I ask him?'

Phin grunted as he tried to close the delicate clasp. 'Why are these always so fiddly? Yes, I do. In fact, I intended to suggest the very thing. He will advise you and indeed may set an investigation in train. There, that should do it.' He bent and kissed her neck. 'We can bring it up over coffee.'

'But even if the police look into the girls' disappearance, I should like to investigate myself. Mary has placed her faith in me, and I don't want to let her down. She has been so loyal all these years, despite what I... we have put her through,' she said, waiting to see his reaction.

'I completely agree, and I'm sure if we all put our minds to it, we may discover where those two young girls have gone. Let's see what Inspector Ryan has to say, my dear. Perhaps you should warn Mary to stand by. It's likely he will want to speak to her. Now, if you're ready, let's await our guest in the drawing room.'

George announced the detective inspector a short while after, and Phin rose to greet him. The inspector stepped forward to shake Phin's hand. 'Thank you, sir, for the invitation.'

'Not at all, Fergus, you're very welcome. And this is Lucy, my wife,' Phin said.

Lucy proffered her hand and smiled. 'Good evening, Inspector.'

His eyes were full of humour as he returned her handshake. 'It's a pleasure to meet you, Mrs Stone, and thank you for including me this evening. I'm sure it's not every evening you entertain the police at your dinner table.'

Lucy chuckled. 'You'd be surprised, Inspector. Some of our best friends are police officers.'

She liked the way his eyes crinkled when he smiled, and reckoned he was only in his early thirties, despite the silver threads at his temples.

'Sit, man,' Phin said, handing him a drink. 'You look as though you would benefit from this.'

Ryan sat down beside Lucy. 'Yes, thank you. It's been a long day.'

'A trying case?' Lucy enquired.

'A murder, yes. Very tragic. It happened yesterday evening,' Ryan said.

'I say, don't give Lucy any details or she'll be off to solve it for you,' Phin piped up with a grin.

Lucy made a face at him just as Ryan cast her a quizzical look. 'Is that so?'

'Yes, and she's good, too,' Phin added.

Lucy threw Phin a dirty look before turning to the inspector. 'It's true that I've helped Phineas on a few of his cases.'

'And she's dying to come out of retirement,' Phin said, sitting down.

'Please ignore him, Inspector,' Lucy spluttered. 'He likes nothing better than to tease me.'

'But I'm intrigued,' Ryan said. 'If you were successful, why did you give it up?'

'Marriage and motherhood. Twins.'

'And how old are they now?' he asked with a warm smile.

'Five. Bash and Ellie.'

'Bash? That's an unusual name,' he said.

'Oh, he was baptised Harold, but he's a boisterous little boy, and somehow Bash seemed... appropriate and has stuck. Why, only today he ran straight into a young lady on the street, one of our neighbours. Almost knocked her over. I was mortified.'

'A neighbour?'

'Yes, poor Mrs Carver. I'm sure she was horrified by his wildness.'

'Not Olivia Carver?' Ryan asked, setting down his drink on a side table, his expression eager. 'Are you acquainted with her?'

'No, not really. It was our first meeting and not one she is likely to forget.'

Ryan leaned forward. 'I wonder, Mrs Stone. Can you give me any insights? What kind of person is she?'

Lucy was taken aback. 'I don't understand why you're asking me. Do you know her?'

'In a sense. I only met her this morning, too. She provided an alibi for my chief murder suspect which has thrown my investigation into disarray.'

Lucy narrowed her eyes, ignoring the warning glance from Phin. 'Your murder suspect lives two doors away? Now that is intriguing.' But Ryan quirked his mouth, and she guessed he was regretting telling her as much. Lucy homed in, her pulse quickening. 'For some reason you doubt her testimony, is that the issue? I am not acquainted with her at all, but I sense she's an unhappy young woman.'

The inspector glanced at Phin who shrugged. 'How sharp you are, Mrs Stone. Yes, I'm sure she was lying to me, but I don't know why,' Ryan said, taking up his glass once more, his face set. 'I hoped that if you were acquainted with her, you might give me some insight into her circumstances and why she would protect him.'

Lucy smiled. Fate was working in her favour for she knew just how to help him. 'I would love to help you. As yet, I don't know her well, Inspector, but I liked her and intend to cultivate the friendship which may help you...' He nodded in understanding. This was perfect.

There was a deal to be done.

Conversation over dinner centred around the supposed threat to rob the crown jewels. Ryan looked surprised when Phin brought up the subject, but Phin had stated that they were free to speak of it in front of Lucy. She beamed back her thanks to Phin and entered the discussion as much as her scant knowledge would allow. She was biding her time, however, and intended to corner the inspector when they retired to the drawing room for coffee.

Lucy withdrew to leave the men with the port and checked on

the children. Both were sound asleep, and Jenny, the nursery maid, looked as if she were fit to collapse into bed herself. After bidding her to do just that, Lucy left the nursery and went back to the drawing room to await the others.

Shortly after, George and Mary entered with the coffee and tea things. Despite being chiefly a lady's maid, Mary often took on multiple roles in the household. In the early days, it had been because of Lucy's impoverished state, but now, when they travelled, it was easier to have just the essential staff with them and to hire additional servants only if they needed them, such as the cook they had employed for their stay in Dublin.

Lucy caught Mary's eye and beckoned her over.

'Yes, ma'am?'

'There is a DMP inspector here for dinner this evening. I'm going to ask him what to do about your missing cousins. It's possible he will wish to speak to you, so stay close by.'

Mary cast her a sad smile. 'I will, ma'am. Thank you.' Shoulders slumped, she turned and left the room. George watched the maid leave, looking concerned.

Then he cleared his throat. 'Mary has told me about her family trouble. Ma'am, if there is anything *I* can do to help in the matter, you have only to say.'

'Thank you, George. I know Mary would appreciate any help you can offer. My plan is to discuss it with the inspector, and I'll let you know if you are needed,' she said, just as voices were heard out in the hall. 'You may go for now. I will hand out the coffee, George. Thank you.'

'Very good, ma'am,' he said, holding the door open for the gentlemen to enter.

Once Lucy had served everyone their coffee, she made a beeline for the vacant seat beside Ryan.

'Thank you for dinner, Mrs Stone—'

'Lucy, please. We don't stand on ceremony at home,' she said.

He smiled, and Lucy thought how handsome he looked as the years dropped away.

'Thank you, and you must call me Inspector,' he quipped, his eyes lighting up with mischief.

Lucy laughed. 'I think we will get along famously, *Inspector*.' He acknowledged this with a grin and a nod.

'And how do you like Dublin so far?' he asked.

'Very well. It's wonderful that everywhere is within walking distance. A pleasant change from London. We only arrived a week ago, so there is plenty more for us to explore. If you have any suggestions, please let us know. In particular, if there is anywhere the children might enjoy.'

'I would be happy to, Lucy.'

They drank their coffee and chatted about various beauty spots close to Dublin, and then the politics of the day. Ryan's intelligence and confidence impressed Lucy. Despite how different their circumstances were, there was no awkwardness. He was articulate and came across as compassionate, with liberal views, much like their own, on many of the topics they touched on. During the course of the evening, she grew confident that he would help with Mary's problem.

'I was wondering if I might ask a favour, Fergus? Well, I suppose it is more in the line of advice I require.'

'Certainly, if it is within my power,' he said.

'An unfortunate situation has arisen. My lady's maid, Mary, is from Dublin, and she visited her mother recently. However, the family is in turmoil. Her young cousins travelled to Dublin recently, only to disappear. This isn't typical behaviour, so everyone, including Mary, is anxious to find them. Mary and I visited Westland Row Station yesterday to see if anyone would remember the girls' arrival. Luckily, a young woman on the cigar stall recognised the girls from the photograph we had with us. She told us she had directed them to Irishtown, which is where Mary's mother lives.'

'But they never appeared there?'

'Correct.'

'Mrs—sorry, Lucy—there is, unfortunately, a seedy side to

Dublin. Young women arriving from the country are often too naïve to realise the danger they are in. They are easy prey.'

'Yes. The stationmaster explained all about that to us. But what should we do to find them? I'm unsure of where to begin.'

'You say you have a picture of the girls?'

'Yes, indeed.'

'Perhaps I might borrow it. I can ensure it is circulated throughout the different districts and in particular the... ah, notorious locales. You never know, we might be lucky and find them if they haven't been in the city too long.'

'Thank you. That's reassuring,' Lucy said before she rose and tugged the bell at the side of the fireplace. Seconds later, Mary's head popped around the door. 'Mary, can you fetch that photograph for the Inspector, please?'

Mary stepped into the room, pulling it from her apron pocket. 'I have it here, ma'am,' she said, holding it out to the inspector.

Ryan sat forward and took it. He stared at it for some time, tilting it this way and that. Then he frowned.

'What is it, Fergus?' Phineas asked, standing up and joining Lucy by the fireplace.

Ryan didn't answer the question; instead, he looked across at Mary. 'Miss, could you tell me your cousins' names, please?'

Mary walked towards him, all colour draining from her cheeks. 'Bridget and Peggy O'Reilly, sir. From Wexford town.'

Ryan glanced up at Lucy, his expression turning her stomach.

'What is it?' Lucy asked. 'Please. Something is wrong, I can tell.'

To her astonishment, Ryan stood, and escorted Mary to the sofa, before sitting down beside her. 'I'm sorry, Mary. I regret to say that I saw one of these young girls only last night.' His voice was gentle, but Lucy's stomach twisted. She sensed what was coming and reached out for Phin's hand.

Mary grabbed the inspector's arm. 'Are they well? Where are they, the silly widgeons?'

'I'm very sorry,' he said, his finger tracing a circle around one girl. 'But I believe this girl—Peggy—has been murdered.'

ELEVEN

The unsavoury location was the first thing Lucy observed as her cab drew up at the front door of the Dublin city morgue. A couple of seedy hotels and tenement buildings graced the opposite side of the street, and some individuals who lurked about the place made her uneasy. This feeling increased as she noticed their close surveillance when she stepped onto the path. She clutched her reticule tightly.

The second thing of note was the foul odour. Whether the smell was from the nearby River Liffey or the morgue, Lucy wasn't sure. Perhaps it was a combination of the two. Beside her, Mary stalled as she alighted, putting a handkerchief to her mouth as she threw Lucy an anguished glance. All Lucy could do was shrug.

Lucy regarded the austere façade of the morgue with mixed feelings. Once before she had visited a morgue, and that had resulted in nothing but trouble. So, standing here triggered a flood of memories, as she recalled that fateful day, eight years before, when she had been summoned to Vine Street mortuary in London. On that occasion she had entered blithely, convinced it was all a huge mistake, only for it to be confirmed that her husband, Charlie, was dead. He had lain broken on a marble slab, the wounds that had killed him all too obvious. That had only been the beginning, as an avalanche of revelations about his life poured forth from his grave, driving her close to penury and almost into the clutches of the gang Charlie had fallen in with. It was also the first time she had come face to face with Phineas. It hadn't been an auspicious start, and she could not have imagined how their lives would eventually entangle. Although she gave thanks daily that they had done so.

This morning, however, her intuition told her this was no fool's errand. Mary knew it, too; her red-rimmed eyes and the dark circles beneath were evidence of a night of weeping and little sleep. Lucy only hoped that the sight they were about to behold wasn't too grisly. She gave her maid an encouraging smile and ushered her up the steps.

They followed the arrows to the mortuary room. As they advanced down a narrow corridor, Lucy spotted Inspector Ryan, who awaited them before an open doorway. His countenance the previous evening, as he had examined Mary's photograph, had been enough to convince Lucy that his murder victim and one of Mary's missing cousins were one and the same. And now, at Inspector Ryan's request, Mary was here to help identify the dead girl. A formality, but a devastating one for Mary and her family.

'Ladies,' he greeted them. 'Thanks for coming in. If you would follow me, please.'

Mary shivered, and Lucy squeezed her arm. 'It will be over soon, Mary. Stay strong,' Lucy whispered. 'There is nothing to be afraid of.' Mary's answering look was full of doubt.

The room they entered was unpleasant. Once-white walls with peeling paint, and ugly white tiles on the floor, were the backdrop to a gruesome sight. Five slabs, three of which were occupied, stood in the centre of the room. Each had a sprinkler above, spraying water continuously. Lucy presumed it was to slow down the decay of the corpses and to smother the odour. Unfortunately, due to the warm July weather, the system was inadequate. Lucy had to look away, trying to catch her breath. The solitary window, high on the wall, was open. A fly banged against the glass, as anxious to escape the bleak scene as Lucy. But escape was impossible. For the sake of Peggy O'Reilly's distraught mother, they had to go through with this. From the corner of her eye, Lucy spotted an elderly man appear in the other doorway to the room, looking half-dead himself. Ryan introduced him as the registrar cum caretaker.

Then, Inspector Ryan gestured for them to follow him further into the room. Lucy averted her eyes from the other occupied slabs they had to pass, deeply regretting having partaken of breakfast before they left the house that morning.

Ryan came to a halt at the base of the last slab. A dark-haired young woman lay on it, a sheet drawn up to her neck; a bizarre attempt to protect her modesty, Lucy thought, as the sodden linen revealed much of the thin body beneath. The girl's face held no colour, and her wet hair clung to her skull, a gash to her temple making Lucy suck in a breath. Lucy wondered if that had been the fatal blow. There were no other visible signs of injury. However, it wasn't a question she could ask Ryan with Mary present. Despite the sad sight the girl presented, she had been a pretty girl, an unfortunate circumstance that had marked her out as prey and had sealed her fate. A surge of anger made Lucy grit her teeth. How she wished she could get her hands on those scurrilous men who preyed upon these young women.

As she drew closer to Ryan, she realised Mary had stalled once more. She turned to encourage her, but Mary was shaking her head, backing away.

'Mary, we've come this far. It's essential you do this. We agreed. Your mother is too elderly and upset to come here.'

'I thought I could, ma'am, but I can't. I don't... want it to be her,' the maid said, her head turned away.

Lucy threw Ryan a pleading glance.

'Miss O'Reilly, I know this is difficult for you, but we need a family member to identify her. Then we can release her body, and she can have a decent burial. Otherwise, it will be an unmarked plot in Prospect Cemetery in Glasnevin. You don't want that for her, I'm sure. Please,' Ryan said, holding out his hand as he walked towards her. He turned Mary around and guided her to the slab.

Lucy threw him a grateful glance as she bit her lip to hold back her tears. Mary drew in a shaky breath and stepped forward, her face now a mask of misery. One brief glance was all she took of the dead girl before she fell sobbing into Lucy's arms.

'Please, Miss O'Reilly. Is this Peggy O'Reilly, your cousin?' Ryan asked.

Mary mumbled something into Lucy's shoulder.

'You must say it, Mary, nice and clear for the inspector,' Lucy said, easing the maid away from her.

Mary blew her nose and nodded. Then: 'I'm sorry, ma'am, sir. Yes, it's our Peg, the poor cratur,' she exclaimed before succumbing to tears once more. 'This'll kill Aunty May and me mother. How will I tell them?'

'There, there,' Lucy said, rubbing her back. 'I'll help you in any way I can. We will go to your mother from here and break it to her gently. At least the poor girl will get a decent burial now. You are not to fret over anything.'

'Thank you, Miss O'Reilly,' the inspector said, with a brief glance at the registrar. 'You'll note the identification in the official register, Mr McCarthy?'

'I will, sir, I will,' the old man said before shuffling away once more, muttering the unfortunate girl's name repeatedly under his breath.

Outside the morgue, Lucy urged Mary up into the waiting carriage. 'My dear, try to calm down before we see your mother. You must be strong for her or how else will she cope? I'll be with you in a moment, but first, I wish to speak to the inspector.' Mary nodded and blew her nose as she sat back against the squabs, the picture of misery.

Lucy swung around to Ryan with a meaningful glance. He

moved away, and Lucy fell into step with him as they headed to the corner towards the bustling Liffey quays. They stood in silence for a few moments. Across the road, dockers were unloading crates from a vessel onto a cart at the quay.

'Poor girl, that was hard for her,' he remarked.

'Extremely. If only we had arrived a week earlier, we might have found Peggy in time.'

'You can't know that with certainty,' he said. 'Will Mary be alright?'

'I think so. At the moment, it's the shock of it all, but she is strong.' Lucy turned to face him. 'Such a senseless act, Inspector. Why kill her, and in such a brutal way?'

'We may never know, but my guess would be that she refused the client.'

Lucy inhaled sharply. 'And paid a heavy price for it. He must be a beast.' Ryan grunted in agreement, and Lucy took the bull by the horns. 'I noticed the injury to Peggy's head. Is that how she died?'

The inspector's brows shot up, and Lucy feared he would prevaricate, assuming she was squeamish. 'The specifics are a tad gruesome...'

'Inspector, I cannot help you if I don't know the details,' Lucy said.

Ryan opened his mouth to speak, then shook his head. 'Your husband was right about you.'

Lucy gave a dismissive gesture with her hand. 'What do you think happened in that brothel?'

'We believe it was a client who killed her. The woman who runs the place, the flash-house keeper, has named the man she believes is responsible. One of her employees has also stated Myles Carver was Peggy's last client.'

'I see, but your problem is that Olivia Carver has given him an alibi for the time in question?'

'Yes, she has. However, I suspect she was being forced to provide it. But whatever hold Carver has over her is strong.'

'You must persuade her to be truthful.'

'I shall do my best.'

'And the attack itself?'

'As you spotted, someone struck Peggy on the head. The doctor believes the first blow was to the back of her head which would have stunned her, then a blow to her temple which would have cracked her skull and caused her death.'

'How cowardly.'

'Yes. She must have turned to defend herself, but the second impact finished her. We found her lying on the floor on her back. She had some defensive wounds on her arms, but she was slight, so someone could have overpowered her with ease.'

With dismay, Lucy envisaged the scene. 'What will happen now?'

'I will inform Peggy's family in Wexford that she has been formally identified, and we will arrange for her burial in Glasnevin Cemetery.'

'Oh, no, Inspector,' Lucy said, 'she must return to her family.'

'The DMP cannot cover the cost—'

'I will bear any outlay. Mary is not only my maid; she is a friend who has stood by me in my darkest hours. The poor girl's family will want Peggy to be buried at home. Please make the arrangements and let me know the final bill.'

'As you wish,' he said. 'That is very generous of you.'

Lucy accepted this with a nod. 'So, now you must tell me. Your case. Where does it stand?'

'As I told you, my chief and only suspect is Myles Carver. Until I can break his alibi, there isn't much we can do. If I could only find the cabbie who took him from the brothel to his home, I would have some chance of disproving his claim that he wasn't in The Monto, but so far no one is prepared to speak out.'

'Well, you will forgive me for saying so, but that isn't really good enough. You may not find this cabbie or any other witnesses. Are you happy to let this brutal killer go unpunished? What if he strikes again?'

A flicker of anger crossed his features. 'I am powerless to act, Mrs Stone. There are procedures I must follow. I'm further inhibited because The Monto residents hate the police.'

'The Monto? That's where it happened?'

'Yes, it is a large area close to Amiens Street Station and the docks. Every second house is a house of ill-repute. It has proved impossible to police, I'm ashamed to say.' The colour rose in his face. 'Influential people frequent it...'

'Ah, I understand. So, the businesses, for want of a better word, are protected so the DMP cannot act.'

'Correct,' Ryan said. 'The last thing they will do is cooperate with us. If we raid these premises, the madams claim they are boarding houses so unless we catch clients... well, we are stumped. At best, we charge them for the illegal sale of alcohol, one of their many lucrative sidelines.'

'Even though in this case you are dealing with a murder?' Lucy was incredulous.

'The history in the area is unfortunate, and now the brothel owners and the gangs rule the place,' he said. 'Violence is an everyday occurrence. They are immune to it.'

'Then you will have to accept my help. I am not prepared to let this Carver fellow go scot-free.' She cast him a fierce glance. 'You are sure it was Carver...?'

Ryan shifted. 'The madam who owns and runs the flash-house swears it was him. I don't believe she has any reason to lie.'

'She's hardly a reliable witness or of good character.'

'No. But she knows I won't let her reopen until we have made progress. Celine Burton is ruthless and grasping. She'll cooperate if it's the only way to entice clients back into her house. At the moment, her clients find a burly constable standing on her front steps a bit of a turnoff.'

Lucy smiled. 'How wily of you, Inspector, to place him there.' He shrugged. 'However, Peggy's sister Bridget is still missing. A matter of grave concern to us all, and now my priority. We must trace her before she, too, meets a ghastly end. Have you put anything in train yet?'

'I have, Mrs Stone. We have distributed the photograph you gave me throughout the city. I'd be confident, if she's still in Dublin, we will find her.'

'Good. But the sooner, the better. It would be ghastly if she were to suffer the same misfortune as her sister. Have you considered searching that awful house? What if Bridget is being held there against her will?'

'Burton denies any knowledge of her, but I intend to instigate a search when I have enough manpower.'

'Good, though I would suggest you do so as quickly as possible. They might move her.'

He grunted in response.

'Last night we made a bargain, and I intend to fulfil my end of it this afternoon.'

'And what do you intend to do?' he asked, his brows raised. 'I'm almost afraid to ask, but is what you propose legal? I cannot condone the use of thumbscrews or the rack on Olivia Carver.'

With a suppressed grin, Lucy said: 'You've been listening to Phin, I dare say.'

'What he has divulged was interesting. You have a fascinating history.'

'Hmm. Well, it won't come to torture, I can assure you. You will have to trust me to find out what I can. From my brief encounter with Olivia yesterday, I am convinced she is under considerable stress. Perhaps her father-in-law put her under duress to provide that alibi.' Lucy paused. 'Or it might be down to the long hours she tends Edith Carver. Constant attendance in a sickroom would blight the happiness of any soul, and particularly a young woman who I suspect is lonely. But let me worry about that. I have already set things in motion. At first, I thought I'd return Olivia's visit, but I imagine she will not open up to me within the confines of that house. So, I sent a note to her this morning, suggesting we meet for a stroll in Merrion Square gardens this afternoon. She has accepted. If possible, I will... encourage her to speak out.'

The inspector quirked his mouth. 'Thank you. That sounds like a workable plan. You will let me know how you fare?' he said as they turned back towards the carriage.

'I promise I'll send you a note this evening.'

'If you fail, I shall have to contrive to meet with her away from Carver's influence,' he said. 'I must break that alibi.'

Lucy smiled. 'I don't intend to fail, Inspector, but if my first attempt should flounder, I shall arrange that meeting for you at our house.'

Ryan handed Lucy up into the carriage, shut the door and stood back. As the carriage waited at the corner to turn onto the quays, Lucy looked back. The inspector was walking along, lost in thought. Lucy shared his frustration. Although Mary's identification of her cousin was a positive step, and they could speculate about what had occurred on the evening of the murder, it brought them no closer to breaking Carver's alibi. It only made Lucy more determined to extract the truth from Olivia that afternoon.

But first, Irishtown, to break the bad news.

TWELVE

Merrion Square

On her return to Merrion Square some hours later, Lucy found Phineas in the library, his head stuck in a book. Raising his eyes to her, he smiled and snapped the book shut. 'My dear, you're back. How did you fare? Was it Mary's cousin, as we feared?'

Lucy sat down opposite as he laid his book aside. 'Yes, it was terrible, Phin. The morgue is a dreadful place. And yes, Inspector Ryan was correct—it was Peggy O'Reilly. Afterwards, we went out to Irishtown, and I've left Mary at her mother's house. The poor woman was distraught when Mary broke the news. As I didn't want to intrude on their grief, I left, but I've told Mary to stay with her mother and to accompany her down to Wexford for the funeral. I can manage without her for a few days. And I have offered to pay for the transport of the young girl back to Wexford by train. It felt like the appropriate thing to do in the circumstances.'

Phineas nodded. 'Well done. It's what her family would want. Poor Mary. How is she coping?'

'Not well, and we are still left with the hunt for the missing sibling, Bridget. Mary is now fearing the worst, no matter what I say. To be honest, I'm concerned, too. The underbelly of this city is nasty; it swallows people whole.'

'As is the case in any large city,' Phin said. 'What does Ryan say? What are the DMP doing to find the girl?'

'He says they are doing their best. They have circulated the photograph hoping someone recognises her. I suggested, strongly suggested, that an immediate search of that awful woman's property should be carried out.'

'And what do you propose to do? I know you too well to imagine you will leave this in the poor inspector's hands.'

'Do you rate him?'

'I do, actually. His reputation is excellent.'

'Not another Kincaid then,' Lucy said, remembering another DMP officer they had crossed paths with years before.

'Definitely not. Don't you like him?' he asked.

'I do, yes, but—'

'You are impatient to see progress,' he said.

'Yes, indeed. Where is that poor girl, and what is she being subjected to?' she said.

'What is your plan, my dear?'

'Well, I was thinking about it on my way back from Irishtown. This area where the brothel is—it's known as The Monto—must hold the key to both the murder and Bridget's disappearance. Ryan says that people there hate the police and that no one will cooperate, but I've been thinking.'

Phin's eyes lit up. 'Oho, now we're in trouble.'

'Don't be mean.'

'I'm merely speaking from experience, my love. Pray, continue.'

'The police aren't welcome, but the clergy might be,' Lucy said. 'If I can convince the local Catholic priest to help me, we might make some progress. The women who work in the brothels may speak to him. Perhaps even be willing to meet me if he is present.'

Phin nodded. 'That's a very good idea, Lucy. But please be careful. If you wish to venture into such a dangerous neighbourhood, please take one of us with you. In fact, I insist upon it.'

Lucy bit her lip. 'Funnily enough, I was going to ask if you could spare George.'

'That goes without saying... and he is anxious to help. He is very fond of Mary. But you will keep me up to date on your progress?' he asked. 'I'm hoping to act as a consultant, at least.'

'Most definitely,' she said. 'If we all work hard on this, I hope we can restore Bridget to her family alive.' Lucy stood. 'But first I must try to help our favourite Irish detective.' With a glance at the clock, she continued, 'Wish me luck. I'm due to meet Olivia Carver in fifteen minutes.'

Phin's brows were drawn together.

'What is it?'

'It occurs to me that Ryan might not be considering all possibilities in relation to Peggy's murder.'

'What do you mean?' she asked, sitting back down.

'What if Carver was there but wasn't the murderer? That he is being set up. This madam seems very keen that he is blamed, and Ryan doesn't appear to have considered anyone else, which, frankly, surprises me.'

'But he's sure Mrs Burton is telling the truth so that the case is closed quickly and she can reopen.' Phineas shrugged. 'So, you think Olivia isn't lying?'

'I think we should consider it a possibility.'

'But if not Carver, then who killed Peggy? Another client?'

Phin nodded. 'Or someone else who was part of the household. My understanding is that there are bully boys located on the doors to deal with unruly clients and disobedient women. Perhaps a punishment got out of hand.'

Merrion Square Gardens

Only the residents of Merrion Square had access to the green oasis of the private gardens. Lucy was pleased to see, on unlocking the gate and stepping down onto the path, that only a handful of people were to be seen. An elderly gentleman sat reading a newspaper on a bench on the far side of the central lawn, and a harassed nanny was standing, hands on hips, scolding her charges, further along the path. Then, with little ceremony, the nanny marched her charges out through the eastern gate. The fewer people around, the better, Lucy thought. Olivia would be more likely to confide in her.

Admiring the perimeter trees and shrubs, which ensured the residents' privacy, Lucy strolled along the boundary path. Occasionally, she would look across the lawn toward the southern gate. As the minutes ticked by and there was still no sign of Olivia, Lucy feared the young lady had changed her mind. Or perhaps her father-in-law had prevented her from leaving the house. But why would he? He was unaware of the link between Peggy O'Reilly and the Stone household.

She found a bench with a convenient view of the gate and sat down to mull over what approach she should take. Revealing the connection was out of the question for now, for she didn't know if she could trust Olivia with the information. It would be best to cultivate a friendship, slow as that might be, to gain Olivia's confidence. But every day that passed without finding Peggy's sister, Bridget, was a worry. Where was the young girl? Had this madam, Peggy's so-called employer, also trapped her into working for her? From what Mary had told her the sisters were very close and would have stayed together if possible. Might poor Bridget still be trapped in that awful place? But how was she to gain access to such an establishment? No, that was a doomed notion. Ryan would have to handle that aspect. Her original plan to find a go-between made more sense.

Phin's parting words worried her a little. Could Ryan be jumping to conclusions too quickly? But Lucy's gut was telling her he was on the right track. And now, she was committed to helping him break Carver's alibi. Something in Olivia's world was off kilter, she was sure of it, and reading between the lines from their last meeting, it centred around Olivia's father-in-law.

So engrossed in her thoughts, Olivia's sudden appearance startled Lucy. 'Good afternoon. My apologies for being late, but Edith was poorly again.'

Lucy patted the seat. 'Not at all. I'm so sorry. Is there any way I can help?'

Olivia smiled at her as she sat. 'That is kind of you, Lucy, but my maid Sally has promised to sit with her while I'm out.' She glanced away for a moment. 'However, I'm afraid I cannot stay long.'

'Are you concerned your mother-in-law is getting worse?'

Olivia licked her lips, nodding her head. 'I don't understand it. Sometimes, she perks up and is her old self, and I think her medicine is working, and then... Oh dear, I'm sorry. I have no wish to burden you with my worries.'

On the contrary, I wish you would, Lucy thought. 'My dear, if it helps to share your concerns, I am more than happy to listen. I know all too well how it feels to be isolated, even within your own family.'

This earned Lucy a sharp glance. 'Really?'

Perhaps if she shared some of her family history, it might encourage Olivia to open up.

'Yes, indeed. My mother, brother, and sister-in-law treated me as a pariah the last time I visited our family home. It was some time ago, but it still rankles.' Lucy grinned. 'My eloping at eighteen might have had something to do with it, however. I was not a model daughter because I married for love—what I thought was love at least—not money. My father had hoped that a rich husband might save the family's shaky finances. My Charlie's talent, however, was spending not making money.'

Olivia's eyes popped. 'I see.'

'Now, that is a tale for another day.' Lucy slipped her arm through the young woman's. 'You were very upset yesterday, and I know it was something I said that caused it. Please. If there is anything I can do, even if only to listen...' Lucy waited, hoping she had said enough to elicit a revelation of some kind.

Olivia did not respond straight away. Instead, she plucked at her gloved hands. 'Well... there is something that has been worrying me. When Edith first fell ill, the doctor was called in, and he claimed that the type of heart condition she had was very treatable. Despite that, she became bedridden within a matter of weeks, and I think the doctor is as confused as I am about the speed of her decline. Not that he would ever admit or discuss it with me, you understand, but I know by his expression that he is worried. When I realised my father-in-law had no intention of hiring a nurse, I stepped in. As was only right, and believe me, Lucy, I am happy to do it. Edith has always been so very kind to me. So, I administer her medicine twice a day as per the doctor's instructions. And I am very careful about the dose and log it in a book the doctor left.' Olivia's brow wrinkled. 'He often consults it, as if he doubts my word. But...' She trailed off, and Lucy tried not to react.

'But?'

Olivia looked about before she spoke in a voice so low, Lucy had to lean towards her to hear. 'Something isn't right, and I overheard the doctor say it to Mr Carver. That was a few weeks ago. Then Edith rallied, and I was once more hopeful. Then, about a week ago, she went into a decline once more.'

'And the medicine isn't helping?'

'Not that I can tell. I asked the doctor if we should increase the dose, but he said no, that might prove fatal.' Olivia stared down into her lap.

'There is something else?' Lucy probed.

'My father-in-law cannot abide illness and avoids the sickroom except for first thing in the morning. He insists on sitting with Edith after he has his breakfast, before he leaves for the bank. If he is home in the evening, he does not go near her, even to wish her goodnight.'

'Hardly the loving husband,' Lucy remarked.

'No. I am convinced that he no longer cares for her. Then one morning, I thought he had left for the bank and entered her room. I found him standing at the end of her bed, staring at her with such an expression on his face. It was pure hatred, Lucy. It was horrible.'

Olivia shivered. 'When he saw me, he was so angry and roared at me to get out. His temper is foul, and he frightens me, so I dare not enter the room in the mornings until the maid assures me he has left.'

'Are you saying,' Lucy began, trying to choose the right words, 'that he may be tampering with her medicine with ill intent?'

Olivia nodded, suppressing a sob. 'Am I wicked to think it? But what else could cause her marked distress and weakness during the mornings after he has left. She hallucinates and becomes so confused. Then, by evening, she appears to recover. Lucy, I check the dose carefully, and I have even marked the bottle so that I can check it hasn't been tampered with. The level does not change between the doses I administer.'

'Olivia, are you saying that you believe your father-in-law is overdosing Edith?'

Olivia nodded, her jaw quivering. 'But I have no idea how he's doing it.' Olivia turned tearful eyes to Lucy. 'And if she dies, might they blame me?'

'Good Lord, I don't know. Perhaps you should protect yourself and go to the police,' Lucy said. 'I would, in your position.'

'Oh no. That's impossible. I have no evidence against him, no proof, as I haven't seen him give her anything he shouldn't. Besides, he would cast me off. Lucy, I have nothing. I depend totally on Myles Carver's benevolence.'

THIRTEEN

Fergus stood to attention in his superior's office, trying hard not to show his impatience. Chief Inspector Malone was muttering and rifling through Fergus's progress report. The office overlooked the deserted Lower Yard of Dublin Castle. Like most of the DMP offices, the windows were so old and caked with layers of paint, it took superhuman strength to open them. Apparently, it was something the chief inspector lacked and, combined with whatever scent he had drowned himself in that morning, the atmosphere in the room was making Fergus queasy.

At last, Malone looked up, and his hand came down on the front page of the report with a slap. 'What is this supposed to be, Inspector? I see nothing but a litany of excuses.'

'I'm not sure what you mean, sir.'

'Why on earth did you not arrest this fellow...' Malone gazed down at the report, pushing his glasses up his nose, and running his pudgy finger down the page. 'Carver?'

'Well, sir, he has an alibi provided by his daughter-in-law and his servants. He is adamant that he was at home that evening.'

'Pah! Women are notoriously unreliable witnesses. They could be lying for him,' Malone said with a derogatory wave of his hand.

'They most certainly are,' Fergus answered.

'What?' blustered the chief inspector. 'And you didn't haul them all in?'

'With respect, sir, I believe that would serve no purpose. He has a hold over them. Until I know what it is, I will not shake them from their stories.'

'So, you intend to let the man walk free?'

'No, sir. I intend to break his alibi. As we speak, my men are trying to trace cabbies who may have conveyed him either to Mecklenburgh Street or from there to his home on Merrion Square. We are also trying to track down other men who might have been at Burton's place that evening. Sergeant Hughes is interviewing his bank employees to see if they know anything. I suspect Carver isn't generally liked. I believe we will have no difficulty in obtaining some interesting information from them.'

'All of which you should do anyway. And what good will all of this do if the ladies in his life won't tell the truth?'

'If faced with strong evidence of his guilt, I believe Mrs Carver will retract her statement and the others will follow.'

'And you base that on what, Inspector? Your famous intuition? Pretty thing, is she? Do you hope to charm her into changing her story?' He laughed. 'Bring her in here and you'll soon get the truth out of her. Did you explain how serious it would be to aid and abet a murderer?'

'She is a lady, sir, and an intelligent one at that. I realised she was letting me know she was under duress.'

'Poppycock!' Malone exclaimed and then stared at him. 'What about these other witnesses who place him in the flash-house?'

'Again, sir, they pose a problem. Any defence barrister would annihilate Mrs Burton in the witness box. With her record, she would be discredited, and her testimony would be worthless. The porter, Mulcahy, is a brute of a man who can hardly string two words together. Pit them in court against a gentleman of Carver's standing and the jury would acquit him. I am convinced he did it, sir, and I want him convicted. But all we have is the word of two of the most disreputable characters in The Monto.'

Malone narrowed his eyes. 'You better know what you are doing, Ryan. You have until the end of the week to break that alibi, otherwise I will send Inspector Burke to bring Carver in.' Fergus clenched his teeth. Burke's methods were suspect, and he was Malone's protégée. He had been snapping at Fergus's heels for years.

'And what progress have you made regarding this threat to the jewels?'

'I will be visiting my source soon. I hope they will give me more information,' Ryan answered.

Malone quirked a brow. 'And Mr Stone. What is he up to?'

'He is only interested in the security aspect here in the castle, sir. He has stated explicitly that the Fenian threat is DMP business, and he has no wish to be involved.'

'Is that so? Doesn't want to get his hands dirty, no doubt. Well then, you'd best get on with it.'

Fergus turned for the door only to be hailed once more.

'And if you have any idea what that Mr Stone is really up to, you come and tell me at once. This jewel business is only a cover story, I'm convinced of it. He's here to spy for London.' Malone scowled at him. 'DeWinter will hound me for information, so make sure you root it out.'

Fergus almost smiled as he turned away. The paranoia of his superiors was no surprise, but he had no desire to become embroiled in their political machinations.

Mulling over his earlier conversation with Mrs Stone, Ryan felt a little guilty. He hadn't given the missing girl much attention, his focus on Carver and Peggy's murder. While Lucy tried to work her magic on Mrs Carver to break that damned alibi, he should at least investigate if Bridget had been or still was in Burton's flash-house.

Ryan entered his office to find Sergeant Hughes waiting for him. 'Good man, I was hoping you were still around. This missing girl, Bridget O'Reilly.'

'Yes, sir?'

'Anything in from the stations?'

'No, sir. No trace of her so far. I've gone through the reports from the various districts only this morning.'

'Then I think we should pay Mrs Burton a visit with a few constables. Give the place a thorough search, and hopefully rattle her. I don't want another dead girl on my hands. They might be hiding Bridget O'Reilly there or, worse, have the body stashed on the premises until the coast is clear.'

'I'll make the arrangements, sir. When do you wish to do it?'

'Why, this afternoon. No time like the present.'

The Monto

Celine Burton was not pleased to see Fergus, despite his cheery greeting. Lounging on her sofa, glass in hand, she rolled her eyes as he came through the door.

'Good afternoon, Celine,' he said. He glanced at the glass. 'A bit early, surely, even for you?'

'None of your business, polis. I hope you've come to remove that constable from my doorstep. He's a bloody nuisance.'

'What a pity,' he said with a smirk. 'But I'm afraid he or one of his colleagues will be a feature for a while yet.' He rubbed his chin. 'Murder investigations are notoriously long... drawn-out affairs.'

'You can't do that. You'll ruin me business,' she shouted, as she wriggled into a sitting position. 'It's not fair.'

'Fair? Is it fair that young Peggy O'Reilly was murdered? A mere child you snatched off the street.'

'You can't prove anything... That had nothin' to do with me, Ryan.'

'It had a lot to do with you. She should never have been here at all,' he ground out.

'I can't help it if these young 'uns want somewhere to stay. Begged me to take her in. I's helpin' them out. No one else does.'

'Helping them to line your pockets, more like,' he said, attempting to keep his temper in check.

'Piffle!'

He didn't trust himself to respond.

Meanwhile, she continued to glower at him. 'So, what do you want? More stupid questions, is it?'

'There will be plenty of questions, Celine, but right now, my officers need to search the house and the yard out back.'

'What? Why?'

'Peggy's sister is missing. Bridget O'Reilly. Ring any bells with you?'

'Never 'eard of 'er.'

'The girls were inseparable and arrived in Dublin together, so I reckon she was here at some stage as well. And let me tell you, if I find her here, or worse, her corpse, I'll haul you in and you'll rue the day you were born.'

'I know nothing about no sister,' she said with a sneer, sitting back once more. 'Search if you want, darlin'.'

Fergus took in her smug face and knew he was already defeated. He'd still search, he had no choice, but he knew they wouldn't find anything.

FOURTEEN

In Mary's absence, Lucy sought the cook's help to find out which Catholic parish The Monto belonged to. Just after eleven-thirty she left Merrion Square alone in a hired cab to travel across the city to the pro-cathedral on Marlborough Street. She had considered bringing George, but as she only intended to visit the parish church and not venture into The Monto itself, she decided against it.

On arrival, however, a large crowd was descending the front steps of the church. Lucy surmised a church service had concluded, so she waited near the foot of the steps. The mass-goers filed past; a mixed-looking congregation of the well-dressed and those who looked to have fallen on harder times. To her surprise, although many of those who passed threw her curious glances, their smiles were open and friendly. It seemed to be the way of Dubliners in general and a stark contrast to London.

Resolved to carry out her mission, she mounted the steps and entered. The small entrance hallway was dark, providing a welcome break from the midday heat, and the church interior was cooler still. Unfortunately, it appeared to be empty. Had she missed her chance to catch one of the priests in situ? Where would they be outside mass times?

It was a beautiful church, and vast. For several minutes, all she could do was stand and stare. As she marvelled at the interior, she turned and looked up, for above the entrance door was a large organ gallery. It, too, was vacant, however. Undeterred, Lucy strolled down the mosaic-tiled aisle, her footsteps echoing in the silence. Before her, the altar formed a large platform above which was a half-dome decorated with figures in relief, depicting the Ascension. It was as fine a church as Lucy had ever seen, and she wondered about its history.

It was only when she reached the altar that she realised there were two side-altars. And her luck was in. Before one altar, on which stood the statue of what looked like a bishop, was a figure in a black cassock, kneeling. As she watched, the priest lit a candle, which he placed in a brass candleholder before bending his head. Hearing his whispered prayers, Lucy sat in a pew a couple of yards away to wait for him.

Her thoughts strayed to Mary and her poor murdered cousin. Lucy glanced at her watch and reckoned the O'Reilly family were well on their way to Wexford on the train with their sad cargo. They had visited Mary and her mother in Irishtown the evening before, only to discover the family were waking Peggy in their tiny home. Lucy had been embarrassed, feeling they were intruding, but Mary's mother, Kate, had insisted they were most welcome, and had plied Lucy with tea and Phineas with something far stronger.

Eventually, the priest rose, then genuflected before the altar. When he turned away, he caught sight of Lucy and approached. He was small of stature, erring on the plump side with a forehead that was chasing his hairline in a battle long lost. A pair of grey eyes assessed her, and she was almost on the point of categorising him as a severe-looking man when he broke into a smile, which lit up his face.

'May I be of assistance, madam?' he asked in a melodious voice. 'I'm afraid we are not hearing confessions until this evening.'

Lucy rose and stepped out onto the aisle, pulling the piece of paper from her pocket on which the hired cook had written the name of the priest she should ask for. 'Thank you, but I'm not of your flock, Father. I was hoping someone might help me with a personal matter,' she said. 'I'm looking for Father McGuinness.'

The smile broke forth once more. 'I am he.'

'That is most fortunate, Father. I'm Lucy Stone,' she said, holding out her hand. 'Could you spare me a few minutes of your time?'

He returned the handshake. 'I'd be delighted. The parochial house is next door. Perhaps you would care to join me for a cup of tea, Mrs Stone?'

'Thank you,' Lucy said. 'Tea would be perfect.'

Lucy did her best not to show her astonishment when Father McGuinness guided her to a Georgian three-storey over basement house, next door to the church. However, he must have guessed her thoughts, for he turned to her as he put his key in the latch. 'It's not only me living here, Mrs Stone. There are four of us clergy and a housekeeper.'

He pushed the door open, ushering Lucy inside. 'Mrs Clancy?' he called out. 'I have a guest with me. May we have some tea in the front parlour, please? And maybe some of those gingersnaps you made yesterday?' He winked at Lucy. 'There're very good.'

A voice answered from the bowels of the house. 'Right-ho, Father. No problem at all.'

They stepped into a fine parlour, sunlight streaming in through the long narrow casement window. The furniture, though old-fashioned, was beautifully kept, and the smell of furniture polish made Lucy's nose tingle.

'Please take a seat,' the priest said, indicating a chair beside the fireplace. He took the facing seat and smiled at her in an encouraging way. 'Now then, how can I help you?'

She explained who she was, then dove straight in. 'My maid's cousin was the young woman murdered last Thursday in The Monto. Peggy O'Reilly.'

Father McGuinness's brows drew together. 'Ah, yes. Very sad,' he said. 'My condolences. It was a dreadful and shocking crime. I was called to the, ah, premises, but there wasn't much I could do but lead some prayers for the poor soul. It was too late to perform the Last Rites. She was only a child. I hope the police find out who did it.'

'Yes, indeed. Had you by any chance met the girl in question before?'

'No, sadly. Many of the young women—well, locally they are known as "the unfortunate girls"—do not come to the church often. Too ashamed.' He shook his head. 'We try to reach out to them. Persuade them to give up that life, turn back to God, but the kip-keepers and the gangs have them terrified. That particular kip-keeper, Celine Burton, is among the worst. A vicious woman and shameless with it. I tackled her once. The next day, someone smashed in all our windows.'

'You have my sympathy, Father. The difficulty I have is that I wish to speak to someone who works in that house, anyone at all. Obviously, I cannot venture into that area. I would stand out and raise suspicion. The police are not tolerated, so I, a total stranger, would get nowhere. They would not speak to me.'

The priest nodded. 'You are correct, and it would be far too dangerous. But why do you wish to speak to them, may I ask?'

'Because another young woman is missing. You see, Father, Peggy travelled to Dublin with her sister, Bridget. They were very close, and everyone believes they were not easily separated. It was sheer luck we discovered the fate of Peggy, but Bridget is missing. The police are certain she is not in that house. The inspector in charge of Peggy's case even visited it on Saturday to carry out a search to make sure, but Mrs Burton claims she knows nothing about her. She is probably lying.'

'Nothing more certain. She is not an honest woman,' he said. The priest got up and walked over to the window, deep in thought.

There was a tap-tap on the door, and the housekeeper entered bearing a tray. She smiled and nodded to Lucy and set the tray on the table.

'There you are, Father. Drink it now while it's nice and hot.'

'Thank you, Mrs Clancy,' the priest said. 'You might be so good as to keep lunch for me. I won't be too much longer.'

Lucy's heart dropped at his words. Was she about to be dismissed? Perhaps she had overstepped the mark.

'I will, Father,' the housekeeper said. Her gaze swept over Lucy before she slipped from the room.

'Please,' Father McGuinness said, indicating the tea tray. 'Will you join me?'

Lucy did as she was bid, watching the priest as he poured out two cups and passed her the plate of biscuits.

'Father, can you help me?' Lucy asked after several moments of unnerving silence.

He drew in a long breath, and those grey eyes bore into her. 'I can, or perhaps to be more truthful, I shall try. There is a lass who works in that house who might talk to you. She has reached out to me before due to certain circumstances which I'm not at liberty to share. I believe she trusts me. I shall contact her, and if she is agreeable, I will send you a message.'

Lucy beamed back at him. 'Thank you.'

'Not at all. That unfortunate girl's family must be frantic. I will try to persuade Ginny to meet you. Now tell me, what's your assessment of the gingersnaps?' he asked, breaking one in two before popping it into his mouth.

FIFTEEN

Thomas Street, later that afternoon

The Sleepy Druid public house leaned against its neighbours, exuding the aroma of decades of stale tobacco and spilt beer. Fergus hesitated outside, his heart sinking. He hated the place and kept his visits to a minimum. He looked up with a sigh. Ignatius Byrne's name was emblazoned in gold letters across the sign above the entrance. As Fergus had explained to Phineas Stone, Byrne ran an empire. The Druid was only one of Byrne's many hostelries scattered throughout the city. G Division knew him well, his moneylending and smuggling being legendary. But Ignatius was clever enough to have others do his dirty work. Much to the DMP's frustration, and Fergus's in particular, he remained a free man.

Fergus almost turned on his heel. Coming here to learn more about the so-called Fenians and their plans was a fruitless task. The informant must have had their own agenda and Fergus suspected it was a tall tale. His time would be better spent on Peggy's murder case, especially with Carver still a free man.

Most of all, Fergus wasn't keen on dealing with Byrne directly. Mostly because the man was his relative, a fact no one in G Division knew, and Fergus wanted to keep it that way. It was highly inconvenient for him to have a relative, albeit a second cousin, who featured prominently in underworld circles. If the chief inspector ever found out, Fergus's career would be over.

He braced for the inevitable battle ahead and pushed through the door. He heard the clink of glasses coming from the far end of the narrow saloon bar. Lizzie, his cousin, was standing behind the bar cleaning and stacking glasses. She spotted him and smiled.

'Well, look who the cat dragged in,' she said, dropping her cloth and skipping around the bar counter to bestow a peck on his cheek. She was a dainty young woman of about twenty-six and worldly-wise, her father having put her to work in the pub at a very young age. Fergus always wondered how such an ugly old codger as Byrne had produced such a pretty and vivacious daughter.

'It's good to see you, Lizzie. How are you?'

She did a twirl, then tilted her head and gave him one of her looks. 'Just grand.'

'Is himself in?'

'Indeed, he is. Sure, he'll be delighted to see ye.'

'I doubt it. This is an official visit,' he said.

Lizzie sucked in a breath. 'Ooh, I'd hate to be in your shoes, so,' she said in a singsong voice. Pulling out a bar stool, she hopped up on it and swung her legs gently. 'Tell me,' she said, 'how is life treating my favourite and most handsome cousin?'

'Same as ever.'

'That bad, eh? Maybe police work ain't your thing. You should come work for Da. You know he'd love that.'

Fergus shuddered. He looked around the bar and dropped his voice. 'Don't go reminding him, Lizzie. He'll not get his claws into me. Ever.'

'You can run, but you cannot hide, cousin dear. Half of Dublin is under his thumb. Eventually he will get his way,' she said, raising her brows. 'He always does.'

Fergus rolled his eyes. Ignatius's lack of a son and heir was a constant source of aggravation between them. For some reason, Ignatius considered Fergus the heir apparent. At first, Fergus had found it amusing, but since a close shave with the grim reaper earlier in the year, Ignatius was putting renewed pressure on him. Fergus had given up trying to persuade him that there was nothing about the proposition that would entice him to abandon his police career.

'How's your father doing?' Lizzie asked.

'Not too bad. The winter was the hardest when he was stuck indoors.'

'God love him, sure that would drive anyone mad,' Lizzie said, shaking her head. 'Can't believe it's only nine months since the accident. I often think of your Ma and Kathleen, God love them.'

Fergus reached out and squeezed her arm. 'Thanks, Lizzie, I miss 'em something terrible. You know, Da would love to see you.'

'Ah, you know I can't, Fergus. Himself would kill me, he would,' she said, tipping her head towards the back of the premises. 'Him and your Da never got on.'

'True, but no one would tell Iggy. Certainly not me.'

Heavy footsteps coming through from the rear brought their conversation to an abrupt close. A heavy-set man with a shock of white hair emerged through the door behind the bar. He stood staring at Fergus, leaning on his walking cane. Lizzie slid off the bar stool and winked at Fergus.

'There ye are,' Ignatius grunted. 'Haven't seen you in months. Have you been avoiding us?'

Fergus smothered his irritation 'Good afternoon, Iggy,' he said. 'I'm a busy man.'

His cousin's beady eyes narrowed. 'As am I. What'd you want?'

Fergus drew himself up. 'Police business, Iggy.'

'The devil take ya,' Byrne spat at him. A standoff of staring ensued. Fergus knew he'd won when his cousin's gaze dropped. 'Lizzie, lock the door. You, follow me.' Iggy turned and waddled back towards the rear of the pub.

'Good luck,' Lizzie whispered. 'Ye'll need it.'

Fergus shrugged and made his way towards his cousin's office. Ignatius's lair, as he liked to think of it, was a tiny airless room. His cousin's relationship with hygiene was a very loose one, so being confined in this tiny space with him was always a trial. The grubby window looked out onto the backyard, where he saw the outline of stacked barrels. Jake, his cousin's potman and a giant of a man, was out in the yard, hauling crates.

'Shut the door,' Iggy barked at him.

Fergus pulled it over, but it was so warped with age that it stuck.

'Leave it so,' Ignatius said, wiping his face with a grubby handkerchief. Then he gestured towards a pile of wooden boxes and told him to sit. The only other chair in the room was home to an enormous grey cat, notorious for her temper. Fergus half sat, half leaned against the boxes, crossed his arms and tried to breathe as shallowly as possible.

'Well, polis, what is it?' his cousin barked.

'Fenians.'

'What of 'em?'

'I hear tell you've been hosting them here,' Fergus said.

'Can a working man not have a pint wherever he wants?' his cousin asked, pushing his straggly hair back behind his ear. Fergus noticed the ear was swollen. Iggy must have been in a fight.

'Aye, as long as he leaves his politics at the door. It's when they start planning mischief that I have a problem with it.'

Ignatius guffawed. 'I can't control what my customers talk about. What has ye in such a pucker?'

'An informer—'

'Who?' Ignatius roared.

Fergus scowled at him. 'I'm not going to tell you that.'

'No customer of mine would dare.'

'Well, that's where you are mistaken. Someone did dare,' Fergus said. He was happy that Ignatius suspected the informer was a customer. It was, in fact, his daughter Lizzie who had sent Fergus the note warning of the Fenian plan, but Fergus had to protect her from her violent and unpredictable father.

Ignatius clenched his fists, as he scowled at the clutter on his desk. 'If I find out...'

'That's your problem, not mine,' Fergus cut in. 'I want to know who's involved in this hare-brained scheme to steal the Irish Crown Jewels.'

Iggy burst out laughing. 'Do you, now? Well, that's the first I've heard of it. I know nothing. Sounds like a lot of nonsense to me. Only a fool would attempt it.'

'You know *nothing*?' scoffed Fergus. 'That's a shame because that would leave me with no alternative but to post a few of my officers outside the door every night for the foreseeable to check who is coming and going. I'd imagine that would be detrimental to business.'

'You wouldn't dare.'

'Try me.' But it was an empty threat. Fergus tried not to imagine Chief Inspector Malone's face if he mooted such an idea. But Byrne didn't know the idea would be shot down in flames without hesitation.

Byrne's breathing grew laboured as he struggled to control his temper. At last he said, 'Billy Murphy and Gavan O'Neill.' He shook his fist at him. 'But they were messin'. There's nothing in it.'

Fergus knew both men. Murphy was, in fact, one of his informers. 'Anyone else?'

'No,' Ignatius snapped. 'And you didn't get those names from me. Understand?'

'Oh, certainly. Thanks. I'll leave you in peace now, cousin. It was a pleasure, as always.'

As he put his hand on the doorknob, his cousin called out. 'Wait.'

'What? Can we make this quick? I'm in the middle of a murder investigation,' Fergus said.

A rumble that might have been a cough came from Ignatius. 'It's that malarkey I want to talk to you about,' he said.

'I can't discuss it, and you should know better than to bring it up,' Fergus answered.

'Get off your high horse, Fergus. I'm family. Doesn't that count for anything at all?'

Fergus grunted then remained silent. It was best not to poke around in the quagmire of their family history.

'Why hasn't there been an arrest yet? We can't have murderers walking the streets, boy.'

He wondered why his cousin was so exercised about this case in particular. He had never expressed any interest in the other members of the criminal fraternity before. Fergus straightened up, giving him a stern look. 'The matter is under investigation, and that is all I'm willing to say. Unless you have information that you would like to pass on. I know how keen you are to fulfil your civic duty.'

'I'd sooner die than be one of your informers,' Byrne snapped, with a twist to his mouth. 'Word is you know who the bastard is. Why haven't you acted?'

'The suspect has an alibi. Anyway, who told you about it?' Fergus asked, trying to control his rising temper.

'A friend,' his cousin said with a smug smile.

Fergus shook his head. 'I might have known you and Lady Muck were acquainted,' he said. 'Associating with kip-keepers now, that's just lovely. That could tarnish your image, damage business. Do your God-fearing customers know about this?'

'Mind your tongue, Fergus boy. My relationship with Mrs Burton is a business one. All this furore is hurting her. She needs to reopen.'

Fergus grinned, putting two and two together. 'We were wondering who her liquor supplier was. Thanks for the information.'

Byrne wagged his finger at him. 'All above board,' he said, narrowing his bloodshot eyes.

Fergus snorted. 'Sure it is. A match made in heaven. You do know she doesn't have a licence.'

'It's for her personal use,' Iggy said.

'Yep, and I'm the King of Spain,' Fergus said with a shake of his head.

Ignatius struggled to his feet, with a great deal of wheezing and puffing. 'I have nothin' to hide. You know well, I'm a respectable businessman, Fergus, and I find your attitude offensive. I am concerned about you for I'd hate for you to mess up your career like you have your personal life. Anyone can see police work is not for you. Even your father found it hard to stomach when you signed up, and he's an idiot.'

'Oh dear. Is your relationship to me hurting your business? I am *so* sorry,' Fergus said.

'Haven't I always been the heart of the family? Looking out for all of you? Devil a bit of thanks I've had for it over the years.'

'Oh yes, a regular patriarch.'

Byrne clutched the side of the desk, his knuckles white. 'That's right, mock me, but where would you be without me and Lizzie, eh? We're the only family you have left, except that cripple of a father of yours.'

'Leave Da and Lizzie out of it,' Fergus snapped.

'How can I?' Byrne wheezed and made an expansive gesture with his hands. 'When they finally put me in an eternity box, all of this will come to her, and she'll need help... unless...'

'No. You know that is impossible.'

'You always were a stubborn little brat. My poor cousin had her hands full with you and your sister. And she'd be alive today if it wasn't for you and your damned pride,' Ignatius spat at him, his face crimson with rage.

And there it was. It always came down to Ignatius playing on his guilt.

Suddenly the space seemed even smaller, and Fergus felt as though he was suffocating. 'I'm leaving. Good day to you,' he said, whipping around and charging out the door. His stomach churned in disgust. How had he allowed Iggy to draw him into the same old argument? As he made his way out towards the bar, he was astonished to feel someone grab his arm. It was Iggy, and he was breathing hard with the effort of catching up with him.

'That blackguard Carver is guilty. Do your duty,' Iggy shouted.

About to pull himself free, Fergus froze. 'How do you know his name?'

'Celine told me.'

'Can the woman not keep her mouth shut? I told you already. The man has an alibi.'

'He can't have,' Byrne said. 'The blaggard was there. Everyone says so.'

Fergus felt the hair rise on his neck. 'What do you know, cousin?'

'I know you are not doing your damned job,' Ignatius roared.

The impact of Ignatius's fist to the side of Fergus's face pushed him back against a door architrave, winding him. But it was the blow to his stomach that sent him crashing to the floor. And all to the sound of Lizzie screaming his name...

<h1 style="text-align:center">SIXTEEN</h1>

Merrion Square, Tuesday, 24th July

Lucy kept vigil at the window of the front parlour, but it was late morning before she saw Myles Carver climb into a cab and head towards the city centre. With haste, she made for the hall, pulling on her gloves. She picked up the basket of fruit, which she had requested the cook to put together, and was about to open the door when George appeared from the rear of the hall.

'May I be of assistance, ma'am?' he asked. 'Would you like me to hail a cab?'

'Not at all, George. I'm going to pay a call on Mrs Carver at No. 83. You might tell cook I hope to be back for lunch.'

George stepped up, opened the door and stood back. 'As you wish, ma'am.'

Lucy paused on the threshold. 'And if I don't return within the hour, I may have encountered a... difficulty. Come fetch me.'

'I understand, ma'am,' he said, a slight smile playing about his lips. 'You are on a mission.'

'Of sorts. Do you disapprove, George?'

He smiled. 'On the contrary. I hope you will not think me too forward if I say I'm delighted to see the bounce back in your step.'

Lucy was still chuckling as she pulled the bell at No. 83, but she composed herself before a stern-faced, middle-aged maid opened the door.

'Good morning, I'm Mrs Stone,' she said, handing over her visiting card. 'Would Mrs Carver be at home?'

The maid glanced at the card and then at Lucy. 'Mrs Carver is ill. She's not receiving any visitors this long time, and I dare say she shan't ever again.'

Slightly stunned by this extraordinary speech, Lucy said, 'My apologies, I should have clarified. Mrs *Olivia* Carver.'

The maid's expression lightened for a moment. And to Lucy's astonishment, she leaned out the door and scanned the street before stepping back and beckoning Lucy inside. *Who was she looking for? Did she fear Mr Carver might return? How bad were things in this house?*

'If you take a seat in here, madam, I'll see if she is at home.'

Lucy was shown into a library, which smelled of books and cigars. The room was dark and austere, a brown flocked wallpaper adding to the gloomy aspect. Much like the man himself, Lucy thought from what she had seen of him. How Phin would scold her for making judgements based on appearance, but from Olivia's revelations, Lucy suspected Carver was a cheerless individual with an overbearing manner.

An ancient grandfather clock, which stood in an alcove next to the fireplace, punctuated the silence of the house. Lucy decided it wasn't a room she'd like to spend much time in. It was far too gloomy. However, with nothing else to do while she waited, she perused the books on the shelves but found nothing to her taste.

It was several minutes later that Olivia entered the room. 'Lucy, how kind of you to call.'

'Not at all. I don't wish to intrude but I hoped this small gift might lift Mrs Carver's spirits,' she said, indicating the basket of fruit she had left on the desk.

'How thoughtful of you. Thank you.' Olivia sucked her bottom lip as she examined the contents of the basket.

'How is your mother-in-law today?'

'No change, I'm afraid. Perhaps...?'

'Yes?'

'Would you like to see her?' Olivia asked. 'Though I'd understand if you'd prefer not. It's just I'd value your opinion on the matter we discussed the other day.'

'Certainly, but only if it would not disturb or upset her,' Lucy said.

'It won't. She's in one of her deep sleeps. It's such a shame, for I know she'd like you. Her illness has isolated her so. No one ever visits.'

'Does your father-in-law discourage it?'

'His instructions to the servants are to turn all visitors away. It's so unfortunate, because before she was ill she loved to socialise. I believe she would welcome the company, but perhaps he is right. It would only remind her of happier times. Besides, some of the time she doesn't even recognise me.'

'That is sad. Am I correct in thinking your father-in-law is not at home?'

'That's right, so he cannot object,' Olivia said as she led Lucy back out into the hallway and up the stairs. Lucy considered this statement encouraging. Perhaps Olivia had a tiny bit of rebellion in her. 'I don't expect him back until late this evening. He's dining at his club.'

They entered the sickroom. A tiny bird-like woman, grey of hair and face, lay against a bank of white pillows. The curtains were almost fully closed, and the lack of light together with the overpowering smell of various medicines made the room a melancholy place. Lucy longed to fling open the windows to let some air in. It wasn't a healthy atmosphere for the poor woman or for Olivia.

Olivia approached her mother-in-law, bent down close and then righted herself. With a shake of her head, she whispered, 'I'm sorry, she is sound asleep.'

Lucy pointed to the various bottles on the nightstand. 'That's a lot of medication.' She homed in on a blue bottle. 'This is the one you mentioned you were concerned about?'

Olivia glanced at the door, blinking rapidly. 'Yes. Digitalis for her heart. And that's the book I enter the doses into.'

Lucy picked it up and flicked through a few pages. Olivia had noted the date and two doses a day which she signed off with her initials. It all looked to be in order. She laid it back down and picked up the bottle of digitalis. Lucy removed the stopper and sniffed. She drew back. 'Good Lord, that smells vile. I can't imagine it tastes nice either.' Olivia remained standing at the other side of Edith's bed, wringing her hands. Seeing how anxious she was, Lucy put the bottle back down. 'I've been thinking about what you said on Saturday.'

'Oh, Lucy, no!' She cast a meaningful glance at the sleeping woman. 'We can't discuss that here. She might hear and become upset. Come across to my room.'

Lucy followed Olivia across the hall.

'I'm sorry. But I must be careful,' Olivia said as she closed her bedroom door. 'Edith might say something to Myles and there'd be the devil to pay.'

Lucy sat at the dressing table. Olivia plonked down onto the bed and covered her face with her hands.

'My dear, tell me what troubles you,' Lucy coaxed. 'Is it Edith's illness or is there something else worrying you?'

Olivia blinked at her. 'No, no. Just Edith. I feel so helpless. Yesterday, she was so ill I thought she was going to die. The doctor was called, but he said... there was nothing more he could do.' Olivia wiped away some tears with a handkerchief. 'If she lasts another week, it will be a miracle. But you can see for yourself how she is. It is no life, lying there day after day, so confused and ill. Her passing would be a blessing at this point, I believe.'

'I'm very sorry. I realise how distressing this is for you. But tell me, was Mr Carver with Edith early this morning?'

Olivia nodded, her chin trembling. 'Yes, his usual early morning visit.'

'And you are sure you gave her the correct dose?'

'Yes, absolutely. I even checked the level in the bottle twice. I have become paranoid about it. Two drops in a glass of water is the correct dose.'

'I don't doubt that you are being extra careful. I would be the same in your position. But don't you see? If he isn't using the medicine in her room to overdose her, Mr Carver must have his own supply, and when they are alone, he administers it. Does a servant go to the apothecary to buy her medicine?'

'No. He does.'

'Does he now? So, the apothecary would know him well. Carver would only have to say that the bottle had broken or some such and get another without raising any suspicion.' Lucy stood. 'So he must have it hidden somewhere in the house so he can access it with ease. There is nothing for it, Olivia. We may not get another opportunity. We must search for it.'

All the colour drained from Olivia's cheeks as she swallowed hard. 'What? You can't be serious.'

It took ten minutes of reasoning before Olivia agreed to search Carver's room for the hypothetical extra digitalis tincture bottle.

'He will throw me out if he finds out,' she moaned. 'What if he comes home early and catches us?'

'Is that likely? Does he ever come home early?'

'No,' Olivia conceded.

'And you said he was dining at his club. Would he come home first to change?'

'He doesn't usually do that.'

'Then we are fine. We have all day, in fact.' Lucy gave her an encouraging smile. 'Let's not waste time. And don't worry, he won't find out. If the worst should happen and he does, you must pack a bag and come directly to me. We will give you sanctuary.'

Olivia stood, sucking her bottom lip. 'Maybe.'

Lucy, now frustrated with Olivia's stalling, paced the room. 'Can we trust the servants?'

'My maid, Sally, yes. The others... they are an unhappy lot. He pays them a pittance, but they dare not complain lest he lets them go without a reference. However, I don't trust any of them. I think they are spying on me, at his behest.'

'What a charming man Mr Carver must be. I almost wish I could meet him,' Lucy said, but Olivia didn't look amused by her flippancy. 'Very well, ring the bell for your maid. Best not to lose any more time in case he should decide to come back.'

The maid summoned, they waited in silence. Lucy had no clear plan other than to find the extra supply of medicine, which would explain Edith's deteriorating condition. But if they found it, what should she do? Give it to Inspector Ryan? Somehow, she doubted Olivia would willingly incriminate Carver. She still hadn't admitted to Ryan she'd given Carver a false alibi for Peggy's murder, so Lucy concluded the man had a powerful hold over her.

The maid, who had answered the front door to her earlier, appeared at last.

'Come in, Sally,' Olivia said. 'And shut the door, please.'

Sally cast Lucy a look laced with suspicion. 'What can I do for ye? Is Mrs Carver worse?'

'No, no, Sally, she's asleep for now. But we need your assistance. Mrs Stone will explain.' Olivia's voice shook.

Lucy outlined her theory, and as she did so, the maid's face lit up.

'Sure, I've had it in mind to do the very same,' the maid exclaimed. 'Something's not right, and that man is wicked enough to do that poor woman harm. And do you know what I think?'

'Do tell,' Lucy said.

'I reckon he has a mistress... and that would give him a motive. Mark my words, when that poor woman is no more, he will move the fancy woman in.'

Too curious not to ask, Lucy said, 'What makes you think he has a lady friend?'

The maid wrinkled her nose. 'State of his clothes, for one. His valet, as was, told me he smelled cheap perfume from his shirts. Coming in at all hours as well, and his missus slippin' away, God love her. 'Tis wicked.'

Olivia's shoulders slumped, and she sat down. She fidgeted with her skirts with trembling hands. 'Oh dear. This is all so distressing. I don't know what to do.'

Lucy shared a conspiratorial look with the maid. 'You need to be strong, Olivia. If we are successful, it may well result in your escape from this dreadful house.'

The young woman appeared much struck by this notion, her hands going still. 'Escape?'

Lucy turned to the maid. 'Sally, you must act as lookout. We don't want any of the other servants to know what we are about.'

'Or Mr Carver,' Sally said.

'Lord, yes, especially him.'

The maid responded with a shrug of her shoulders before she said, 'He's unpredictable, mind you. But never fear. I'll stand at the head of the stairs and repel all boarders.'

'Excellent,' Lucy said, warming very much to the maid and wishing Olivia had half her courage. 'Come along, Olivia. It shouldn't take us long if we search separately.'

A large four-poster with white bedlinen dominated the master bedroom. An armoire and two chests of drawers, in a chinoiserie style, took up one wall, and on the other, a door led into a dressing room-cum-bathroom. There were plenty of potential hiding places for a small bottle.

Lucy turned in the bathroom doorway to find Olivia standing at the main door of the room, twisting her hands. Her pallor was alarming, but Lucy had already guessed she wasn't the adventurous type. The woman was terrified of her own shadow. How on earth was she going to get Olivia to admit she had lied to the police? But if this poisoning matter was cleared up, she might learn to trust Lucy and be guided by her.

'Why don't you search this bathroom? It won't take long,' Lucy said, 'and I'll do the bedroom.'

Olivia headed into the bathroom, and soon Lucy heard drawers and cabinets being opened and closed. After a deep breath, Lucy started her own search. Apart from a collection of risqué postcards hidden in a drawer of starched white shirts, she found nothing suspicious. But it wasn't long before she heard Olivia gasp and call out to her.

'What is it? What have you found?' Lucy asked, peering into the bathroom.

Olivia turned around, and in her hand was a blue bottle with digitalis tincture on the label. 'This is what I feared, but I hoped I was mistaken,' she cried. 'What do we do now?'

Lucy took the bottle and removed the stopper. One sniff was enough to confirm it was the same medicine as in Edith's room. 'We must remove it.'

'No,' Olivia cried. 'You can't do that. He'll know it was me, and the game will be up.'

'Why do you fear him so?'

'Please. Don't press me,' Olivia whispered, her eyes welling up. 'But I have good reason to fear him.'

Lucy stared at the bottle in her hand. 'Well, we have found the evidence. We cannot ignore it. We either remove it, or we must neutralise the harm.' Olivia just gazed at her, eyes bright with tears. Lucy wanted to shake her. Such timid acceptance of her situation was irritating. *She* would have to act. With that, Lucy poured the contents down the sink and ran the taps to rinse the greeny-brown liquid away. Olivia stood staring down at the sink, horrified.

'Why have you done that? Oh, Lucy, I will be in such trouble. He will figure out it was me.'

'No, he won't, because we will replace the liquid with something innocuous, don't worry. Hopefully, he won't realise. Here, hold the bottle while I consult with your maid.'

Lucy hurried to the landing, where she found Sally standing at the head of the stairs. 'Sally, we found it,' she whispered. 'I've disposed of the medicine and now I need some liquid, preferably brown, to replace it. Any ideas?'

Sally pulled at her chin. 'Brown, you say?' Lucy nodded. 'Would tea do?'

'It might. Do hurry and don't let the others see you take it,' Lucy said.

The next ten minutes crawled by, but eventually Sally appeared with a small jug, which she handed to Lucy.

'Watch the door, there's a good woman,' Lucy instructed the maid.

Then Lucy topped up the bottle with the tea to the same level as the medicine the bottle had contained. She checked the smell. The residue of the medicine disguised the odour of the tea. Lucy replaced the stopper and handed the bottle to Olivia with a grin. 'Put it back exactly where you found it.' She let out a slow breath as she watched Olivia do as she was instructed.

'That's a good morning's work. I think we have earned our lunch, don't you?'

'You have nerves of steel, Lucy. Let's just hope he doesn't discover the trick.'

Lucy suspected he would soon realise something was amiss when his wife's health remained stable, but she didn't voice it. Time enough to rescue Olivia from her prison. For now, she was more use to her and Inspector Ryan in situ.

SEVENTEEN

Late afternoon sun streamed in the window. Fergus sat back, his gaze unfocused. Another interminable meeting with Malone an hour before had resulted in a headache. The chief wasn't happy, not something new, but it was grating on Fergus's nerves. He knew himself to be a good detective, but there were days, like today, when it felt like an uphill battle. Peggy O'Reilly's case was going nowhere. With a sigh of deep frustration, Fergus reread Lucy Stone's note. His hope that she would persuade Mrs Carver to rescind her statement and tell the truth appeared to be in vain.

Olivia Carver. Since Friday, she had been in his thoughts far too much. So much hinged on her account, yet he was confident she was under duress to give that alibi. Why was he so reluctant to challenge her? Malone was right for once. He should bring her in for questioning. A little pressure, the intimidating atmosphere, and she would be sure to confess and tell him the truth. But the thought horrified him. There had been something in her gaze. A plea for understanding? Or had he imagined that? He could no longer deny that he was attracted to her, making objectivity a challenge. Perhaps he should call on her in Merrion Square. Catch her unawares. If Carver was out of the house, at the bank, she might talk to him.

He glanced down at the dinner invitation for the following evening which had accompanied the note Lucy had sent. What was the point of going? Surely, if she had other news relevant to the case, she would have included it in the note. Did she not realise how urgent it was? He twirled the invitation between his fingers, unsure he wanted to go. Yes, they were hospitable, but the Stones's life was far removed from his own, he thought, as the image of his father that morning supping tea from a cracked cup, popped into his head. The cup Da had found in the rubble of their former home. The new cups Fergus had bought were pristine where they sat, untouched, on the shelf. Da was getting worse. A fighter all his life, somehow the fire had gone out. No longer being able to work and losing Ma and Kathleen accounted for it. But it was as if he had lost Da, too, that night their home turned to rubble.

Fergus touched his cheek. It was still tender from when Iggy had hit him, and he was developing a spectacular bruise. As expected, he had received a ribbing from his fellow officers on entering the building that morning. He did not divulge the details of his altercation with Iggy for fear of drawing attention to the connection, instead putting it down to a tussle with a vagrant.

But Iggy's words from the day before floated into his mind, and he growled aloud. He couldn't help it. God, the man was such a bastard. Always rubbing his nose with the accusation that it was Fergus's fault that his mother and sister had perished. It didn't help that there was some truth in it. Iggy had offered to find them a new place to rent, one of his many properties, when Fergus's mother had complained about the rats in the tenement where they lived. Big as a cat they were, she had claimed. But Fergus, not wanting to be beholden to Iggy, had refused on the family's behalf. And then, nine months ago, part of their tenement had collapsed in the middle of the night. Fergus had managed to get his father out, but the bystanders had prevented him from going back in to rescue Ma and Kathleen. It was futile to attempt it as the gable wall had buried them. From the street, Fergus had been aghast to see the building fall. Their rooms had been on the top floor, under the eaves. They hadn't stood a chance...

Fergus wiped his forehead with his handkerchief and was contemplating tackling the window to let in some fresh air when Sergeant Hughes walked in. Fergus perked up. Perhaps he had some news. Unfortunately, hot on his heels was Inspector Burke, Malone's pet. Burke grunted a greeting, not even making eye contact, as he passed Fergus on his way to his desk at the far end of the room. Sergeant Hughes's gaze flicked between them, but he was wise enough not to comment.

'Afternoon, Sergeant. Any developments?' Fergus asked.

'Well, sir, we have completed the interviews in The Monto. Either they tell us little or nothing, or fear prevents them from talking at all. Their statements are far too similar in my view. I'd detect Lady Muck's hand in that.'

'And Mulcahy, no doubt. A conspiracy of silence?'

'Oh, aye. The usual, sir. Though...'

Fergus cocked his head. 'Go on. There was something.'

'Maybe. It may not be significant, sir, but the girl'—he consulted his notebook—'Ginny O'Mara. Her room is below Peggy's. She said she heard a loud thump from the room above but thought nothing of it at the time.' He tilted his head as he read from his notes. 'She says some clients are quite rowdy, especially if they've been drinking.'

Ginny? But she had said to him on the night of the murder that she knew nothing. What was she playing at?

'Did she say what time she heard this? It might have been the attack she heard,' Fergus said, sitting up.

With a shrug, Hughes answered, 'She wasn't sure but thought it was at least twenty minutes before seven. It was just a thump. I asked if she had heard anyone cry out or scream, but she was unsure. Well, except for an hour later when all hell broke loose when Lady Muck and Peggy's next client entered Peggy's room and found the body.'

Fergus absorbed this with a frown. 'But hold on. Celine said that Carver had arrived just before seven. If he did, he can't be responsible.' He rummaged in the drawer of his desk and pulled out his notebook. With a quick flick through, he found the entry he wanted. 'Yes, she said "about seven".' Fergus rapped his fingers on the blotting pad on his desk. 'But I don't suppose it exonerates Carver. Celine might have been mistaken about his time of arrival. How did Ginny know the time, anyway? I doubt she owns a watch.'

'She'd returned to her room from the kitchen to prepare for her next client. As I say, she wasn't sure. Only that it was before her own client arrived.'

'And her client arrived at seven?'

Hughes nodded.

'And still no luck finding a cabbie who might have dropped or picked up Carver?'

'No, but he might have walked,' Hughes commented.

'From the bank on Dame Street? I don't think that's likely. Not someone of his standing. Besides, the local lads would have attacked and robbed him walking around The Monto in evening dress. You might as well have a "rob me" sign on your back. My money is on his using a cab. Keep looking.'

'Will do, sir. I've asked my friend over at Store Street station to give me a list of cabbies based in that area. They are more likely to have picked up a fare in there.'

'Good thinking. Right, we'd better see if we can find our so-called Fenians, Murphy and O'Neill, and drag them in for questioning. I'll give you their addresses. You might organise a couple of constables to do the necessary.'

'Oh, I can save you the trouble, Ryan,' came Burke's heavy Cork accent from across the room. 'The chief has asked me to take over that case. You're making so little progress, and it being so important, like.'

For a moment, Fergus went rigid with anger. Malone. He'd

love to string the man up. To his disgust, Burke sauntered over to his desk, smug as you like.

'I understand Murphy is one of your informants. Didn't you know he was a Fenian troublemaker? Oh dear. Not like you to slip up like that, Ryan. You being our *star* detective.'

'I didn't slip up, Burke. Murphy is no more a Fenian than I am which you'll soon find out. You'll be wasting your time for I don't trust the source of the information, but since the chief expects it to be followed up on, I suggest you get to it,' Fergus said with what he hoped was a patronising grin.

Burke flushed but clamped his mouth. With deliberate slowness, he walked to the coat stand, pulled his hat and coat off, and swept out the door without a backward glance.

Hughes's mouth twitched.

'I can see you are tempted, but say nothing. Well, I suppose this is a blessing. It gives me more time to work on the O'Reilly cases.' Fergus picked up Lucy's invite. 'I'm heading to Merrion Square, Hughes. I have to drop in a reply to this dinner invitation from Mrs Stone.'

Hughes's eyes widened. 'No need to go all that way, sir. One of the messenger boys could do that for you.'

'They could, but I also wish to call at the Carver house. Seeing as I'm now free of the Fenian hunt, it's about time Mrs Carver and I had another wee chat, and she started telling us the truth.'

EIGHTEEN

Merrion Square

Having handed in an acceptance for Lucy to the butler at No. 81, Fergus headed to the Carver residence. The hatchet-faced maid, who had greeted him on his earlier visit, answered Fergus's ring of the bell. Her eyes narrowed as she recognised him. 'Yes?'

'Good afternoon, may I speak to Mrs Carver... Mrs *Olivia* Carver,' he corrected in time, remembering the existence of the older lady.

'I doubt she's receiving, sir,' the maid answered with a dead stare. 'Perhaps another time?' The door started to close.

Fergus stopped it with his foot. '*Perhaps* you would be good enough to do your job and pass on my request to see her, miss. It is *police* business. Alternatively, I will have to insist she accompany me to the castle, which will be far more disruptive to her day and yours, I'm sure you'd agree...'

As he hoped, this had the desired effect. She opened the door fully and beckoned him in. With a nod of her head towards the library, she barked, 'Wait in there, please... sir.'

As he entered the room, he chuckled to himself. *Cerberus himself could not have been as fierce a guard.* He was only glad she had just the one head. But the question was, why did Olivia need a sentinel? Had she warned the maid to keep him at bay?

Fergus wasn't really prepared for his reaction when Olivia joined him in the library. His stomach did a strange somersault. It was bizarre. Despite puzzling over this, he observed her pallor, and he could have sworn she had grown thinner in the few days since last they spoke. She was under considerable stress, he'd put money on it. That damned father-in-law of hers was the likely culprit. It made his blood boil to think of this poor young woman being preyed upon by such a man. And now, here he was about to put her under more pressure, but the job had to come first. There was no room for sentimentality in a murder case. And then she spoke, her voice low and melodious, and his resolve almost melted away.

'Good afternoon,' she said upon sitting down. Then her eyes widened, and he guessed she was wondering what had happened to his face.

Feeling self-conscious, he touched his cheek and cleared his throat. 'Good afternoon, Mrs Carver.'

'What can I do for you, Inspector?'

He noted her trembling hands as she smoothed down her skirts. Then she tucked a strand of hair behind her ear. 'I have some further questions for you. Is Mr Carver at home?'

'No, he is at the bank today.'

Fergus offered her a smile as he sat down. 'Then we may speak freely.'

If anything, the colour in her pale cheeks drained even further. 'I don't understand you, sir. I thought our interview last week concluded the matter.'

'Mrs Carver, I will pursue every lead until we catch the killer. In that light, and on reflection, is there anything you'd like to change in the statement you provided to us last Friday? Perhaps you have remembered something, or the events are a little clearer?'

Her hands clenched. 'No. I have nothing to add.'

'Is there any chance you are mistaken about the night we are talking about? Is it possible you were confused?' He was offering her an excuse, but would she grasp the opportunity to alter her statement?

'It was only a few days ago. I recall the events of that evening with absolute clarity.'

He didn't miss her irritated tone, so he decided on a different tack. 'You must understand that providing a false alibi to someone, particularly in a murder case, is a serious offence in itself. It would amount to perjury in court if the case goes to trial.'

There was a flicker of fear in her eyes. 'I... I have nothing to add.' It was almost a whisper, and he saw what it cost her.

But as much as he sympathised with her situation, his frustration was growing. 'My problem is this, Mrs Carver. There are several witnesses who have placed your father-in-law at the scene of a murder last Thursday evening. He was a regular visitor to the establishment, and they are certain of his identity. In a nutshell, I have several people whose testimonies contradict yours. So, I ask again. Do you wish to add to or amend your statement in any respect?'

Olivia bent her head.

'Are you under duress?' he asked, half exasperated.

Her head flew up. 'Is it not enough that you have those other witnesses? Why do you need me to...' She waved her hand in a flustered gesture as she trailed off.

That surprised him. Was it a sign that she had given the conundrum some thought and saw this as a way out for herself? 'Possibly. But I cannot ignore your statement. It is on the record. For me to act on their testimonies, you must withdraw or amend yours.' This wasn't strictly true, but he hoped it would jolt her conscience.

Her chin went up. 'Both options are impossible, Inspector, because I can only tell the truth.' Suddenly, she rose to her feet, and he had to follow suit. 'I hope you find whoever murdered that girl, but I can be of no further assistance in the matter. I'll bid you good day.'

Defeated for now, Fergus could only fume in silence. Whatever hold Carver had on this woman was too tight. It would take more than his powers of persuasion to sway her. But he was certain her statement was a lie.

He followed Olivia out into the hallway. The maid was nowhere to be seen, however, so Olivia advanced toward the front door to let him out. But something caught his eye. Beside the coat stand was a large brass cane holder, which held several umbrellas and an unusual wolfhound-headed cane. Fergus pulled it out, admiring the carving.

'Does this belong to your father-in-law?' he asked.

Olivia walked back towards him. 'Yes. He is extremely attached to it. It was a present from his wife.'

'Does he use it most days?'

'Yes.'

Fergus ran his fingers along the shaft and then weighed the carved head in his hand. The back of the dog's head was round and the right size... a perfect weapon, in fact. The image of Peggy's bashed-in temple flashed into his mind. If they found traces of blood on it...

'I'll take this with me,' he informed her, tucking the cane under his arm.

'Oh, no, you mustn't. He will be furious,' she said, clutching his arm.

He shook her off, angry now. 'I think, madam, you have obstructed me enough for one day,' he said as he brushed past her towards the door. He heard her gasp, but he didn't turn around as he exited for fear of what he might see in those beguiling green eyes.

NINETEEN

Hedgelong & Peavey Booksellers was a Dublin institution on Grafton Street, the city's premier shopping thoroughfare. Standing on the corner of Duke Street, the bookstore had been serving Dubliners for decades. It was also Fergus's favourite bookshop to visit when he had a free hour. With his father invalided, Fergus put aside a little of his salary each month to buy him a book. Prior to the tragedy which had claimed his leg, Fergus's father had been a teacher. Now, stuck in their lodgings, and with Fergus working long hours, his father often succumbed to melancholy. Books were his escape. These days, he had few other pleasures, and the sight of a new book, preferably about some aspect of Irish history, was guaranteed to cheer him up.

How Fergus envied the likes of Carver with his vast library, and it galled him that it was all for show. He guessed Carver had bought the entire collection at an auction, and as Fergus had speculated on that first visit to the Carver household, rarely opened any of them.

If only Fergus had half the space to store books, but as it was, his purchases, once read, were brought to a second-hand bookseller and cashed in, bar one or two that he could not bear to part with. Someday, Fergus swore, he'd have a library of his own and he'd read every damn book in it, many times. As would his father.

As Fergus browsed the shelves near the front window of the bookshop, he happened to look up and out onto Grafton Street. As usual, the street was busy, with carriages and carts jostling for road space, and the pavements were thick with a mix of pedestrians from all walks of life. Finely dressed shoppers strolled past, some with servants trotting behind them, carrying their parcels. Street urchins often shadowed these unsuspecting shoppers on the lookout for an opportunity to relieve some careless citizen of their wallet or purse. Fergus knew the street and its environs well, for his first beat on joining the DMP had been around this area. Consequently, he knew most of the shops on the street were high-end, and their produce unattainable on a police inspector's pay. Except for the books, thank goodness.

And then he saw her and caught his breath. Instinct kicking in, he stepped back in case she spotted him. Olivia Carver. Looking as lovely as ever. As she walked past the bookshop, she tucked a stray strand of hair behind her ear, a mannerism he found enticing. He couldn't help but watch her, for she moved with such grace. He wondered where she was going. Was she on an errand for her mother-in-law perhaps or shopping for herself? The temptation to follow her was strong, to bump into her, but after the events of the previous day, and the manner of their parting, meeting him was likely the last thing she wanted. Once again, he cursed Myles Carver's antics for placing him in a difficult position with her. If only they had met under different circumstances. But deep down he knew she'd never be interested in him, for their worlds could not have been further apart. Fergus's good mood shifted. His chances of befriending Olivia were as unrealistic as his hopes of owning a library. That was his reality.

Glancing at his watch, Fergus groaned. He needed to stop dawdling, choose a book and hurry back to work. Soon after, he spotted *Cromwell in Ireland*, which looked interesting. He knew his father would love it. He'd grumble and rant to Fergus as he'd read it, thoroughly enjoying himself as he castigated the infamous Englishman. Fergus plucked it from the shelf and headed to the counter to pay. As he waited for the lad behind the counter to write out a receipt, Fergus's mind was already back on the case. He hoped Doc Peters would have concluded his tests by now and sent a report. If there was blood on that cane, it would be enough evidence to pull Carver in, *and* it would be a reason to visit Merrion Square, and an excuse to see her again. The thought brought a smile to his face. But it was important for the case too, obviously. Surely, such evidence would be enough to convince her to be truthful at last.

Fergus left the shop and turned north towards Trinity College. Only a few yards down the street, however, he suddenly spotted Olivia again on the far side. Fergus ducked into the entrance of a milliner's shop, half turning to look into the curved window with its display of hats. Unable to help himself, he glanced across. Olivia was speaking to a couple standing outside Pope & Baker, the military outfitters. Even from his side of the street, Fergus noticed that Olivia was animated, chatting away and looking up at the gentleman, her eyes wide. She paid little or no heed to the lady who was in a bath chair. The invalid wore a wide-brimmed hat, which hid her features, and her head was bent as if she were studying the pavement. The gentleman was tall and in uniform, and was, presumably, about to enter or leave the outfitter's premises. As Fergus watched, the man glanced down at the bent head of the lady, then reached out and touched Olivia's arm so quickly Fergus could have missed it. Then the conversation ended abruptly. The officer nodded to Olivia before turning the bath chair around and pushing it back up the street, away from Olivia.

So, Olivia must have some acquaintances in Dublin, Fergus mused, as he wondered who the couple were. Perhaps they were brother and sister, because that lightning touch had an intimate quality to it. His mood plummeted once more. Which was ridiculous. Why would it bother him? She was a widow, her period of mourning ending soon, which meant she was free to start over.

But then he realised Olivia had not moved a muscle. Instead, she stood watching the couple disappear into the crowd. But it was the look on her face that shocked Fergus.

It was pure desolation.

Fergus stepped further inside the entranceway, into the shadows. How very odd, he thought. And then almost as quickly, Olivia's face softened, and she clutched her parcel to her chest. She half turned, but was unable to resist a final lingering gaze in the direction of her acquaintances, even though Fergus was sure they were well out of sight by now. Then Olivia must have realised she was blocking the path, for she spun on her heel and walked away.

Merrion Square

An excited yelp followed by a whoop drew Lucy's attention away from her book and out to the back garden. Ellie was doubled over, giggling, and Bash was running around in circles, waving his cricket bat above his head. They were supposed to be playing cricket on the lawn, supervised by Jenny and George, but as usual it appeared to have degenerated into something else altogether. Lucy raised a brow, and George shrugged and gave her a reassuring smile. George's endless patience with the children was a godsend. They, in turn, adored him.

A sudden commotion out in the hall pulled Lucy's attention away, and seconds later, Mary burst in the door.

'I'm back, ma'am, so I am,' the maid said, barely drawing breath. 'Thank you ever so much. We gave her a grand send-off. Such a big funeral. Sure, the whole county must have been there. Mind you, a few old biddies didn't turn up because of the circumstances. People are fierce cruel sometimes. Poor Aunty May was hurt about it, but me Ma said they weren't worth the trouble.' Mary paused for breath. 'If only poor Bridget could have been there, too.

Aunty May is so grateful to you and Mr Stone for all you've done for us, and bid me tell you so.'

'I'm only too glad to help, Mary, and I'm delighted to have you back again. You must be exhausted after the journey, and hungry, too. Ask cook to get you something.'

'No, ma'am, I'm fine. I'll have something later. I was anxious to tell you... before I left Wexford, I told me aunt that if anyone can find our Bridget, it will be you.'

'Oh, Mary, I hope you didn't give her false hope. I will do my best, we all will, but it's weeks now since anyone saw her.'

Mary quirked her mouth into a woebegone smile. 'Sure I can't sleep with worrying about what has happened to her, but she was always the cleverer of the two, so perhaps she made her escape. I was thinking maybe she was too ashamed to go home and is hiding somewhere. But how will she survive with no money or friends to help her?'

'I have no idea. That worries me, too. They have heard nothing down in Wexford?'

'No. Not a dickybird, ma'am. Me poor aunt has said several novenas, but alas, it doesn't seem to be working.'

Lucy knew it would take hard work on their part as opposed to prayers to find the missing girl.

'Do sit, Mary. Please. You will be glad to hear I haven't been idle while you were away. I have some news.' Lucy waited for the maid to sit and then told her about her visit to the priest. 'And not an hour ago, I received a message from him. A young woman by the name of Ginny is prepared to meet us this very afternoon at the priest's house.'

'That's wonderful, ma'am. I mean, she wouldn't agree to meet us if she didn't know something.'

'My thought exactly.'

'I pray she knows where our Bridget is,' Mary said.

'So do I, or if not, that she might have information that will lead us to her. The last I heard from Inspector Ryan, they had circulated the photograph of the girls, but it hasn't generated any clues.

The DMP searched Burton's house from top to bottom on Saturday, but they found no trace of Bridget, and everyone there denies ever seeing or hearing about her. They are lying, I'm sure of it, but how does one prove it? However, the inspector is joining us for dinner again tonight, so he may have more news for us then.'

Mary's lip turned down. 'At least they tried, I suppose. But our Bridget ain't important enough for them polis to do more to find her. If she were highborn, they'd be doing more.'

'To be fair to the inspector, Mary, I believe he is doing his best. His priority must be finding Peggy's killer before the man strikes again.'

'Maybe.' Mary stared down at her closed fists and then looked up, her eyes bright with tears. 'But I'm putting me money on you and no mistake.'

Marlborough Street, later that afternoon

The priests' housekeeper, Mrs Clancy, showed Lucy and Mary into the front parlour of the parochial house, explaining that Father McGuinness had been called away to a dying parishioner and sent his apologies. Mrs Clancy then offered to make tea for them while they waited for their visitor.

'Thank you, Mrs Clancy.' However, the housekeeper hesitated in the doorway, her lips clamped in a hard line. 'Was there something else?' Lucy asked.

'Just a warning, Mrs Stone, for Father is too polite to say it, but the women from that place are not fit company for you... liars, thieves and heathens, the lot of 'em. I wouldn't trust this young one, if I were you. She'll be coming here to make mischief, if not for you, for Father.'

Lucy took a calming breath to quell her irritation, treating the woman to a hard stare. 'Thank you, Mrs Clancy. That will be all.'

'Huh,' the housekeeper muttered and trotted out the door.

'Maybe she's right, ma'am. I feel awful bad about involving you in all this. You're not used to the likes of these women.'

'Mary, you seem to forget both of us have had dealings with Coffin Mike over the years. You don't get shiftier than him.'

'It's true for you, ma'am. I did,' Mary said with an exaggerated shudder. 'There's few souls as bad as him and no mistake.'

'We must do this, Mary. We can't do anything more to help poor Peggy, but there's a good chance that we can find Bridget.' With a sympathetic smile, she continued, 'We can't give up now.'

A smile trembled on Mary's lips. 'Thank you, ma'am. But what if this woman doesn't come or knows nothing useful, or spins us a tale? It's not safe for either of us to venture into that place, especially for you. My, what a scandal that would cause. What would the master say?'

'I'd do it if I had to. As would he,' Lucy declared with a toss of her head. 'There is a conspiracy of silence about what goes on in there. How could the police have let it get to the point that they fear to enter? There can be only one explanation.'

'What's that, ma'am?'

'The men who frequent the brothels are well-to-do and influential, and are determined to keep their *activities* secret. All of which is going to make our job more difficult.' Lucy glanced at the clock on the mantelpiece. 'But don't give up hope, Mary. The woman is only a little late. It may not be easy for her to get away. From what Inspector Ryan told me, the women in the brothels have little freedom. We must make allowances, for she's risking a lot to come and talk to us.'

A few minutes later, Mary grabbed her arm while looking out the window into the street. 'Look, could that be her?'

A young woman, dressed in a navy coat and matching hat, had stopped outside and was looking up at the house. She was so thin, her gaunt cheekbones spoilt what would otherwise be a pretty face. Mary's grip on Lucy's arm tightened as the woman climbed the steps of the house and rang the bell.

They waited. Outside the parlour door there was a whispered conversation. Lucy and Mary exchanged concerned looks.

'And don't you forget. You're dealing with quality. None of

your nonsense or Father McGuinness will deal with you,' they heard Mrs Clancy scold.

The parlour door opened, and Mrs Clancy entered, the woman in navy close on her heels.

'Your *visitor*, madam,' Mrs Clancy said, her lips pursed, and her stony gaze fixed on the young woman as she stepped forward. 'Virginia O'Mara.'

Lucy stood. 'Thank you, Mrs Clancy,' she said as she offered her hand to the visitor. 'Thank you for agreeing to meet us, Miss O'Mara. We are *extremely* grateful to you for coming to see us today.' Then she stared hard at the housekeeper, who sniffed and exited, snapping the door shut. They shook hands, and the woman nodded to Mary. 'Please won't you sit down? I'm Lucy Stone and this is Mary O'Reilly.'

'Thank you, ma'am,' Miss O'Mara said. Her posture was rigid and Lucy suspected she was nervous.

'Tea, Miss O'Mara?' Lucy asked.

'Ginny, please. Everyone calls me tha',' Miss O'Mara said in a strong Dublin accent. 'And yes, please. I'd love some tea. I'm parched after the walk. It's roastin' again today.'

'Excellent,' Lucy said, pouring three cups and handing them out. Lucy was shocked. The young woman's pallor was striking up close, contrasting with the purple smudges beneath her eyes. Lucy knew a prostitute's life must be a hard one, but this woman's body screamed illness.

'We won't keep you long, Ginny. We have a couple of questions, and Father McGuinness thought you might help us.'

A wary expression settled on Ginny's features. 'Maybe. Depends, don't it?'

'On?'

'What youse want to know.'

'That's a fair point,' Lucy said. 'I'll let Mary explain.'

'Well, I'm Peggy O'Reilly's cousin—the young girl who was murdered—'

'I knows nothin' about it,' Ginny exclaimed.

'That's all right, Ginny. That's not why we're here,' Lucy interjected.

Biting her lip, Ginny said, 'Sorry for your loss, God rest her soul. The poor chiseller didn't deserve it.'

Mary flicked an anxious glance at Lucy before she continued. 'Thank you. Well, me and Mrs Stone are trying to find out where her sister Bridget has disappeared to. They would have been together and yet there's no trace of her. The police asked after her where you, ah, work, but everyone denied ever seeing her.' Mary pulled out the photograph of the sisters and shoved it across the table. Ginny picked it up. 'She's the one on the right.'

After a few moments' scrutiny, Ginny placed the picture down on the table. 'Yeah, I saw her. Look, you must understand. It's dangerous for us to talk. The consequences for squealing are dire.' She paused, looking down at her thin hands. 'I'm sorry about your cousin. None of us will forget that night. I didn't know her well. Girls come and go, but she seemed nice... though a bit dim-witted for getting herself into Lady Muck's clutches, if you don't mind me sayin'. Young, too, but then Lady Muck likes them that way. There are clients who only want them like that. She has her bully boys snatch them off the street. Country girls mostly, or girls like me that get into trouble and have nowhere to turn... have no choices left.'

'But you saw her? In The Monto?' Lucy asked. Ginny nodded. 'That's something. You see, we traced them as far as Westland Row and we believe someone approached them at the station. We are sure they planned to visit their aunt, Mary's mother, but they never made it.'

'Sounds about right. Lady Muck has bully boys hanging around there looking for likely girls to pluck,' Ginny said. Then she took a shaky breath and stared out onto the street. 'Look, I don't know her history, but she didn't deserve to die like that. Me and the other girls were upset.' Her gaze swung back towards them. 'Mulcahy is supposed to protect us.'

'Who's that?' Lucy asked.

'Lady Muck's chief bully boy. He's on the door and is supposed to screen the clients. And if us girls don't toe the line, she has him give us a slap or two. Word is that the client who killed your Peggy was a regular, so Mulcahy would have let him in, no questions asked. They could be some swanky toff or a sailor, he don't care once they have money. Then Lady Muck plies them with drink and charges them a fortune. Violence of some kind is often the result.'

'Good lord, Ginny, that sounds horrific. So, you have no protection?'

'None.'

'Sorry. Who is Lady Muck?' Mary asked.

'Mrs Burton. She owns half the kip and flash-houses in The Monto. She's vicious.'

'But she has told the police who the likely killer is.'

Ginny scoffed. 'She's not what you'd call kind-hearted. You can be sure she has her reasons.'

Phin's warning echoed in Lucy's head. 'Is she lying to protect someone else? A different client?'

Ginny just shrugged. 'Or she's helpin' the DMP so she can open up again as soon as possible.' She sniffed. 'She's losing a fortune.'

Lucy's instincts were urging her to probe further, but the main reason they were here today was to trace Bridget. She'd report this conversation to Ryan as it might help him. Perhaps Olivia wasn't lying, and Carver was innocent after all. As Phin had pointed out, they hadn't considered that possibility.

'Do you recall the day the girls arrived in The Monto?' Lucy asked.

Ginny's eyes strayed to the photograph once more. 'Yep.'

'Do you know where Bridget is now?' Lucy asked.

'Please,' Mary said. 'We need to find her. Her mother is terrified she'll end up like Peggy. We're desperate.'

Ginny finished her tea and set her cup back on the saucer. Her hand shook. 'I don't want no trouble, see. Narks end up dead around here. The likes of me has few choices. Most of us end up in the Westmoreland Lock Hospital... then Glasnevin Cemetery, or as we call it, "The Monto Terminus".' She ended on a dry laugh, which sent a shiver down Lucy's spine.

'I think you're a good person, Ginny. In fact, I know you are— why else would you come and see us today? If you can help us, we will do what we can for *you*,' Lucy said. 'Please help us. We must find Bridget before she comes to harm.'

The young woman gave her a sidelong look. 'I've had enough, and I want out before TB or worse finishes me off. I nearly have the fare saved for the boat to England...' Her voice trailed off, but Lucy now knew what she wanted.

Lucy sized her up. She had to take the risk. 'Fine. I'll give you enough for your fare and money to get you to London if your information is useful. A friend of mine runs a charity for lost young women. She may be able to help you find a position in service.'

Beside her, Mary gave a little gasp, her eyes round as saucers.

'That sounds acceptable.' With a slow nod, Ginny held out her hand. Lucy shook it, shocked to feel the bones in Ginny's hand so easily.

'Where is she, Ginny?' Lucy asked.

Ginny quirked her mouth as she looked at Mary. 'Of the two, your Bridget must have been the one with brains. She point-blank refused when she realised what kind of house it was, even tried to make a run for it, but Mulcahy put a stop to it. Peggy was whisked off, crying her eyes out. In all honesty, I thought Bridget was in for it. I mean, Burton is handy with a knife when she doesn't get her way. But your cousin's luck was in. Burton's booze supplier was there, and he persuaded Burton to let him have her.'

Her words made Lucy's blood run cold. 'What do you mean, "have her"?'

'Byrne owns pubs around the city, and he was looking for a good-looking girl to work behind the bar. He took a fancy to your Bridget.'

Lucy breathed out slowly with relief. 'So, not another flash or kip-house.'

'No. But don't be thinking she's having an easy time of it. Byrne is even worse than Burton. I hear he's a right old bastard, forgive the French.'

Lucy dismissed this with a wave of her hand.

'Which public house is she working in?' Mary asked, leaning forward.

'I heard it was The Sleepy Druid, Thomas Street. You know it?'

'In the Liberties, isn't it?' Mary asked. Ginny nodded.

'Thank you, Ginny,' Lucy said. 'We will check it out. Provided your information is correct, I'll leave a message with Father McGuinness and make arrangements for you to travel to England. Is that acceptable?'

Ginny sat back and gave each of them a measured look before breaking into a weary smile. 'I reckon so. Pleasure doing business with you, Mrs Stone.'

TWENTY

Merrion Square, later that evening

It was a lovely evening and still daylight as Fergus approached the Stone residence on foot. Straightaway, he spotted Olivia Carver descending the steps of her home as he crossed the road from the park side of the street. She, however, did not notice him but turned and walked away. She wore a deep burgundy dress with a paisley shawl instead of her usual lilac, which made him wonder. Such evening attire surprised him—where was she off to?—for he'd imagined her social life was as barren as his own. Could she be meeting that couple she had met on Grafton Street? Deeply curious, he was tempted to speed up and find out, but he hesitated. It was possible she was still angry with him for taking the cane, not to mention his attempt to coerce her into modifying her statement the previous afternoon.

It was only afterwards, when he returned to his desk at Dublin Castle, that Fergus had considered how Carver might react when he discovered the cane was in his possession. Through his servants, he would know about Fergus's visit and would blame Olivia. He felt guilty about that. Would the brute take it out on her? Might he be violent towards her? Look what he had done to poor Peggy

O'Reilly. Still, he had to do his job. He could not have ignored such evidence. Such opportunities had to be seized when they arose.

There had been only one thing to do, and that was to summon Dr Peters. All too aware of the man's fascination with forensic analysis (having sat through a lengthy monologue on the topic and his purchase of his microscope one evening in a public house), Fergus wanted Peters's expert opinion on the cane. Luckily, the doctor had been only too willing to give it. He agreed with Fergus that the head of the cane might be the murder weapon, and he took the cane away to examine it further. Fergus hoped if traces of blood were found on it, it would provide him grounds to arrest Carver.

As he was leaving the castle this evening, a note had arrived from Peters detailing his findings. Using Schönbein's test, applying hydrogen peroxide to detect the presence of blood, Peters confirmed that the hydrogen peroxide had foamed, and therefore he was satisfied that blood was present in the grooves of the wood. Fergus had punched the air when he read that. Carver had to be guilty; why else would there be such damning evidence? First thing in the morning, he would bring the new evidence to Chief Inspector Malone and proceed to arrest Carver for Peggy's murder. The only sticking point was Olivia's statement. But if he told her about the blood on the cane, she would have no choice but to tell the truth.

Fergus couldn't help himself. He slowed down so that he might observe Olivia as she walked away from him. However, to his astonishment, she didn't go far. She climbed the steps to the Stone house and rang the bell. Was she also a dinner guest? His heart rate jumped, and he smiled. This was Lucy's doing and for his benefit. What was Lucy up to now? Intrigued, he increased his pace and mounted the steps as the Stone butler opened the door.

'Good evening, madam... sir,' the butler said.

Olivia spun round, her face registering shock as she met his gaze. Her colour rose as she nodded to acknowledge him before she stepped inside, handing her shawl to Lucy's maid. In her agitation, she dropped her reticule and scrambled to retrieve it before either Fergus, the maid or the butler, had a chance to help.

Was it a guilty conscience that was making her act so jittery? Fergus struggled to find the right words to say to her, particularly in front of the servants, but the opportunity was lost as Lucy's maid, Mary, caught his eye and approached him.

'Sir, I'm glad to have a chance to speak to you in person. I wanted to thank you again for all you did for our Peggy. The family is very grateful. We gave her as good a send-off as was possible in the circumstances.'

'My pleasure, Mary, but I think most of your thanks are due to Mrs Stone,' he said.

'Yes, sir. She's very good.'

Olivia stood listening to this exchange, with a frown. Could it be that she didn't know the connection between the murdered girl and the Stone household? But if she did, she'd not be brazen enough to attend a dinner party under those circumstances. Lucy must have withheld the information for her own ends. Clever of her, if so. Gain Olivia's trust first, then reveal the details of the incident and the Stone connection and apply pressure. If only his own colleagues were half as strategic. Though with the recent evidence from Peters, Fergus didn't think he'd need Lucy to turn the thumbscrews. But how was he to get Olivia alone this evening? Offer to escort her home later, perhaps?

'Mrs James Carver and Inspector Ryan, ma'am.' A few yards away, the butler was announcing them to Lucy and Phineas. Dismissing his thoughts, Fergus approached Olivia, extending his arm. 'Shall we?' Avoiding his gaze, she rested her arm on his, her face devoid of expression. He was not forgiven.

Once the dessert dishes were cleared, Lucy rose from the table, Olivia's cue to follow her to the drawing room. She ushered Olivia ahead, then stuck her head back around the dining room door and said, 'Enjoy your port and cigars.' When she was sure Olivia was out of earshot, she whispered, 'But don't be long.'

She exchanged meaningful glances with Phin and then Inspector Ryan. Matters were coming to a head, Lucy was certain. Olivia had been almost silent throughout dinner and had eaten little. Breaking point was not far off. If they were to persuade her to reveal the truth, tonight was their best chance. Lucy hated to put the poor woman in such a position, but the memory of that visit to the morgue was too fresh in her memory. Out in the hallway, Lucy had only to see Mary's downcast features for her resolve to harden. Carver had to be held accountable for killing Peggy. Olivia *had* to tell the truth.

Lucy entered the drawing room to find Olivia pacing the floor. 'My dear, what is the matter? You were very quiet during dinner. Has something happened?'

Olivia squeezed and twisted her hands. 'Oh, Lucy, yesterday evening was dreadful. A servant told my father-in-law about your visit, and he was livid.'

'Why so? Did he notice anything amiss with that bottle of digitalis?'

'No, he never mentioned that.'

'What did he say? Do please sit down.' Lucy waved to the seat opposite.

'He said that Edith wasn't up to visitors and that you were a stranger and had probably upset her. That I had done it deliberately, too. I'm so sorry, but I'm not allowed to admit you again.'

'But that's nonsense. The poor woman slept through my entire visit. My dear, it seems to me that man wishes to keep you and his poor wife isolated. Have you no other friends or relatives who might help you?'

'No one in Ireland, Lucy. No one I can trust.'

'Except us.'

'Yes, I... yes.'

'Well, I'm glad you came to us tonight. How did you get away?

Did you say you were coming here? I can't imagine he'd be pleased about that.'

'It didn't arise, Lucy. He left for Cork this morning, and he will be away for several days. Otherwise...' Olivia glanced at the clock, then back to Lucy. 'Thank you for the invitation, but I won't stay much longer. I'd like to look in on Edith before I retire.'

Lucy knew a scared rabbit when she saw one. Olivia must suspect they were going to gang up on her. She needed to keep her talking. Where were the men? 'Ah, I see. Is Sally sitting with her? I have to say, she impressed me. You appear to be as lucky with your maid as I am.'

'Yes, she has been with me since I was seventeen. I was so lucky that she agreed to come to Ireland when I married. I'd be lost without her.'

'Then if Sally is standing in for you, stay a little longer. I suspect you don't have many opportunities to socialise. It's early yet, and the men will join us soon.' Lucy watched as a myriad of emotions danced across Olivia's face. Ryan's presence was troubling Olivia, she was sure of it. 'Did Mr Carver visit Edith this morning before he left?'

'No, he left the house for Kingsbridge straight after breakfast to catch the first Cork train.'

'Then he wouldn't have had any opportunity for mischief. How did Edith fare during the day?'

'She was calm, but she slept for most of it. The strange thing was that when she woke, she kept complaining there was a yellow hue to everything in the room, even me.'

'That sounds odd,' Lucy said. 'It might be a sign of poisoning. Perhaps you should consult the doctor about it. It would be an ideal opportunity with your father-in-law away.' Olivia's nod was perfunctory, Lucy noted, so she plunged on. 'All of this confirms, does it not, that your father-in-law is up to something on the days he visits her in the morning? He must be giving her extra doses.' Olivia answered with a shrug, a hint of misery in her eyes. 'Well, we have neutralised his mischief for now, my dear.'

'I hope so.' Olivia lapsed into silence.

'Perhaps...' Lucy began, and Olivia glanced at her, wide-eyed. 'Perhaps we should tell the inspector about your suspicions.'

'Oh, no, Lucy. I have no definite proof.'

Lucy sat forward on her chair. 'But I can back you up. What reason could he have for possessing that second bottle of her medicine? Ryan should investigate.'

Olivia's chin trembled and Lucy feared she would cry. 'No, no. If there is a problem, the doctor will notice and... take action. I don't want to cause trouble.'

Lucy wanted to shake her. Why was this woman so afraid of taking responsibility for anything? She was running out of patience with her.

Prior to their guests' arrival, Lucy and Phin had discussed the best approach to persuade Olivia to tell Ryan the truth. Olivia had never mentioned the inspector or his visits to the house, let alone her giving her father-in-law an alibi for murder, which was telling in the circumstances. She had shared her fears about her mother-in-law being poisoned, but why not the equally grave situation of giving a false alibi? Throughout the meal, Olivia had acted as if she had never met Ryan before, yet Lucy knew he had interviewed her at least twice. Olivia was wary of him, Lucy was sure, but if she would only confess, they were best placed to help her, whatever the aftermath might be. Lucy had little doubt that Ryan was enamoured. His gaze had not strayed far from Olivia the entire meal. He had addressed her several times, attempting to include her in the conversation. Olivia had responded only in monosyllables.

Lucy decided to push her. 'What *do* you think of Inspector Ryan? He is charming and Phin and I like him very much. He strikes me as a consummate professional and a fair-minded individual. Have you ever encountered him before?'

Olivia blanched and jumped up. 'I must go. If Edith wakes up and I'm not there...'

Lucy almost panicked but Phin and Ryan walked into the room at that very moment. Lucy threw Phin a beseeching glance.

'You're not leaving us so soon, Mrs Carver?' Phin asked with a smile. He took her hand and guided her back to the sofa. 'You must at least have some tea before you go. Look, here's George with the tea and coffee now. What will you have?'

Olivia stared at him for a moment, and Lucy thought she was going to bolt. Then Olivia swallowed hard. Would she resist Phin's charm offensive? But good manners overcame her instinct to flee, much to Lucy's relief. 'Tea, please.'

'Excellent,' said Phin, winking at Lucy. 'And I'll have coffee, please, George.' Then he sat beside Olivia.

'Very good, sir,' George said and set about pouring and handing around the various orders.

Lucy mouthed 'Thank you' to Phin and relaxed back into her seat. After a sip of her tea, Lucy turned to Ryan. 'Inspector, when we last spoke, you gave us an update on that dreadful murder last week. Have there been any further developments?'

Ryan stood before the fireplace, directly opposite Olivia. One eyebrow shot up. 'Yes, indeed, Mrs Stone. Only this evening we have had it confirmed that the suspected weapon used, a gentleman's cane, is now in our possession. Along with witnesses who swear he was there, we have enough evidence now.'

Olivia's eyes widened. 'Oh!' Her cup rattled on its saucer.

'So, you now know who the culprit is? There is no doubt?' Phin asked, relieving Olivia of her tea things with a gentle smile.

Still with his gaze fixed on Olivia, Ryan answered, 'No doubt. An arrest is imminent.'

Lucy feared Olivia would faint, she was so white-faced. 'Olivia, my dear, I'm sorry but there is something I must explain to you. My invitation to you and Inspector Ryan this evening wasn't entirely motivated by a desire for your company, excellent as it is. You see, I'm afraid that the murder victim in The Monto was the young cousin of my maid. Her name was Peggy O'Reilly, and she and her sister had only arrived here in Dublin to find work. Unfortunately, someone lured the girls into working in a house of ill-repute. So, you see, my dear, providing your father-in-law with an

alibi for that night is misjudged. We understand you are in a difficult position and that Mr Carver pressurised you into lying.
However, now you know the truth, you must help the police. It is
the only right course of action open to you.'

'You tricked me,' Olivia said, her gaze flicking between them
all. 'I trusted you. You should have told me why you asked me here
tonight.'

'And your trust is not misplaced, believe me. We understand
your situation. But we can help you; even give you refuge here if
necessary. Once the police arrest your father-in-law, he cannot
harm you any further.'

'What Mrs Stone says is true,' Ryan said, moving towards
Olivia. 'Please tell me what happened last Thursday night.'

'You don't know what you ask,' Olivia cried, dropping her head
in her hands. 'He will kill me if I tell you.'

'No, I won't let that happen,' Ryan answered as he moved to
stand before her. 'Mrs Carver, please listen to me. The evidence is
compelling. Blood was detected on the cane I removed from the
house yesterday afternoon. Carver's cane. You must rescind your
statement. I promise you will not come to any harm. You or Mrs
Carver, senior.'

Lucy held her breath, her eyes flying to Phin, who was
watching Olivia intently.

Olivia's lip wobbled, and she wept. Phin whipped out a handkerchief while Ryan took a step back and watched her with a helpless expression as she held it to her face. Lucy motioned for Ryan
to move back further, and she sat on the other side of Olivia. Ryan
returned to stand at the fireplace, his eyes fixed on Olivia.

'Now, my dear. Inspector Ryan is right,' Lucy said, rubbing
Olivia's back. 'Tell us what happened. You will feel better when it
is all out in the open.'

It took several minutes before Olivia was calm enough to
speak. Lucy's heart went out to her, for she looked wretched.

'I'm s-sorry,' she stuttered. 'You can't imagine what it is like
living in that house. He hates me. I was never good enough for his

precious son. He idolised James, but he was blind to his faults. James was a charming profligate. By the time he had drunk himself to death, he had gambled away my dowry. My family didn't want to know, so I was stuck here in Dublin, living with Myles and Edith.'

'You have no income at all?' Lucy asked.

'Myles was very clever and my brother neglectful in the extreme. The marriage settlement they brokered stated that if James died before our tenth anniversary and we had no children, I'd be disinherited. We were only married for five years when he passed. My circumstances are intolerable, and I have dreamed of escaping. I've even considered trying to find work, but then Edith fell ill. Myles refused to hire a nurse for her. Said it was my duty to step in and care for her. You must understand that I am very fond of her anyway, so I couldn't leave her. But when Edith dies, we will take our chances, me and Sally. We will not stay in that house. As Sally told you the other day, we are certain Myles has a mistress waiting in the wings.'

Lucy glanced over at Ryan, who raised his brows.

'And last Thursday, Olivia. What happened?' Lucy asked.

'He arrived home in a foul temper. At first, I thought something awful had happened at the bank or at his club. But then he claimed some bad people would make false accusations against him.' She glanced at Ryan. 'He didn't say it was a murder, so I agreed to help him. Well, I had little choice. But once I made my statement, I was too scared to change it. If Sally and I didn't do as he asked, he threatened to throw us out.'

'And what did he ask?' Lucy urged.

'That we say he was home much earlier. He forced all the servants to give false statements, too.' Olivia took a trembling breath and looked across at Ryan. 'I'm sorry, but I had no choice but to lie.'

'I had a feeling that was the case. So, what time *did* he arrive home?' Ryan asked.

'About half past seven,' Olivia said at last, before breaking down in tears once more.

Lucy wasn't sure if the timing fit Ryan's theory. 'Does that help you, Inspector?'

'Very much so. It would only take about fifteen minutes to travel here from The Monto,' he said. He took a step towards Olivia, his eyes full of concern. 'Thank you, Mrs Carver.'

But Lucy doubted Olivia even noticed or heard him through her tears.

TWENTY-ONE

Dublin Castle, Thursday, 26th July

Lucy looked down into the Castle Yard and watched Valentine DeWinter hop up into a waiting carriage. *What a tiresome man. How does his wife put up with him?* she wondered. He had dropped by to get an update from Phineas on his security inspection of the Bermingham Tower. The encounter had been interesting to observe, with DeWinter trying to ascertain what Phin's final recommendations would be, and Phin's determination not to reveal them.

'He's gone,' Lucy remarked and turned back to Phin, who was seated behind the desk, grinning like a Cheshire cat. 'What a dry stick that man is.'

'Don't worry, my dear. My report is almost complete, and once it is, you won't have to meet him again. In fact, I daresay he'll shun us completely.'

'Is the situation that bad?' Phin nodded. 'Thank goodness. I couldn't stand another evening of Caroline DeWinter and her superior friends. I was in fear that he might proffer a dinner invitation for this evening so he could interrogate you more. Will your report be very critical of him?' she asked.

Phin's lips clamped. 'It will. He won't be happy. The PM, on the other hand, will probably be delighted. I suspect it will give him the leverage he wants. So, if you wish, we can plan to go home.'

Lucy sat down. 'Oh, no. Not while Peggy's murder isn't solved. And we still must find her sister, Bridget.'

'You are determined to see these cases through?'

'Yes, and if you had the time and were more involved, you would be, too. Besides, what is the rush to return to London? We have the house until the end of August. I'm enjoying my stay here, and the children are having a wonderful time. To return early would only upset Seb. He'd think you didn't have faith in his abilities.'

With a shrug, Phin said, 'Perhaps.'

'Now, Phin, you know he is happy to run the agency for you while you are here. Did you not receive a glowing report from Beck Insurances about him only last week?'

'True. He handled that case well. The responsibility has been good for him.'

Lucy threw him a mischievous smile. 'And won't do him any harm in Lady Madeline's eyes.' Lady Madeline was her friend Lady Sarah's youngest sister, and Lucy had great hopes in that direction.

Phineas chuckled. 'Stick to crime solving, Lucy, and leave the matchmaking to the mamas.'

'Hmm. That's all very well to say, but you know how tongue-tied Seb is around her. He likes her very much. I'm smoothing the way when I can. Sarah is, too. She's as keen on the match as I am.'

Whatever Phin was about to say in response was cut short by a knock on the door. 'Come in,' Phin called out. 'Ryan, good morning to you.'

Inspector Ryan nodded to them both. 'Good morning.'

Lucy waved to a chair. 'Do sit down, Inspector. How did you get on with Olivia last night? Was she able to tell you anything further when you escorted her home?'

'Not really. She was distressed, as you know, when we left your house. Eventually she calmed down enough for me to take her revised statement. Her maid helped a great deal. A very sensible woman.'

'Yes, I have found her so, too,' Lucy said.

'Then between us we encouraged her to drink a small brandy, after which the maid took her off to bed. Luckily, the maid also provided me with an additional statement, which agrees with Mrs Carver's. As we suspected, Carver had threatened to throw them both out on the street if they didn't give him that false alibi.'

'Do you have enough to arrest Carver now?' Phin asked.

'Yes. Mrs Carver believes he is due in from Cork at around one o'clock tomorrow. We will be waiting for him at Kingsbridge Station.'

'That is such a relief, Inspector. Thank you,' Lucy said. 'Mary will be overjoyed when I tell her. However...'

Ryan held up his hand. 'Yes, I know. The sister.' He paused and rubbed his chin. 'Despite our best efforts, she seems to have disappeared without a trace, which worries me a great deal.'

'Well, Inspector, I think I may have some information that may shine a light on it all.'

His eyes widened, and a slow smile formed. 'Indeed? You never cease to amaze me, Mrs Stone.'

'Thank you. Mary and I have been doing a little investigating of our own,' she said, then filled him in on her meeting with Father McGuinness. 'He was keen to help and set up a meeting with a woman from Mrs Burton's establishment. Miss O'Mara—'

'Not Ginny O'Mara?'

'Why, yes. Are you acquainted with her?' Lucy asked. Ryan nodded. 'Is she reliable?'

'More than most of the girls. But I would imagine she would only tell you what was safe for her to reveal. Celine Burton and her bully boys are vicious. Ginny would not risk getting into trouble if the information might be traced back to her.'

'She said as much to us, but she confirmed she saw Bridget at the house and was able to tell us that Bridget was taken away and set to work in a public house instead.'

'Good gracious. What's the name of this place?' he asked, taking out a notebook and pen from inside his jacket.

'The Sleepy Druid.'

Ryan stared back at her, his pen poised mid-air. 'No!' Then he placed the notebook and pen on Phin's desk, blowing out his cheeks. 'I don't believe this.'

Lucy exchanged a glance with Phin. 'What is it? Is there something awful about this public house?'

With a mirthless laugh, he answered, 'In a way, yes. I am related to the owner. I... this isn't common knowledge, and I'd prefer this information stayed within this room.'

'To be sure. You have our word,' Phin said, leaning forward, his chin resting on his steepled fingers. Lucy recognised the glow in his eyes. Phin was intrigued.

'The man who owns the pub, and several others, is a cousin on my mother's side. He is a notorious moneylender, and I recently discovered that he is Celine Burton's alcohol supplier. It does not surprise me he's mixed up in this, but my connection to him is not something I can acknowledge around here.'

'Indeed,' Phin said, his brows drawing together. 'And, if I recall correctly, the informer who triggered this warning about Fenian mischief mentioned that public house.'

'Yes, I'm afraid so. Supposedly, the men in question were overheard talking about it there. The informer was my cousin, Lizzie, Iggy Byrne's daughter.'

'Why would she do that? Implicate her father, or at least his business?'

Ryan shrugged. 'I don't know. It makes little sense to me, either. However, when I challenged him, my cousin told me the names of the two men. Mind you, he claimed it was the drink talking, which I'm inclined to believe.'

'Well, I can see that this puts you in a difficult position,' Lucy said. 'But we must locate the girl before she comes to harm.' She glanced at Phin. 'I'd willingly visit the establishment and investigate, but I fear someone like me going in there and asking questions would be seen as suspicious. They'd clam up.'

Ryan gave her a sheepish look. 'Absolutely. And it would be highly dangerous, Mrs Stone. Please don't contemplate such a plan.'

'She won't,' Phineas said, giving Lucy a stern look, which she ignored.

The inspector rubbed his chin. 'I'd better tackle them.'

Phineas harrumphed. 'Perhaps not, Inspector.' His eyes briefly met Lucy's. 'I sense you have a plan brewing, my dear.'

'Yes, I do. Mary.'

'Mary?' Phin raised an eyebrow.

'Yes, my dear. I'm certain she'd be willing. She is desperate to find Bridget. My idea is that she goes to this pub and pretends to be looking for work. Mary's a native Dubliner and so won't raise any suspicions. If she is successful, she can then worm her way in, look for Bridget or ask questions. If we are lucky, she might even find Bridget and be able to get her out.' Lucy turned to Ryan when he objected. 'Yes, I know. That might be difficult. They're unlikely to let Bridget go without a fight. So, how about this? If she finds out anything, we will let you know, and you can send in the cavalry at that stage. Would that be acceptable to you?'

'That might work,' Ryan said. 'Unfortunately, my men barging in now would trigger panic. The locals know the constables by sight, and Ignatius, Lizzie's father, would whisk Bridget away and hide her at the first sign of trouble. Besides, I'd be reluctant to send them in without being certain that Bridget had been seen in there. I hate to admit it, but neither of my cousins would tell me anything if I questioned them. So, yes, I like this idea, and your maid comes across as a practical young woman.'

'Oh, she is, Inspector. She might complain a lot when things get, ah, sticky, shall we say? Goodness knows she's had reason to over the years, but she is both brave and determined. I'll talk to her later today and let you know.'

'Very well,' Ryan said, rising. 'I'll hold off on doing anything at my end until I hear from you.'

TWENTY-TWO

As if the heavens were in accord with Fergus's fractious mood, the current spell of glorious weather broke with yet another violent thunderstorm. Dubliners scurried along the pavement, heads bent against the driving rain and wind. Fergus, however, was preoccupied as he stared out of the police carriage. In his pocket was the telegram from the RIC, the police force in Cork, confirming Carver had boarded the Dublin train that morning.

Traffic on the quays was moving at a snail's pace due to the rain, ratcheting up Fergus's anxiety. If they missed the train, Carver might get to Merrion Square before they intercepted him. The last thing Fergus wanted was to have to arrest Carver while Olivia was there. She was distressed enough.

So, they were headed to Kingsbridge to intercept and arrest him.

Fergus was so het up, he didn't even mind being squashed inside the confines of a malodorous police carriage with three burly constables, handpicked by Sergeant Hughes. Jackson, Moore and Geraghty were a formidable threesome of DMP constables, feared throughout the city, with just cause. Jackson, or to give him his street-name 'The Paw', was a native Dubliner like himself. Standing well over six foot, he had been known to pursue suspects for miles on foot before his mighty hands would descend on the poor unfortunate and they were hauled off to the nearest police station. No, Fergus was confident Carver had no chance of eluding his men. However, when he glanced at his watch and saw the time, he groaned. The train was due on the hour, and it was five minutes to already.

Thankfully, the traffic eased, and they swept past the black entrance gates of the Guinness brewery at St James' Gate, and soon, despite the deluge, the imposing granite façade of Kingsbridge Station loomed on the horizon. The forecourt was busy with a tight press of cabs, carriages and trams close to the entrance. Large groups of people were gathered under the portico, sheltering while porters procured their cabs. Anxiety nipped at Ryan. What if they missed Carver in the crush?

The carriage pulled up, and they piled out, dashing for the cover of the front portico of the station building. Fergus was aware of the wary expressions of onlookers, some of whom moved to stand further away, even risking getting wet. Oh, the power of a police uniform.

'Now, lads, we can't afford to mess this up,' Fergus said, eyeing them each in turn. He patted his pocket. 'We know he's on the Cork train. When I spot him, I'll point him out. He won't be expecting us, so we have the advantage of surprise. However, we must nab him before he breaches the barriers and disappears into these crowds.'

'Sir,' the officers replied in unison.

Fergus hailed a passing porter. 'Which platform for the Cork train?'

'Number four, sir,' the man said, pointing to the far right of the interior of the station. 'Due any minute.'

'Follow me,' Fergus ordered, striding off into the melee of the ticket hall, adrenaline pumping. The anticipated satisfaction of removing a tyrant from Olivia's orbit, and catching Peggy's killer in one stroke, was driving him forward.

As Fergus and his officers arrived at the designated platform, the barriers remained down, with several ticket inspectors standing just inside it, chatting while they waited for the train to arrive. To Fergus's relief, a few hundred yards away, a steam locomotive was only just entering under the station canopy. With an ear-splitting screech of brakes and a blast of steam, the engine came to a stop. To Fergus's consternation, the billowing steam obscured the immediate area from view. His heart rate rocketed. He couldn't see a thing. But within a few seconds, the steam dissipated, and passengers emerged, porters trailing behind with wagons of bags, trunks and suitcases. The barrier went up. Fergus tensed but tried to remain calm, scanning the faces as they passed through the barrier after showing their tickets. Most moved toward the front exit.

Then, suddenly, halfway down the platform, he spotted Carver at the same moment Carver noticed him. Carver froze, the panic of recognition crossing his features, his hand going to his heart. Their gazes locked.

'Sir?' Jackson, standing beside him, said, breaking the spell.

'That's him, Jackson. Go get 'im,' Fergus said, pointing Carver out.

Jackson pushed past the ticket collectors and broke into a run, passengers scattering to the sides to avoid a collision. For Fergus, it was as if time slowed down. As he watched, Carver turned and took off to his left. What the hell? Fergus shouted a warning to Jackson, but he had already veered off after Carver. Constable Moore grabbed Fergus's arm.

'Sir, there's an exit on that side of the building. Out towards the river.'

Fergus turned to the two men beside him. 'Damnation! I'd forgotten about that. Geraghty, stay here in case he doubles back. Moore, go back out front and try to cut him off that way. He mustn't get over King's Bridge.'

Fergus sped after Jackson and his quarry. Keeping Jackson's helmet in view, he manoeuvred his way through the throng of people towards the arched exit way. He saw Jackson swing out the doorway and go left. Fergus followed and found himself out on a roadway that bordered the river. In the distance, he saw Carver with Jackson in close pursuit. Jackson was gaining on the older man. Fergus picked up speed, ignoring the rain driving into his face.

'Stop, police!' Jackson yelled, pulling out his truncheon.

Carver chanced a glance behind, then appeared to get a second wind. He kept running.

But up ahead, Fergus knew it was a dead end. The road led directly to the gates of Islandbridge Barracks, home of The King's Dragoon Guards. As Carver drew closer to the barrack entrance, the gates opened, and a cavalry troop emerged. Carver skidded to a halt and turned, fear in his eyes. Jackson pounced and wrestled him to the ground to the cheers and jeers of the officers on horseback. Fergus caught up, panting hard, but he didn't need to assist Jackson. Carver was no match for the constable. As they trotted past, the Dragoons saluted Fergus with cheeky grins and some choice ribald comments. Fergus ignored these and watched with satisfaction as Jackson hauled Carver to his feet. They'd got him.

DMP Headquarters, Dublin Castle

So far, Carver had refused to answer any questions, and now they were waiting for his solicitor to arrive. Fergus almost felt sorry for the man. Carver sat across from him in the interrogation room, his clothes soaked through and a nasty bruise forming on his cheek where he had hit the cobbles during his arrest. However, it was clear Carver was not intimidated. He glared at Fergus, pure hatred twisting his thin lips. It was no wonder Olivia feared him, Fergus thought, clenching his fists in his lap under the table.

At last, his sergeant entered the room, followed by a rangy middle-aged man in a black suit and a stiff collar so high it was in danger of cutting into the man's jugular. He greeted Carver, who shot him a filthy glance. Carver crossed his arms and sneered across at Fergus. 'You may begin,' he said, with a challenge in his eye.

'Most kind,' said Fergus, leaning back. With a tilt of his head, he invited Hughes to sit next to him. 'My sergeant will take notes.'

'He may dance a jig, for all I care,' retorted Carver.

Fergus bristled. 'Mr Carver, you are facing a serious charge, which may, in due course, result in a death sentence. Perhaps a little less levity in the circumstances?' A quirk of the mouth was the only response. 'The reason for your arrest today is that additional evidence has come to light, which casts doubt on your assertion that you had nothing to do with the murder of Peggy O'Reilly. We have two witnesses who place you at the scene—'

'Ridiculous. Any defence lawyer would annihilate those two reprobates in the witness box,' Carver scoffed.

'So, you know who I'm talking about. Now, that is interesting, Mr Carver, if you say you know nothing about that flash-house.'

Carver actually growled. 'I deny all knowledge, but someone is determined to pin this murder on me, and it is safe to assume that whoever they are, they are the worst kind of scum. That area is a cesspit. Everyone knows it. Anyone who hails from it is a liar and a thief. I'd hazard one of them did it, and they are using me as a scapegoat. It's the only logical explanation.'

'Why would they accuse you of this murder if they've never met you... sir?' Fergus asked. 'Did they pluck your name out of thin air?' He didn't wait for him to answer but plunged on. 'And your daughter-in-law has amended her statement to the effect that on the night in question you did not return home until half past seven.'

'Olivia is a featherhead. She's confused, or you have coerced her into altering her testimony. There's something sneaky about her. I've never trusted her.'

Fergus stiffened, outraged that Carver was casting aspersions on Olivia. It was disgusting. 'The housemaid has also amended her statement,' Fergus added.

'Another chancer. I should have kicked the pair of them out long ago.'

'And then there are the traces of blood found on your walking cane, a cane your servants and family claim you rarely leave the house without. A cane also described by the flash-house doorman.'

Carver's face drained of colour. 'Someone must have smeared it on... probably that Burton woman or her henchman.'

The solicitor coughed, but it was too late.

Fergus smiled. 'So, you admit you know these people by name, and you *were* there?'

After a few deep breaths, his mouth trembling, Carver nodded. 'Alright. I have frequented the establishment... on occasion. My wife is ill, dying... I have needs.'

Carver's words made Fergus's skin crawl, and he added Edith Carver to the growing number of Carver acolytes he had sympathy for. It required significant effort not to let his emotions show. '*Were* you there on the night of Peggy's murder?'

Carver jumped to his feet. Hughes responded in kind. 'Yes, damn it. I was there in that hellhole.' He slapped his fist down on the table. 'But I tell you, the girl was already dead when I entered that room.'

'Sit down, sir,' Fergus said, holding eye contact until the man obeyed. 'You'd best tell me what happened. From the time you arrived.'

A flash of distaste crossed Carver's face. 'Burton usually greets me and escorts me to the room but had someone with her. Another client, I suppose. I could hear arguing. Anyway, the doorman sent me up to the room on my own. You see—it had to be a setup. Unsuspecting, I went in expecting some... entertainment... and was greeted by the most stomach-churning sight. The little whore was sprawled on the carpet, and there was blood everywhere. I got such a fright I dropped my cane. That's how there's blood on it. But I thought I had cleaned it off...'

'If you didn't kill her, why didn't you raise the alarm? Why did you flee?' Fergus asked.

'Because I knew that bitch Burton would try to blame me. We'd had a falling out a few weeks ago when I complained about the price of her brandy. She had threatened to bar me. I've been waiting for her to contact me.'

'What? Burton?'

'Yes. It was all a setup so that she might blackmail me. I'm sure of it.'

'But Burton hasn't done so?'

'Not yet. But she will. And she'll find I'm not such an easy mark.'

Fergus suspected Carver was throwing this out as a distraction. 'Mrs Burton swears the girl was alive before you arrived.'

Carver smashed his fist down on the table again. 'Lies, all of it. The girl was dead. I did *not* harm her.'

'What time did you arrive in The Monto?'

'It must have been almost seven o'clock.'

'We haven't been able to find a cabbie who can verify that,' Fergus said.

Carver smirked. 'That's because I didn't arrive by cab. A colleague at the bank dropped me off in his gig. He lives out in Clontarf. It was on his way.'

Fergus exchanged a quick glance with Hughes. No wonder they'd had no luck. 'And this man's name? We will need to verify this.'

'I'll not drag another respectable man into this,' Carver shouted.

'I suggest you consider this carefully, Mr Carver, if you do not wish to hang in the very near future.'

Carver growled once more, his face flushed crimson. 'Blanchard, Roger Blanchard. He's a director at the bank.'

'Thank you. We will contact him. In the meantime, you'll remain our *guest* here at the castle... sir.'

Carver turned to his solicitor. 'Say something, man. I'm sure I'm paying you enough.'

The solicitor glanced at Carver over the rim of his glasses. 'I'm afraid there is nothing I can do, sir, at this juncture.'

'Idiot!' Carver cried. 'I'm surrounded by fools. By God, if I ever get my hands on that bitch Burton I'll teach her a lesson she'll never forget.'

TWENTY-THREE

The earlier downpour had left the pavements glistening, and the air was heavy with the smells Mary O'Reilly would always associate with Dublin: hops from the brewery and the dank odour of the River Liffey, the constituents of which it was prudent not to analyse. As she made her way along Thomas Street, she had to avoid the large puddles which threatened to soak her feet through the holes in her borrowed boots. She glanced down with distaste at the old dress and jacket the cook had lent her, clothes that hadn't seen the light of day for some time if the state of disrepair was any indication. But she had to look the part: a woman desperate for work.

Was she mad to attempt this on her own? Most of her previous adventures, as Lucy liked to call them, had been experienced at her mistress's side. Except for that time in Italy when she woke up to find herself trussed up like a turkey, on her own, in a hut in the mountains above Lake Como. She'd survived that by using her wits. Surely what she was about to do was nothing in comparison? This was her native city, and she knew it well, knew the type of characters she was bound to encounter. For all that, her stomach lurched, bringing her to a sudden stop. An elderly lady grumbled as she had to sidestep to avoid running into her back.

'Sorry, missus,' Mary called after her. A roll of the woman's shoulders was all the acknowledgement she received.

Really, this was silly. Being so nervous... She was almost there; she needed to buck up. Everyone was depending on her. Her beloved Lucy, the master and that nice Inspector Ryan who'd spent ages advising her before he'd dropped her off at the bottom of Thomas Street. And all she had to do to repay him was a little side quest...

But she also had to do this for her family. The vision of Aunt May weeping at Peggy's grave flashed into her mind. It was such a cruel thing, having to bury her daughter. Not that it wasn't common. TB, which was rife, saw to that. Her own brother had succumbed to it, not two years since. But Peggy's life had been taken with violence. If she had anything to do with it, Bridget would not meet the same fate. Mary was determined to find her, even if she had to stay on in Dublin after the Stone family returned to London.

With a deep breath, and shoulders back, Mary moved forward, her eyes fixed on The Sleepy Druid's sign swinging in the breeze above the pub door. She hesitated at the entrance, nerves tingling. Once she stepped through that door, there was no turning back.

Although only four in the afternoon, she could hear the gentle murmur of conversation through an open window. She squeezed her eyes shut. *Here goes.* She opened the door and stepped inside.

The smoke-filled taproom was long and narrow with a flagstone floor. The ceiling was low and stained brown from decades of tobacco smoke. Three men, nursing pints of porter, sat at a table inside the door, their chatter coming to an abrupt halt as she entered. They threw her curious glances but did not greet her. Mary moved further along, conscious of the men's eyes following her. There were no other customers in the bar. Her priority was to find Ryan's cousin and beg her for work. If the woman wasn't here, she'd have to come back another day, and that was another day lost in the search for Bridget.

The sight of an enormous grey cat sitting on the bar surprised Mary. As she approached, its yellow-green eyes sized her up. Then the cat yawned, stretched and jumped down out of view. And further down, behind the bar, Mary was pleased to see a dark-haired, petite young woman, who fitted the description Ryan had given her of his cousin, Lizzie Byrne. The woman didn't smile but watched Mary's approach with open curiosity as she dried the glass in her hand with a cloth.

'Miss Byrne, is it?' Mary asked.

'Aye. And who are you?' the woman asked, putting the glass down.

'My name is Mary Cahill, and like, I'm after bar work, miss.'

'What makes you think we're looking for anyone?' Lizzie said, hands on hips.

Mary's heart sank. 'I don't... course I don't... I was *hoping*. You see, I've been trying different pubs all day. And to be honest, I'm just fagged out at this stage.' Mary rooted in her bag and pulled out the fake reference Lucy had written for her. 'I've been in service, see, but I lost my position when the family left for England. I heard the Irish aren't welcome over there, so I didn't wanna go.'

Lizzie reached out and took the letter, scanned the page and then handed it back. 'No call for dressing hair in 'ere. Any experience of actual bar work?'

'Well, in me last job I did everything from cook to lady's maid to parlour maid. There's not much I can't put me hand to.' And a lot more besides, she could almost hear Lucy say.

Lizzie's gaze swept across her, her lips compressed, and Mary knew she was being assessed. 'I suppose I could give you a trial run. As it happens, I do need someone, but I warn ye: I need staff I can depend on, not flighty young 'uns who tear off at the first sight of a strapping fella with winning ways. I expect loyalty and honesty.'

'Don't worry, miss, I'm steady, and reliable,' Mary said, waving the reference. 'Me last mistress was very happy with me work...

said I was quick and a useful person to have around.' Well, Lucy would say that if pressed, Mary was sure.

'A gift from heaven, are you, huh? We'll see about that. Will you be needing a place to kip?'

'Yes, I've been staying with me cousin but it's a bit crowded with her chisellers, so if you had something... till I find decent lodgings nearby.'

'You can have the attic room. Nothin' fancy, mind. Rent will be deducted from your wages.' Mary nodded. This was going better than she had hoped.

'Will I be sharing with another barmaid?' Mary asked.

'No. It's just the three of us. My Da helps out if it's busy, but he's not here often. He has other pubs to look after. There's a potman, Jake, who's working out back.'

Mary was disappointed. This didn't sound promising. No mention of Bridget.

Then Lizzie leaned back and roared through the doorway behind her, making Mary jump. 'Jake!'

'Yes, Miss Lizzie?' a giant of a young man answered moments later, ambling in. He was in his shirtsleeves with a green waistcoat over which he wore a leather apron. Mary couldn't take her eyes off his hands, which were as big as spades and heavily callused. A potman for certain, though he looked more like a prize-fighter. Not someone one would want to face in a tussle. But then, the area was notorious. Every pub in the vicinity would have a Jake equivalent to sort out the troublesome customers at chucking-out time.

'I need you to mind the bar, Jake. This young 'un... Mary, is joining us for a few days till we see if she works out. I'm putting her in the room beside yours.'

'Oh, thank you, miss,' Mary said, smiling at Lizzie and then at the giant, who was gazing at her open-mouthed as if he'd never seen a young woman before. *Maybe he's a bit simple*, Mary speculated.

Lizzie broke into a smile and raised a brow. 'Don't thank me yet. Long hours and eight shillings a week, take it or leave it. And that's only if you prove useful in the next couple of days.'

Mary schooled her features. The pay was shockingly low, even for Dublin, but she was unable to object. 'I'm fierce grateful, miss. I won't let you down.'

'Right, so.' Lizzie pushed up the entrance hatch to the bar and beckoned Mary in. 'I'll show you the room, and you can leave your stuff there.'

Mary gripped her small carpetbag and followed her new employer through the doorway, past Jake who was still staring at her, into a dank and dirty hallway. The cat she'd seen earlier emerged from a room off the hall and wound itself around Mary's legs.

'That's Cleopatra,' Lizzie said. 'You're honoured. She usually hates anyone new.'

Mary was unfazed by the cat but more worried about the potman. She hoped he would not be a problem. She'd have enough to deal with when she snooped around.

'That's me Da's office. Steer clear of it, and him, if you know what's good for ya,' Lizzie said with a nod towards one of the two doors. As she headed for a steep stairway that led up into pitch darkness, she said, 'The other's the kitchen. Privy's out back.'

Two flights of stairs brought them right up under the eaves. Lizzie pointed to a door. 'That's Jake's room. You can have this 'un,' she said, pushing open the other door. Mary wasn't too pleased about having a room next to the potman, but she couldn't really complain. Pasting a smile on her face, she walked in and struggled to hide her dismay. It was horrible and smelled of rotting timber. *I must be getting soft,* she thought, yearning for her lovely bright room back in London. *Oh well, all in a good cause.*

Mary removed her coat and put it, along with her bag, on the cast-iron bed. Besides a shelf, the bed and a chipped chamber pot, the room was bare. A barred window allowed some light through but not enough to cheer the place up. It was the grimmest room Mary had ever seen.

Why would you put bars on an attic window? A flicker of anxiety made her bite her lip. What kind of place was this? Would she be sold into slavery or something terrible?

Calm down, stupid. Nothing is going to happen to you. Just keep your wits about you.

From her quick perusal, there was nothing to indicate Bridget had ever been here, though what she was hoping to see she wasn't sure. But at least she was in the door and could nose around when the chance arose. Mary glanced at Lizzie Byrne, who was standing back out on the tiny landing, tapping her foot, and tight-lipped. Not a patient sort, Mary reckoned, or the most approachable woman ever. Her gut was telling her she was a hard taskmaster. Maybe they had worked Bridget to death and dumped her in the Liffey. No, that was a silly notion for she would have been fished out by now. But if Bridget wasn't *here*, where had she vanished to? Perhaps Jake the potman might be a better source of information if she got through to him.

'Well?' Lizzie asked, breaking into her strategizing.

'Oh, it's grand, thanks. A room of my own. Such luxury,' Mary said, hoping she wasn't laying it on too thick.

'Right then, let's see how good you *are*,' Lizzie said. 'You can start by cleaning the outside privy.'

Mary attempted to smile as her stomach churned. This place was going to test her resilience. If she ever got her hands on Bridget, she'd give her such a scold her feet wouldn't touch the ground.

It was almost midnight, and the street was quiet. As pre-arranged with Mary, Lucy and Phin were waiting for her in a closed carriage, parked up opposite St Augustine & St John's Church on Thomas Street. The Sleepy Druid was further down the street, just within sight.

'I do hope she's not come to harm,' Lucy said, checking the street yet again. 'What if Ryan's cousin suspects something? I should have given her my pistol. Mary has no way of defending herself. No way to raise the alarm.'

'Don't fret so. Ryan spoke to her at length before she went in. Besides, Mary knows how to handle herself,' Phin said. 'If Bridget is there, this will be sorted tonight. But don't be concerned if Mary learns nothing in a day. It may take several days before she unearths useful information, or before the other employees trust her enough to reveal something significant. Don't forget Byrne has other pubs, and Bridget might be in one of those, not here.'

'I suppose so.' Lucy tried to read Phin's expression. 'Is it possible the girl is still there? I mean, with all the fuss over Peggy's murder, they might have moved her on somewhere else. Down the country, even.'

'Or out of it,' he said.

'Oh, I hope not, Phin. We'd never find her. Well, at least there is progress in Peggy's case with Carver locked up. Poor Olivia. She was still very upset when I called on her this afternoon. She's terrified that the police might let him go. I told her if that happens, she is to come to us.'

'Absolutely. How fares her mother-in-law?'

'Sleepy as usual when I looked in on her. Olivia has decided not to tell her anything about Carver's arrest. What would be the point of upsetting the poor woman? That's assuming she'd even understand.'

'Indeed. However, the other servants might discuss it within earshot. Either way, it will come out in time, and once the newspapers get hold of it, they will be besieged by journalists.'

Lucy blew out a long breath. 'Yes, it will be a feeding frenzy.'

'Did you convince Olivia to tell Ryan about the suspected poisoning?'

'No, not yet. I don't understand her reluctance, but she is adamant that we don't have enough evidence of wrongdoing. Foolish girl, I could shake her.'

'Perhaps she feels that his arrest and probable hanging for

killing Peggy will deal with the situation without having to reveal anything else.'

'Or she may be afraid that the police will suspect her instead. But I fear it is a risky strategy to pin all her hopes on Carver being charged with Peggy's murder. I'm not sure I'd put that much faith in the justice system. Carver will hire the best legal counsel he can afford, and juries are notoriously unpredictable. What happens if they acquit him? Olivia will be in a pickle then.'

'It won't go to trial unless Ryan has enough evidence. From what he said earlier, he's almost there. The blood on that cane is pretty damning, wouldn't you say?'

'Let's hope so.' Lucy nodded and consulted her watch. 'Now, what's keeping Mary?'

'Patience, my dear. If she is under observation, she may not be able to leave. They might consider it suspicious if she skives off, especially as she has only arrived. I told her to err on the side of caution and I'm sure Ryan did, too. We don't know what she is dealing with in there. If Ryan is to be believed, and if she's been hired, they will work her hard. If she doesn't turn up, we'll do this again tomorrow evening. That's what we agreed with her. Mary is sensible, and she knew the risks when she agreed to do this.'

'That doesn't make me feel any better.'

Phin grasped her hand and squeezed. 'Trust her. She's had you as her role model these ten years or more.'

It was a quarter past one in the morning, and Lucy had almost given up, when she heard hurried footsteps approach the carriage. The horse whinnied, and the vehicle lurched. Phin pushed the door open on hearing a knock, and Mary tumbled in.

'Oh, ma'am, sir, I'm fierce sorry. It was impossible to get away,' Mary gabbled as Phin closed the door. 'But I've been hired, so that's something.'

'Well done, Mary. I knew you could do it,' Lucy said. 'Any sign of your Bridget?'

Mary glanced at them both in turn, her eyes lit up. 'You will not believe this.'

'Try us,' Phin said with a grin.

'Sure, it was easy to get me feet in the door, like. Inspector Ryan told me how to approach his cousin Lizzie. And as luck would have it, they are short-staffed. I had my story ready, like he told me, and sure she swallowed it all. Even your so-called reference, ma'am.' Then Mary scowled. 'The work is a bit menial, like, but I suppose it won't be for long.' Mary glanced at Lucy. 'You will manage for a few days, ma'am, won't you?'

Lucy nodded eagerly. 'Yes, yes. It's all for a worthy cause. So, you got the job; what about Bridget?'

'Oh, yes. Our Bridgey. The inspector's cousin isn't a talker, but the potman is. A bit simple, he is, but he took a fancy to our Bridget. Turns out she worked there all right. For about a week.'

'But she's gone?'

Mary nodded. 'Aye, she is and all. Scarpered with the contents of the till in her pocket. I'm that ashamed of her, I am. What kind of a way is that to carry on?'

'Don't be too hard on her, Mary. Perhaps she needed it to make good her escape?' Phin said.

'Hmm. Well, when I get hold of her, I'll have something to say about it. O'Reillys are not thieves.'

'Of course not, Mary. But as Phin says, maybe she had little choice. I wonder why she didn't seek refuge with family though.'

'Too ashamed or scared, perhaps? Particularly if she knew about her sister's murder,' Phin said. 'Bad enough having tangled with the Burton woman in The Monto only to fall foul of this Byrne chap. In her shoes, I'd have made a run for it, too. As a potential witness to what was going on, she may have been afraid they'd kill her to silence her.'

'Crikey, sir. I hadn't thought of that,' Mary said, with a worried expression.

'But did this potman know where she went, Mary?' Lucy asked.

'No, but she stole a weekend's takings. My guess is she took the boat to England.'

Phin nodded in agreement. 'That would be the most sensible course of action. Ryan can check the manifest records at Kingstown, Lucy. Don't worry. We will locate her. I'll send a telegram to Chief Inspector McQuillan and ask that they find her and ensure she's safe.'

'Thank you, sir,' Mary said. 'That's awful kind of you.'

'All of this suggests your cousin is out of danger,' Lucy said. 'And you were right. She appears to have been the sister with the lion's share of the brains. Therefore, I don't see any need for you to stay at the pub any longer, Mary. You might as well come home with us now.'

Mary flicked a glance at Phin. 'I'd sooner not. You see, ma'am, I promised Inspector Ryan I'd do a bit of digging around for 'im. He wants to discover what his cousin is up to. Lizzie's father, Ignatius. The inspector thinks he has links to that Burton woman.'

Lucy was irritated. Ryan should have asked her. After all, Mary was her maid, not one of his agents. 'You don't have to, Mary, if you don't wish to. It might be too dangerous.'

'I know, ma'am, but the inspector has been very kind, and if it helps bring Peggy's murderer to justice, then I'm game.'

'He has arrested the man responsible. He told you that earlier today.'

'Yes, but he wants to expose the whole setup. Then hopefully, no other poor girl will meet the same fate. Burton and the like pluck these young girls off the street and treat them like dirt. Then they discard them like worn boots if they become ill or have babies.'

'Yes, Mary. You're right. We should help him,' Lucy said, squeezing the maid's hand. 'A day or two more, but then I want you back safe in Merrion Square.'

'Yes, ma'am. Trust me, I won't stay any longer than I have to. I'll see you again tomorrow evening.' She turned to Phin. 'Maybe make it a bit later, sir. Chucking-out time is around midnight. Say half past?'

Phin agreed, and Mary wished them goodnight before slipping out of the carriage. Lucy watched Mary until she turned in at the public house.

'I hope this Byrne character isn't as bad as Ryan made out,' she said as Phin used his cane to tap the roof.

The carriage pulled out from the kerb as Phin changed seats to sit beside her. 'Yes. It might be wise for us to take some precautions. We need someone else on the inside looking out for her.'

'Who?'

'Why, George, who else? Don't you know it's thirsty work being my valet.'

TWENTY-FOUR

After an early breakfast and a perusal of the morning papers, in which Carver's arrest at Kingsbridge was described in delicious detail, Lucy accompanied Phineas to Dublin Castle. She was eager to share Mary's progress with the inspector and to hear the latest on Carver. Would he still deny involvement in Peggy's murder when presented with the evidence?

'Well done, Inspector. I must admit I'd like to have seen that arrest. High drama indeed. Did he think he'd make good his escape?' Lucy asked as she accepted a cup of tea from Sergeant Hughes.

'It was panic that made him run, I suppose,' the inspector said with a twinkle in his eye. 'I have that unfortunate effect on some people.'

'Only those who are up to mischief, I'm sure,' she said. Then she briefed him on what Mary had discovered.

'Well, that is a relief, Mrs Stone. As you say, Bridget is likely to have used the money to leave the country. Poor girl was probably scared for her life.'

'We will still have to find her. We have notified the police in

England. If she has gone there, we'd like to trace her and offer her help. Our friend in the Metropolitan Police, Chief Inspector McQuillan, can put his people on to it.'

'Hmm, we may put feelers out to the other ports here, too. She may even have gone to Cobh with a view to going to America.'

'That idea hadn't crossed my mind. I hope not. We'd never find her in America. You will let us know if you hear anything?' Lucy said. 'Mary will be anxious to learn where she has gone.'

'I will, don't worry.'

'By the way, Inspector, I'd like to compliment you on your handling of Olivia the other night. I know she appreciated your kindness.' The inspector blushed and was suddenly absorbed by the papers on his desk.

Oh, dear, she thought, *he is smitten*. She quickly turned the subject. 'I understand you have asked Mary to look into some other matters while she is under your cousin's roof.'

'Yes. Iggy is engaged in the illegal alcohol trade and is supplying the brothels, too. I want to put a stop to it. Your maid was kind enough to agree to... well, see if she could find any evidence.'

'I'd be very upset if anything were to happen to her as a result,' Lucy said, with a steely glance.

'I warned her to be ultra cautious, Mrs Stone. And I would not have asked her if I had thought it was too risky. My cousin Lizzie is no threat, but her father is a different matter. I told Miss O'Reilly to avoid him at all costs.'

'Hmm.' Lucy drained her cup and rose. She wasn't reassured, but as they were going to send in George to the pub as a customer, she would not labour the point. 'I won't hold you up, Inspector. But please let us know if there is any news of Bridget.' As she pulled on her gloves, a thought struck her. 'Isn't it odd that your cousin didn't inform the police about Bridget stealing all that money?'

'I think not. After all, if Bridget were found and told us about what had happened at Burton's flash-house, and about the sisters' enslavement, it would only be bad news for the Byrnes as well.'

'True, though I understand it was a substantial amount of cash that she took.'

'As much as I'd love to delve into it further, I have plenty of work on my hands as it is, and more importantly, I can't investigate a crime that hasn't been reported. If I waded in demanding to know why the theft had gone unreported, they would immediately suspect Mary of being an informer. The last thing I want to do is put Mary in danger,' he said, his irritation rising to the surface.

Lucy put it down to the stress he was under, so she moved the conversation on. 'You are right, there would be repercussions. I hadn't considered that. Well, I'm sure the people involved are bound to come to your notice for other crimes in due course.'

'Nothing more certain, Mrs Stone,' he said. 'I apologise. I should not have vented my frustrations to you, but my hands are tied.'

'Not at all. I understand perfectly.'

'When the opportunity arises, and Mary is no longer there, I'll tackle my cousin Lizzie about it.' He treated her to a gentle smile. 'Now, I wonder if I might impose on your kindness, Mrs Stone.'

'That depends,' she said, but smiled to soften the words.

'When you arrived earlier, we were about to set out to The Monto. Would you be willing to accompany us to Lady Muck's flash-house? We need to interview a few of the women again, and I believe they will be more forthcoming with a lady present. Let me assure you, you'll be safe with us.'

Lucy mulled this over for a second or two before flashing him a grin. 'Well, I wouldn't venture in on my own. Phineas would be apoplectic, but I'm sure he wouldn't object if I'm with you and your officers. I can leave a note for him. Perhaps one of your men could drop it up to his office? I believe he is meeting Valentine DeWinter somewhere in the castle as we speak.'

'Of course,' Ryan said.

The sergeant handed her pen and paper, and she scribbled the note. 'I'll pop up and leave it on his desk, ma'am,' Hughes offered, scooting out the door.

Ryan held out his arm. 'Shall we? Hughes will meet us down in the Castle Yard.'

As Ryan handed her up into the waiting carriage, he said, 'By the way, we hope to interview Carver again this afternoon, but it won't do him any harm to stew for a couple of hours in the cells. There are some loose ends I wish to clear up first, you see. The slightest slip-up, and Carver's defence barrister will annihilate us in court. A watertight case is what I'm aiming for.'

'I couldn't agree more for I've seen for myself how unpredictable juries are. We must ensure the evidence is overwhelming,' Lucy said, settling back in her seat. 'And you can explain what you mean by those *loose ends* on the way to The Monto.'

The journey through the city traffic was a tiresome stop-start experience. Lucy kept up general chit-chat as she sensed the tension in Ryan. He couldn't sit still. Phin had been right about him; he was a talented detective, prepared to go the extra mile to ensure he had sufficient evidence. Why else this trip back to The Monto?

However, when she mentioned Olivia again in conversation, it had a startling effect on the policeman. His entire body went rigid for a few seconds, and his eyes widened. Lucy smiled to herself as she chatted away. No matter what Phin said about her matchmaking abilities, she was determined these two lonely souls would find each other. She would have to use every opportunity to throw them together. But for now, her curiosity about something else was foremost in her mind.

'What is Carver like as a person?' she asked. 'I've never met him.'

As she hoped, the question pulled the inspector's attention back to her. 'Arrogant and highly manipulative. I must admit that he has got under my skin. That's why I'm determined to gather as much evidence as possible to seal his fate.'

'For Olivia's sake?' Lucy couldn't resist.

The inspector blushed. 'Yes... No, I mean he must face justice. Peggy's murder was one of the most brutal I've ever seen. That is why we want to interview some of the women again. They may reveal something new. And there is one issue that is worrying me.'

'Your loose end?'

'Yes. Ginny O'Mara. She has now come forward with more information.'

'Oh, the young woman who spoke to me and Mary?'

'Yes. She occupies the room beneath Peggy's and now claims she heard something from the room above on the evening of the murder. However, she says this was about half past six or a little after.' Ryan leaned forward. 'My concern is that on the night of the murder I spoke to her, and she said she had heard nothing.'

'Perhaps her conscience has kicked in, particularly after meeting Mary. And I don't blame her for being cautious.'

'True. Burton rules by fear. But this new information poses a problem. We have several witnesses who say Carver didn't arrive until close to seven o'clock. Even Burton's statement said seven. I want to clarify Ginny's statement for she must be mistaken. I mean, all the other evidence points to Carver.'

'Such as the blood on the cane. Hmm, that's assuming what she heard was the attack on Peggy. It may not have been.'

'True. That's the nub of it, isn't it?' he said, sitting back again. 'We shall have to wait and see what she has to say.'

Ryan had warned her that their reception would be chilly at best, and he had described the main characters they would have to deal with. With Carver's arrest, Ryan had withdrawn the constable from outside the house, so their visit would not be expected but might cause consternation.

A tingle of excitement surged down Lucy's spine. Mrs Burton sounded like a complete horror and her henchman, Mulcahy, a ruffian of the worst kind. Lucy couldn't wait to see them for herself, but she had to hide her excitement. Nice as he was, she doubted the inspector would understand how thrilling this all was for her. Just like the old days.

From the inspector's description, Lucy guessed that the ugly brute who answered the door was Burton's chief bully boy, Mulcahy.

He looked them up and down. When his gaze landed on Lucy, his expression grew wary. 'Yeah?' he grunted at Ryan. 'Whatcha want, polis?'

'Good morning to you, too, Mulcahy. Please tell Mrs Burton I'm here and would like to see her,' Ryan said, stepping past Mulcahy and into the hallway. Lucy remained standing on the top step with the sergeant, unsure if she should follow.

'No can do. She ain't here.' Mulcahy tucked his thumbs into his trouser pockets and leaned against the wall. 'You might as well scarper back under that rock you crawled out from.'

Ryan's answering stare was icy. 'When will she be back?'

'No idea. What's it to you, polis?'

'My business is urgent and cannot wait. Who's in charge in her absence?' the inspector asked, exchanging a knowing look with his sergeant.

Mulcahy grinned. 'That'd be me, mate. You caught that Carver fella yet?'

'He's in custody.'

'So, why are you back bothering us then?' the porter sneered. The inspector didn't reply but headed down the hallway. Lucy held back, sticking close to the sergeant as he crossed the threshold.

'Oy! You can't go in there,' Mulcahy shouted at the inspector as he opened a door.

Ryan swivelled round, not the least perturbed. 'We will use this room for our interviews, Mulcahy. Come along, Mrs Stone, I can assure you it's comfortable in here.' Then he turned back to Mulcahy. 'Rouse the girls for me, there's a good chap. I want to talk to a few of them, maybe even all of them. Or would you prefer my sergeant here to do the rousing for you?'

Mulcahy's glared at him. 'You can't—'

'Let me put it this way, *mate*. You can cooperate and this will be over in no time, or I can call up a couple of Black Marias and have the lot of you brought to the castle for interview.' Ryan shook his head. 'The process would take most of the day and well into this evening. Which would be bad for business, would it not? Mrs Burton would be very put out, I'm sure, if she comes back and finds the place empty.'

'You can't do that, Ryan. We've only just reopened.'

Ryan's response was a mock-sympathetic smile. Cursing under his breath, Mulcahy threw him a filthy look before plodding up the stairs.

With an exaggerated bow, the inspector invited Lucy to join him. She smiled up at Ryan as she glided past and into the sitting room. 'Nicely done, Inspector.'

'Fergus?' a female voice called from the stairs.

Moments later, Ginny O'Mara appeared in the doorway. Lucy was shocked by Ginny's appearance. It was as if the young woman had aged since she had seen her only days before. There were purple shadows below her heavy-lidded eyes. Was it lack of sleep or something more sinister?

'Hello, there. Back again?' Ginny said. 'Oh, hello, Mrs Stone,' Ginny whispered before scanning the hallway and stepping further into the room.

'Good morning, Ginny,' Lucy whispered back. She assumed Ginny wouldn't want anyone in the house to know they had met before.

'I was hoping to see you, Ginny. I'm here to ask a few more questions. Would you have a minute to talk to us?' Ryan asked.

'Sure. Always good to see ya.'

'You, too. Hughes, mind the door while we have a quiet word with Miss O'Mara.'

'Will do, sir.'

The inspector ushered both of them to seats, however, Ginny hesitated near the door.

'Don't worry, Ginny. Mrs Burton appears to be out. And even

if she returns, my sergeant will keep her away until we are finished.'

'Good.' The young woman sat on a sofa before the window, but her eyes kept darting to the door. 'Don't wanna get on the wrong side of 'er.'

'Any idea where Burton is by any chance?' he asked.

Ginny gave a shrug. 'Haven't seen her since Thursday evening. Hopefully, she's off on one of her holidays. She loves Bray. Well for some, ain't it?'

'And how are your departure plans going?' Ryan asked her as he sat down opposite. 'Anything I can do to help?'

'Thanks, love, but I don't think so. Your friend here has promised to help me.' She flicked a questioning glance at Lucy. 'I can't wait to leave this hellhole. The sooner the better.'

Lucy nodded. 'I'm not surprised, Ginny, from what I've seen and heard so far. I'm glad to have this opportunity to thank you. The information you gave us the other day was very helpful.'

'You found the girl?'

'Not exactly, but she had been working at The Sleepy Druid. She has run away since. We suspect she has left for England.'

'Good for her. I'll be following in her footsteps when I can.'

'Thanks for helping out with that matter, Ginny,' Ryan said. 'However, it's a pity you didn't give *me* that information on the night of the murder.'

Ginny shrugged. 'Ah, now Fergus. Sorry, but I didn't think it was relevant cos I didn't know they were sisters, now, did I? I don't want no trouble with Lady Muck.' She folded her arms.

'I'm sure you don't, but I need to conclude this Peggy O'Reilly case. Have any of the girls said anything to you that might help me? Some detail from that night they may have recalled. Was there anything unusual about the nineteenth? Clients who acted in a strange manner?'

Ginny said, 'Why? Word is you have the bloke who done her in.'

'I hope so, but it is essential we are absolutely sure when the attack occurred and when this fellow we have in custody arrived here at the house.'

'Can't help you there. I never saw 'im that night. And if you must know, the girls have been reluctant to discuss it.'

'Mulcahy?'

'Yeah. We were told to forget all about it... or else.'

Ryan glanced at his notebook. 'That's what I figured. So, how come you've given us this new information, Ginny?'

Ginny licked her lips. 'I'd forgotten about it but when I talked to Mrs Stone... I remembered a bit more... Look, we reopened last night and I've things to do.' The young woman rose and wrapped her arms around her thin body, but she started to cough as she straightened up. Lucy didn't like the sound of it.

'This won't take long, Ginny. Please,' Ryan said, his voice coaxing.

Lucy stood and held out her hand. Ginny hesitated. 'Thanks again for helping us find Bridget.' Ginny's shoulders relaxed, and they shook hands, Ginny allowing a tiny smile to form on her bluish lips. Lucy pulled out her purse and extracted some notes. 'We made a deal. This should cover your fare and expenses. And here is my card. Look me up in London. I should be back there in a few weeks, and I will introduce you to my friend, as we discussed. You did the right thing in helping us. You're a good person.'

With lightning speed, Ginny tucked the notes into a skirt pocket and sat down. 'No, I'm not really. But I did it for 'er. For Peggy. No one looks out for us girls. Mulcahy would as soon hit you as look at you, and as for your lot...' She turned to the inspector. 'Too bloody scared of the gangs to come in here, most of ya. But I don't need to tell you how things are around here or that Mulcahy's a bastard with a nasty temper.'

Ryan's brows creased. 'You don't think *he* might have killed Peggy?'

'No idea, love, but he's capable of it if the girl was silly enough to refuse a client. Lady Muck would never tolerate that... mind you, she's well able to deal with those situations herself.'

Lucy sat down, giving the inspector a quizzical look. 'You didn't suspect Mulcahy before?'

Ryan sat rubbing his hand across his chin. 'Yes, briefly. But Mrs Burton was so sure it was Carver and Mulcahy backed her up.' He gave a little groan. 'My God, I hope I didn't jump too soon.'

Lucy's heart dropped. 'Well, perhaps Ginny here can help us clear up the timing issue at least.'

TWENTY-FIVE

Burton's Flash-House, The Monto

Ginny remained seated with her hands clasped in her lap and her large green eyes fixed on Ryan. Her gaunt, fragile appearance worried Lucy. The woman was definitely ill and, not for the first time, Lucy despaired at how easily these young women ended up in places like this, forced to work for grasping madams, no matter what their circumstances. Society had turned its back on them and left these women and girls no choice. No wonder Lady Sarah had taken up the cause for reform and set up a charity to help the girls escape their awful lives.

Ryan's gaze was full of sympathy. 'Thanks for staying, Ginny. This won't take long. Please speak freely in front of Mrs Stone. As you know, Peggy was her maid's cousin, and Mrs Stone is as anxious as I am to ensure the poor girl receives justice.'

Ginny gave a nod of understanding.

'So, I wanted to ask you a few questions about the night Peggy was murdered. I wonder if you would go through the events of that night with us now?'

'Am I in some sort of trouble for not saying anythin' before?' she asked.

'No, not at all. In fact, I'm very grateful to you.' The inspector leaned forward. 'But first, tell me, has someone threatened you?'

'No, no. Just like a quiet life, me.' She flashed them both a nervous smile.

'Don't we all,' Ryan exclaimed. After a quick glance at Lucy, the inspector pulled out a sheet of paper from his pocket and laid it on the table between them. 'This is the statement you gave my sergeant. Have a quick look at it to refresh your memory.'

She scanned the page, then sat back. 'Yep. That's all right.'

'Can you talk me through that evening, as best you can remember?'

Her expression wary, she twisted the ring on her finger. 'Some of us girls, we had a cuppa in the kitchen around six. Peggy was there.' She glanced at Lucy. 'A fierce quiet young 'un. Looked scared to death most of the time. But I suppose we all were like that at the beginning.'

Lucy's stomach twisted at the thought.

'Did you have much to do with her?' Ryan asked.

'Nah, girls come and go so often... it's not worth getting to know 'em. You need to know who you can trust, like. I have me own mates, girls who started here at the same time, and we stick together... Though I'm fierce sorry for what happened to her.'

'I understand.' Ryan motioned for her to continue.

'Anyway, we both had clients due, so we left the kitchen together and parted on my landing. Her room was above mine.'

'Roughly what time was this?'

'Must have headed up to the rooms around half past six. Yeah, I was keeping an eye on the time and had looked at the kitchen clock as I'd rinsed out me cup. Lady Muck is very particular about timekeepin', she is. Clients can't be kept waitin'.'

'Did Peggy appear to be worried about anything... more worried than usual, that is?'

'Couldn't tell ye. She looked bloody miserable all the time. She didn't say a word to me that evening except goodbye or see you later, something like that, when we parted.'

'And were there any clients around? In the hallway, the corridors or on the stairs? Did anyone pass you or follow Peggy up the next flight?'

'Didn't see no one except Mulcahy on his perch in the hall when we came up from the kitchen. Sorry.'

'That's fine, don't worry. So, what happened next?' he asked.

'I changed and lay down on the bed for a snooze. Me client wasn't due till seven. I was dozing off when there was a thud.'

'From above?'

'Yeah, right above me head. Startled me, like. I thought it was a piece of furniture falling over.'

'Or a person?'

Ginny shrugged. 'Don't know.'

'Did you hear anything else? A cry, a scream, loud voices, angry voices?'

'I thought I did, but I'm not sure. The place can be rowdy at times.'

'But it was unusual to hear a thump like that?' Lucy asked.

Ginny smirked and treated her to a pitying glance. 'Aye. I mean you'd hear other stuff, huffin' and puffin', regular like, if you know what I mean, but this was different.' Her gaze swung back to Fergus. 'You don't think that was when Peggy was attacked? That's terrible.'

'It's possible, Ginny. But did that not occur to you afterwards when you heard Peggy was dead?'

Ginny dropped her gaze. 'No. It was only when I talked to Mrs Stone that I thought what I'd heard might be important,' she said a little too quickly. 'Sorry.'

Ryan glanced at Lucy. 'Thank you, Ginny. But you're sure about the time?'

'Defo. It couldn't have been much after twenty minutes to seven. I'd barely laid me head down on the pillow.'

'One last question. What time did your client arrive?'

'He was a bit early. About ten minutes to.'

'When you answered your door to him, did you see anyone else around? Anyone coming down the stairs?'

'No, but I heard voices in the hallway. One was definitely Mulcahy, but I can't be sure about the other one other than it was a man.' She bit her lip. 'His voice *was* kinda familiar, but I can't place it. Sorry. He was probably a regular client, and he was asking for Lady... Mrs Burton, he was. Kinda high-pitched. Anxious-like.'

'Thanks, Ginny, that's been very helpful. If you should remember who it was, please send me a note. You can go.'

Ginny flitted out the door and closed it after her. The inspector didn't sit down again but paced the floor. 'None of that was in Burton or Mulcahy's statements. There was no mention of an upset client. I wonder who it was? Both Burton and Mulcahy deny seeing Carver leave.' Ryan stopped before her, his face ashen. 'Perhaps he didn't do it and fled to avoid the scandal as he claims.'

'Perhaps, although the blood on his cane proves he was here and in that poor girl's room. But if Barton and Mulcahy lied to you, it suggests they are hiding something or protecting someone.'

He grunted. 'That's the norm around here. I shouldn't have placed so much reliance on their statements. An error of judgement on my part.'

'I wouldn't dwell on it. Carver has acted guilty from the start. So, the way I see it you need to find out who this upset individual was? Maybe it *was* Carver. We should have asked Ginny if Carver had ever been a client of hers? It would explain why the voice was familiar.'

'Yes. I'll get Hughes to check with her before we leave. The trouble is Burton and Mulcahy were very keen for me to believe Carver was the killer. They would have been only too glad to share that little nugget of information with me, and yet they didn't. And another thing. Whoever killed Peggy would have had blood on their clothes. I saw Carver's coat hanging in the hallway of his home the next morning. It was spotless.'

'Oh dear.'

'Yes, but I assumed he had another coat and that he had hidden the soiled one or thrown it away.'

'I should think that would be very possible.'

'And Carver has no valet at the moment. He might have disposed of a bloodstained coat, and no one would know. And it's probably too late to check for it now.'

Lucy suspected the inspector was guilty of the cardinal sin of fitting the evidence to the suspect he wanted to be guilty. It was something most detectives, herself included, had fallen victim to at some point. Hadn't Phin warned her about it? Perhaps in Ryan's case, his judgement was coloured by his feelings for Olivia. Ryan wanted to shield her from a man he saw as a tyrant. It wasn't surprising. Olivia had a helpless quality many men found attractive. Lucy, conversely, was finding it irritating. It spoke of a weakness of character.

'But from what Ginny has told us this morning, I think you may have to consider the possibility that Carver isn't your man, after all.'

Ryan slumped into a chair and screwed up his eyes as if in pain. 'I know.'

'So, what now?' she asked. 'How do we proceed?'

Before he could answer, someone tapped on the door. The sergeant stuck his head around the door. 'Who do you want to see next, sir? They're getting a bit fractious and mouthy.'

Ryan summoned a smile. 'Feeling under pressure, Hughes? Well, you may dismiss them, but get Mulcahy in here right now. You'd best join us, too.'

TWENTY-SIX

It took Lucy a few moments to figure out what it was about Mulcahy that unnerved her. Then she realised it was his eyes; so pale and silvery, so snake-like, that they made her shiver. Reptiles were not her favourite creatures. She couldn't see their appeal. However, Bash had been delighted with the snakes in the Reptile House at the zoo in the Phoenix Park only days before. He'd even asked Phin if he might have one as a pet, a suggestion Lucy had vetoed on the spot, even before the nursery maid had declared she'd leave if it came to pass. Phin, thankfully, had also shot down the idea. Negotiations on an alternative pet were, however, ongoing now that Ellie had also taken up the call. Thankfully, her pet of choice was a rabbit. Lucy predicted Phin would surrender before the summer was out.

That Mulcahy was nervous didn't surprise Lucy. The sheen of perspiration stood out on his large forehead, and the corner of his mouth twitched ever so slightly when Ryan addressed him. He wouldn't look at Lucy directly and refused to sit when Ryan invited him to.

'I need you to go through the events of the night Peggy O'Reilly died, again,' Ryan demanded. Hughes sat down at the table, notebook and pen at the ready.

'Again? Why? Already told you all I know.'

'There appear to be gaps in your statement.'

'Nah. Not possible, mate. I told youse everything.'

Ryan, who was positioned at the fireplace, crossed his arms. 'You were heard talking to a client who was in a distressed state at ten minutes to seven. You neglected to tell us about that.'

Mulcahy snuffled. 'Don't remember that. Whoever told ya must be mistaken.' His eyes narrowed. 'Was it one of the girls? Cos they're awful liars, you know. Can't trust a word they say.'

'Never mind who told me, Mulcahy. Who were you talking to?'

'I told ye, didn't 'appen. Not that I recall. I'm a busy man. Talk to all the gentleman callers I do, when they arrive. Then show 'em in to the boss.' Mulcahy swung his gaze to Lucy. 'Have to ensure the riffraff stay out. Mrs Burton is very particular.'

Lucy's stomach turned at his words, and she cast Ryan a beseeching look. The man wasn't going to tell them anything. This was a waste of time.

'Where is Burton, Mulcahy?' Ryan asked, the exasperation only too clear in his voice.

'Dunno. I'm not her keeper.'

To Lucy's astonishment, Ryan crossed the room until he was nose to nose with the man. 'Don't tangle with me, Mulcahy. Tell me what you know. And just to remind you, I'm still partial to the idea of hauling the entire household to the castle for the fun of it. Where. Is. She?'

Mulcahy stared back at him for several seconds before dropping his gaze. 'No idea,' he mumbled at last. 'Haven't seen her since Thursday night.'

'Did she say she was going away?' Ryan asked.

'Not to me.'

'When she turns up, tell her I want to speak to her. Urgently. And if I hear that any of the women, and in particular any I spoke to today, have come to any harm, I'll make you sorry you were ever born. Is that clear?'

Mulcahy's response was a grunt before he headed for the door. Then he turned. 'She won't be happy about this.'

'Get out!' Ryan shouted at him. As the door closed, he looked towards Lucy. 'Apologies, but the man makes my blood boil.'

'Don't worry, Inspector, I can see why. However, if no one will tell us who the man was, how can you progress the case? Carver is looking less and less likely to be your killer.'

'Don't I know it,' Ryan said as he watched Hughes answer a knock on the door.

Hughes came back to them a few moments later. 'Sir, this note has arrived from the castle. Mr Blanchard has agreed to see us.' He held up a note and passed it to Ryan. 'He lives out on St Lawrence's Road in Clontarf.'

'It's not far.' Ryan looked at Lucy. 'Do you wish to return to the castle, Mrs Stone... or would you like to accompany us?'

'What a silly question. Of course, I'll come with you.'

Clontarf, Dublin

A fifteen-minute carriage ride later, they turned off the main Clontarf thoroughfare onto a tree-lined road. It was a delightful streetscape of modern red-brick houses, of similar design, hugging both sides of the road as it rose steadily away from the sea. Lucy guessed it was an up-and-coming area. Ryan confirmed this when she voiced it.

Sergeant Hughes scanned the names of the various terraces and rapped on the roof of the carriage about halfway up the road, bringing it to a stop. Hughes and Ryan jumped out, then Ryan handed Lucy to the pavement.

'Which house, Hughes?' Ryan asked.

The sergeant consulted the note. 'Number two, Ellesmere Terrace, sir. That one, I believe,' he said, pointing to a house which appeared to be of recent construction. A cart was being loaded with what looked to Lucy like builder's rubble from the front garden. Ryan offered his arm to Lucy, and they made their way down a tiled pathway to the front door.

A young housemaid answered Ryan's tug on the bellpull.

'Good afternoon,' Ryan said. 'Is Mr Blanchard at home?'

'Who shall I say is calling, sir?'

'Inspector Ryan of the DMP and Mrs Phineas Stone. I believe we are expected.'

The maid's brows shot up, but she stepped back and shepherded them inside, before leading them to a smart sitting room, which smelled of fresh paint. 'I shall see if the master is at home,' the maid said and slipped out the door.

Blanchard bustled in a few moments later, his face creased in concern. 'Good afternoon. I was surprised to have a constable at my door first thing this morning, asking questions. What have I done?' he asked with a nervous laugh.

'Nothing, sir. I'm sorry if you were alarmed,' Ryan said before making the introductions.

Blanchard invited them to sit.

'We are sorry to bother you, sir. However, we are hoping you can help us with our enquiries into a vicious murder that happened last week. Mr Myles Carver gave us your name.'

Lucy didn't miss the flash of horror followed by distaste that crossed the man's face on hearing Carver's name. Not bosom pals by the look of it.

'What has Carver accused me of?'

'Nothing at all, sir.'

Blanchard relaxed. 'Then I will help, if I can. Dashed bad business, that murder. I read about it in the papers. Shocking news.'

'Yes, sir, and we are determined to charge the culprit as soon as possible. You see, sir, Mr Carver has claimed that you can support his alibi for Thursday, the nineteenth. He has stated you dropped him off in Mecklenburgh Street on the night in question.'

With a grunt, Blanchard confirmed this. 'I did. Funnily enough, I asked him about the murder a few days later when I saw him at the bank. He said it had nothing to do with him. You don't suspect him, do you?' Lucy noted the gleam that entered the man's eyes.

'He is helping with our investigation at present. Would you recall the time you dropped him, sir?'

'It was almost seven, and I'm sure of that because I checked my watch before we left the bank on Dame Street, and it was a quarter to. I was running late and anxious to get going, but he kept me hanging about for ages. The impudence of the man. Demanding, not asking, I drop him off, would you believe it? Even though he knew I needed to get home. Won't spend a penny unless he absolutely must, and he knew I always had my gig.' He waved his hands vaguely. 'As you can see, the house has only been finished a couple of weeks, and my wife is finding all this upheaval very stressful. I was eager to get home. Not to mention, it was her birthday on the nineteenth, and we had plans to go out to dinner. But that's typical Carver. Got me onto the board, see, so I feel obliged to... entertain his demands.' He glanced at Lucy. 'I can tell you, madam, The Monto was the last place I wanted to go, or to be seen in. Very damaging to one's reputation, so I hightailed it out of there as fast as my poor horse would go. Dashed bad form on Carver's part. Still in my wife's bad books over it.'

'Thank you, sir. That's very helpful. Can you confirm you saw Mr Carver enter a house on that street?' Ryan asked.

Blanchard smirked. 'The brothel, you mean? Oh, yes. He did indeed. Swaggered up the steps as if he owned the place and waved that damned walking stick of his at me. Apologies, madam.'

'Not at all, sir. I can understand how you feel.'

'I say, is it true what's being said in the papers? Arrested at Kingsbridge, what?' Blanchard asked, turning to Ryan, his tone eager. 'Carver's a rum 'un, but murder? I find it hard to believe.'

The inspector rose to his feet. 'The incident is still under investigation. It may be that Mr Carver was in the wrong place at the wrong time. Thank you for confirming the facts for us. We won't detain you any longer, sir.'

It took all of Lucy's self-control not to smile at Blanchard's expression of extreme disappointment. Once back in the carriage, Lucy said, 'You'll be obliged to free Carver now, won't you? Your evidence is all circumstantial if what Ginny says is true. I believed her, Ryan.'

'Yes. Ginny was certain about the time, and what she heard must have been the attack. And it was well before Carver arrived.'

'What about Olivia?' Lucy asked.

'What indeed?' he growled.

'Can't we warn her before you release him? Perhaps it is best if she moves in with me until she decides what to do.'

'You would do that for her?' he asked.

'Yes. After all, between us we convinced her, against her better judgement, to tell the truth. He might not have murdered poor Peggy, and I'm sure he will be relieved not to hang, but he won't be happy about the accusations.' Ryan groaned. 'Isn't it likely he will direct his frustration at her?'

'You're right. Perhaps she would take the bad news better from you?' he suggested.

Lucy wasn't having that. She was determined Olivia would see Ryan as her knight in shining armour. 'On the contrary, it should be you.' She watched the colour rise in his cheeks. 'And the sooner the better, Inspector.'

TWENTY-SEVEN

It was late afternoon by the time the police carriage pulled up outside the Stone residence. To Fergus' dismay, a group of newspapermen was hanging around on the pavement in front of the Carver house. A pall of smoke hung over their heads suggesting they had been there for some time. Some were leaning on the railings. They looked bored but Fergus knew they would have no intention of leaving until they had some titbit for their editors. He pointed them out to Lucy.

'Yes, the vultures. They've been there since early this morning. Only to be expected, after the high drama of Carver's arrest,' she said as they alighted from the carriage.

One journalist spotted them and rushed forward. Fergus recognised him and groaned. O'Farrell was tenacious and a pest, often inventing copy when police refused to comment.

To Fergus's surprise, Lucy gave him a gentle push in the back. 'Off into the lion's den with you. Good luck,' she said with a cheeky grin, before tripping up the steps to tug on the bellpull of her own house. Fergus watched her slip inside. She really was an extraordinary woman and what a lucky man Phineas Stone was to have such a partner. If only he could find someone like her.

'Inspector Ryan?' O'Farrell called out, pen hovering over his notebook. 'Have you charged Myles Carver? Has he admitted the brutal killing of that prostitute? When will we get all the details?'

Seconds later, Fergus was surrounded, questions flying at him. From inside the carriage, Hughes gave him a sympathetic look but clearly had no intention of joining him.

'Excuse me a moment, gentlemen,' Fergus said, walking over to the carriage door. 'Go back to the castle. I won't be long with Mrs Carver. I'll take a cab back.'

'Yes, sir. And Carver? His solicitor is bound to be back, demanding we charge or release.'

Fergus leaned closer and spoke quietly. 'We will have to release him but hold off until I'm back. I'll have to talk to Malone first, anyway.'

'Ah,' the sergeant said. 'A difficult conversation, I'd imagine, sir.'

'Yes, he won't be pleased.' Fergus closed the carriage door and banged on the side. With rueful thoughts, he watched the carriage until it had rounded the corner.

Then he turned back to the group of newspapermen who were staring at him expectantly. Chief Inspector Malone would have his guts for garters if he said the wrong thing, but he had to say something. Best to trot out the standard line.

'Gentlemen, I'm afraid I have no comment to make at present. Our enquiries are ongoing. Now, if you will excuse me.' Fergus pushed through towards the Carver house, the journalists still firing questions at him, close on his heels.

'Why are you going in there?'

'Are you searching for more evidence, Inspector Ryan?'

'Will he hang?'

These were only some of the questions the journalists threw at him from the bottom of the steps, as he waited at the Carver door, praying Sally would hurry and open the door soon.

Thankfully, she obliged within a minute of his knock. 'Inspector, do come in,' she said, scowling at the men still lingering at the foot of the steps. Once Fergus was inside, she made a threatening gesture with her fist to the reporters, but they laughed up at her.

'Are they being a nuisance?' Fergus asked once she shut the door. 'I can have the local constable move them on if you wish.'

'Aye, they're a nuisance alright. No respect and the poor mistress dying up above. They've been pestering us something terrible all morning. But I'm well able to deal with them, don't you worry. Is it herself you want?'

'Yes, please.'

Sally nodded towards the library. 'Take a seat. I'll fetch her now. She's with the mistress.'

Fergus paced the room while he waited. For some strange reason, his heart was pounding. He couldn't explain it. It wasn't as if he hadn't delivered bad news before.

Olivia appeared, looking as pretty as ever, though she was paler than the last time he had seen her. He suspected she wasn't sleeping well. And here he was, about to make things even worse. The blow he had to deliver made him feel like a complete cad. However, Lucy was correct. It had to be done, and it fell to him to do it.

'Good afternoon, Inspector,' she greeted him. He acknowledged this with a nod, and she said, 'Do sit down.' She attempted to smile but failed. Her eyes widened with sudden understanding. 'Something is wrong, isn't it?'

'Yes. I'm sorry, but I do have bad news. Although we had grounds to arrest your father-in-law yesterday, it now appears the evidence is insufficient. I must release him from custody this afternoon. I wanted to warn you in advance so that you would have time to leave, if you wished.'

Ashen, Olivia's hand flew to her mouth. 'No, no. Please God, no.' Then she burst into tears.

He couldn't bear it. Before he knew it, he was holding her close as she sobbed into his shoulder. 'I'm sorry, Olivia. I have no choice.

It looks as though the attack on that poor girl happened before he entered the house.' Her sobs increased, and his grip tightened. 'Lucy Stone says you are to go to her. You and your maid. You will be safe there. There are reporters outside, but we can use the back lane to avoid them. I can help you make good your escape.'

Olivia went rigid, then pulled away. 'No. no. That is impossible. I cannot abandon Edith. She's dying. There is no one else to tend her. *He* won't, nor the rest of the servants, either. I *must* stay.'

'This is madness,' he exclaimed. 'You may not be safe. I have no way to protect you while you remain in this house.'

This resulted in a watery smile. 'You are very good, but you must understand my position. I will not leave a dying woman to such a man's care.' Much to his disappointment, Olivia moved away from him. After a shaky breath, she said, 'When she's gone, it will be a different matter. There will be nothing to tie us here. Sally and I will leave this house for good.'

'But where will you go?' he asked, filled with dismay.

She caught her breath on a sob. 'I have no idea. I may throw myself on the mercy of my brother in England.' She shook herself. 'But I'll worry about that when the time comes.'

It was heartbreaking to see her so miserable. He offered her his handkerchief and watched as she dabbed her tears. Once she was done, he grabbed her hand. 'Olivia, I cannot stand by and see you treated this way. You must know that I have come to care for you deeply.' Colour rushed into her cheeks as she stared at him. But he was sure there was a spark of hope in her gaze. 'I gladly offer you whatever protection I can.'

'You are very kind, indeed,' she said on a sob, 'but I have nothing to offer *you*. I'm virtually penniless. My husband ran through my dowry in a matter of months. I don't even have an allowance from his estate.'

'How cruel of Carver. I have heard he is tightfisted, yet to hold you prisoner almost with no means of support is downright evil. But it doesn't matter to me if you have money or not, Olivia. If you care for me, nothing matters. I wish my circumstances were better, but unfortunately my father is an invalid, and he relies on me for support. However, my prospects are good. In time, I hope to be promoted. It is true we would not live as you are used to, I regret to say, but I can support a wife.' He smiled encouragingly. 'We wouldn't starve.'

'I... I don't know what to say.' She looked away from him, and he knew she was struggling. Eventually, she turned back to him. 'Thank you for your offer. Money means nothing to me, but I must be honest with you... Fergus. I do have feelings for you, too, but my present circumstances are such that I cannot contemplate... at this moment... Not now while Edith is dying. I must stick it out.'

'You are too good, but I understand. Will you at least promise me that when she has passed, you will consider my offer?' he asked, his grip on her hand tightening. 'And if Carver threatens you in any way, that you will go to Lucy and Phineas for protection?'

'Yes, Fergus, I will.'

He leaned in and kissed her cheek. She didn't resist but to his surprise, she rose and went to the window. She glanced out, and he assumed she was looking at the reporters, but when her gaze met his once more, it was unfocused and she was breathing heavily.

'There is something I should have told you before. And now, I feel I can trust you.'

'I can't tell you how glad I am to hear it.' He beamed.

'No. You must listen. It's something awful. Lucy... knows about it, for I confided in her, and she urged me to tell you. But I didn't want to accuse someone in the wrong. That would be wicked, would it not?'

'Yes, but you *can* trust me. What's the matter? Please tell me.'

Olivia clasped her hands. 'Edith's decline has been quicker than it should have been. Even the doctor has been surprised and has questioned it. Her heart is weak, and she is on strong medication. However, I have long suspected...' She paused as if to compose herself. 'I think Myles is poisoning her.'

'What?' His mind raced. Could it be true? 'That is a serious accusation, Olivia. What makes you believe it?'

'At first it was just a hunch. Myles takes tea with Edith every morning, and everyone else is banished from the room. But after he leaves, she is always unwell. As the day progresses, she rallies a little.'

'What medication is she on?' he asked.

'Tincture of digitalis, for her weak heart, prescribed by her doctor. It is my responsibility to administer it, which I do, twice a day. And before you ask, yes, I do check how much is left in the bottle after Myles is with her. It doesn't change.'

'Which suggests you may be mistaken—'

Olivia held up her hand. 'No. When he leaves, she is confused and complains of feeling sick and that her vision is blurred and strange. That can't be right. Sometimes, she does not even recognise me.' Olivia caught her breath. 'Yesterday, she thought I was her dead daughter.'

'To be honest, that sounds more like senility than heart issues.'

'No, she is muddled, I tell you, but only for part of the day, just after he leaves. So, I plucked up my courage, and I voiced my concern to Lucy. Well, as you know, Lucy is a force of nature and was determined to investigate. While Myles was out, we searched his room to see if there was another bottle in the house, which would explain Edith's wavering condition. We found one hidden in his room. Now, why would he have it if not for some nefarious purpose?'

'Is it still there? Can you show it to me?' he asked. 'Don't you see, if we can prove he is poisoning her, it will give me reason to keep him in custody.'

Olivia smiled for the first time. A smile of relief. 'Come then, I'll show you.'

Fergus followed her upstairs and into Carver's suite. She led him into a small bathroom off the bedroom. From under a stack of towels, Olivia pulled out a small blue bottle. She handed it over.

Fergus uncorked the bottle and took a sniff. It smelled strange. Something foul, like rotting vegetation. 'Have you tampered with this in any way?'

Olivia's face fell. 'Lucy removed the digitalis and replaced it with tea. To mitigate...'

'I can understand why she did that, but it leaves us with little evidence of foul play. Any apothecary testing this would likely say these contents are harmless. Would you be willing to go in front of a judge and jury and tell them about this? Explain the circumstances?'

'Yes. As would Lucy, I'm sure. Nothing daunts her.'

'Yes, she's rather brave.'

Olivia looked at the bottle. 'Surely, we would be believed? Why would he have it if not to speed up Edith's demise? Any increase in the dose could prove fatal. The doctor told me so.'

Fergus turned the bottle over in his palm. 'Yes, that is my understanding, though I'm no expert. Digitalis is extremely dangerous at high dosages. Certainly, this extra bottle's existence raises many questions for Carver to answer. I will have to consult my chief inspector, but it is worth a try.'

Olivia grabbed his hand. 'Thank you... Fergus. I'm most grateful.' Again, she smiled as if a great weight had been lifted.

TWENTY-EIGHT

The Sleepy Druid, Thomas Street

Mary sat in the darkness of her attic room. It had been an eventful evening, especially when the police raid had taken place. Such a commotion. Mary had been working at the bar, pouring a pint of porter when the front door had burst open and several burly DMP constables had charged in. The resulting chaos had been like something out of a farce you'd see in a music hall, as customers attempted to escape, knocking over tables and chairs in their haste. Pint glasses hit the floor and shattered. In her astonishment, the pint Mary was pouring slipped through her fingers and dropped. With a muttered curse, she bent down to retrieve the broken glass as the spilt porter seeped through the ancient floorboards. Flustered, she tried to mop it up with a cloth but then gave it up as a lost cause. As she straightened, she noticed Lizzie stood unfazed, a slight smile lingering on her lips, watching the pandemonium as if police raids were an everyday occurrence.

After the initial uproar had died down, a man with a heavy Cork accent hailed them and approached the bar, asking for Lizzie Byrne. Mary directed him to Lizzie with relief. Whatever was going on, she didn't want to be involved. Was this fella a colleague of Inspector Ryan? Why hadn't Ryan warned her? Did this fella know who she was and, if so, might he give her away?

Thankfully, he took no notice of her; instead, he showed his credentials to Lizzie and demanded she talk to him in private. With a pained expression, Lizzie opened the hatch and beckoned him through to the back office, leaving Mary wondering what she was supposed to do. Best to play dumb. So, she stood and watched the constables rounding up the customers before making them stand in a line. Two constables then stood barring the door.

'Is Billy Murphy or Gavan O'Neill here?' a constable with a thick moustache demanded as he walked down the line. 'Speak up now. Don't be shy.' There were murmurs, and a couple of lads shook their heads. 'Well? Step forward if you blaggards are here.'

'Constable, they ain't in tonight,' a skinny young lad at the end of the line piped up.

The constable didn't look convinced. 'Is that so?'

'Ah, now, them two would be down at The Curragh for the racin',' another man added. 'They love the gee-gees. Murphy is always good for a tip... is that why youse are looking for 'im?'

There were a few chuckles, and the constable snarled in reply. He walked back down the line. 'You, there. What's your name?' The constable, to Mary's amusement, had singled out George, who had appeared in the pub an hour earlier. They hadn't acknowledged each other, other than a knowing glance as Mary had handed over his pint. Mary had been delighted to see him and assumed that Lucy and Phin had encouraged him to come to keep an eye on things and keep her safe. How sweet.

'George Rathbone, sir,' George replied.

'That's an English accent I hear, isn't it? What on God's earth are you doing in this hellhole?' the constable asked.

'Visiting family close by, sir, and decided to drop in for a quick pint.'

'I recommend you choose more wisely in the future,' the constable jeered. 'There's bad company to be had in here.'

Hearing voices behind her, Mary looked around to see Lizzie leading the detective back out to the bar.

'Be reasonable, Inspector Burke,' Lizzie was saying. 'I don't care what people's politics are. I can't afford to turn away customers, now, can I?'

'Well, consider yourself closed for the foreseeable future. I'll be back to talk to your father in a day or two.'

'On what grounds?' Lizzie demanded, but the detective ignored her before brushing past Mary and out into the bar area. 'Well, constable, any sign of our Fenians?'

This prompted a few snorts of laughter from the lined-up men. 'Fenians, is it, Inspector? Sure, there's none of that sort in here,' a wag contributed.

'Who said that?' Burke demanded, his colour rising as he scanned the line-up.

Their response was the shuffling of feet and some soft chuckles.

The moustachioed constable stepped up to Burke. 'I am informed that Murphy and O'Neill were at The Curragh today, sir, and haven't been in tonight.'

Burke glared back at him. 'Damnation, Goss, I thought our intelligence... Oh, never mind.' Then he turned his attention to the customers. 'Right, you lot. Out. This pub is closed.'

'What about me pint?' a plaintive voice from the back asked, amid numerous groans and grumbles.

'What about your pint?' roared the inspector. 'I suggest you lick it off the floor, you dirty animal, then get out of my sight.' The detective marched through the doorway, shoulders stiff with anger. One constable stayed behind and held the door open, gesturing for the customers to exit. George shared a wink with Mary before he left.

'Does this happen often?' Mary asked Lizzie as the last customer disappeared through the door, which swung to with a click.

'No, it does not. Me Da won't be pleased. Thank God he

wasn't here,' she muttered in response. 'Fenians indeed. Right.' She waved towards the mess. 'You'd better get started cleaning that lot up.' Mary, well aware that it had been Lizzie who had passed on the information about Fenians in the pub, wondered what her game was.

Mary lit her candle and pulled her watch from her pocket. Half past eleven. The raid had been three hours ago. Lizzie had left for home as soon as Mary had started cleaning, leaving her alone in the pub except for Jake, who had disappeared down to the cellar. He had ignored her pleas for help. Lazy sod. Mary was fed up. The work was hard, and she knew Lizzie was testing her by giving her the horrible jobs. No wonder Bridget had left.

The police raid had been a godsend, however, as it emptied the pub early. And now, she was waiting for the coast to be clear. Tonight, she was determined she would finish up in this awful place. Once she had fulfilled her promise to Inspector Ryan, that she would have a good look around for evidence of wrongdoing, she would scarper back to the safety of Merrion Square and her comfortable bed.

At last, a creak on the stairs told her Jake had come up to bed. She froze. What was he doing? Why wasn't he entering his room? Mary blew out her candle and strained to hear, but all was silent. Was he standing outside her door, listening? She'd suspected he had done so the night before, which was why she had locked her door. There was something unnerving about the potman; he was always staring at her. Luckily, he had been in a more communicative mood the previous day when she'd cornered him down in the cellar and asked about Bridget.

Moments later, she heard his door squeal open on its hinges and then close. Now, all she needed to do was wait for his snores...

· · ·

Forty minutes had passed when Mary finally entered Iggy's office, her heart thumping. Even though the door would not close over, she risked lighting a candle, thinking it was unlikely anyone would disturb her at this hour. If there were anything to be found, she felt the office was her best option. The only other place someone might hide something was below in the cellar. But it was a horrible, smelly place, infested with mice. Lizzie had sent her down there this morning for bottles of whiskey. She had done a quick, cursory search, but found nothing except the conviction she'd never go down there again.

With the light of her solitary candle, she examined the room in dismay, wrinkling her nose at the pungent smell of alcohol, cheap cigarettes and what smelled like rotten food. The room was a jumble of boxes, crates of bottles and various leather bags, all heaped on the floor. There was a desk with a chair and one cabinet crammed into the corner, with papers stuffed into its half-opened drawers. Where to start? The trouble was, she wasn't sure what she was searching for. Ryan said his cousin was mixed up in the illicit liquor trade and suspected he was Celine Burton's supplier. Could she find anything to link them? It felt like a hopeless quest as she regarded the room, but she owed it to Peggy to find something, anything, that might close Burton down and put Iggy Byrne behind bars.

After placing the candle on the desk, Mary sat down, tapping her fingers along the desktop. But she soon snatched them away in distaste, for the surface was sticky, and her stomach turned. If Iggy was anything like his office, she was glad she hadn't met him. Still, to proceed she needed to push down her revulsion at the general state of the place and search the desk. There had to be some kind of record of Byrne and Burton's illegal transactions.

The first few drawers bore no fruit. But as she pulled out another drawer, she heard scratching at the window. Her heart rate soared, and in a panic, she blew out the candle. But to her relief, the silhouette at the window was cat-shaped not human. Cleopatra, the ill-tempered pub cat. Cursing, Mary re-lit the candle, shook her fist at the cat who was staring in at her, its malevolent gaze unsettling, and continued her search.

Two more drawers down, and she discovered a leather-bound ledger. Hoping it was what she was looking for, she pulled the candle closer and opened the cover. It appeared to be an accounts book, and her hopes rose. The pages were full; however, the names and descriptions were illegible, the writing a tiny spidery scrawl across the page. Only the person who had written in the book could decipher the detail. In frustration, Mary leafed through the pages. They were all the same, but upon closing the book, she realised there was something stuck inside the back cover.

An envelope, addressed to Ignatius Byrne. Now why was it stuffed in there?

She felt inside and drew out the letter. It was creased and crumpled as if someone had scrunched it up to throw it away, then changed their mind. It stank of cheap perfume, so she assumed a woman had written it. A billet-doux to Byrne was unlikely to detail illegal alcohol smuggling or price fixing. And it felt intrusive even to open it. But could it be a love letter to Byrne? From the talk in the bar she'd overheard, and Ryan's description of the man, she didn't think he'd be likely to receive them. Mary was on the point of returning the letter to its envelope when she changed her mind. After all, a quick peek wouldn't do any harm. She'd realise straight away if it were a billet-doux and could put it back.

She unfolded it. It was dated the twentieth of July and comprised only a few sentences.

Iggy, you've put me in an awful position. What am I to do? You and your blasted foul temper. The DMP are crawling all over the house. Some of the girls might talk. It's taking a toll on me nerves, so it is. I'm putting me whole business at stake by helping ya. Ryan will soon figure out that Carver didn't do it and he'll be back. We better meet and talk this over. Why should I pay for your naughtiness?? Maybe you should be paying me? Our previous arrangement is at an end. No more free access to my girls. And I want my loan wiped off your books, or else. CB

Mary sat for several moments, shocked at what she had read. Ryan needed to see this letter, and fast. Her heart pounded as the letter's implications crystallised in her mind. The undeniable conclusion was that Ryan had the wrong man, and if she understood correctly, Ryan's cousin, Iggy, was the killer. But would Ryan act or cover it up? Was blood thicker than duty in this instance? Ryan appeared to be a decent man, but Mary's previous experiences with the Dublin police hadn't always been the most pleasant.

Mary checked her watch. She was due to meet Lucy and Phin in twenty minutes. She'd give the letter to them, and they could decide what to do with it. Whatever else Ryan wanted rooting out, he'd have to do it himself, she thought. The vision of her dead young cousin came into her mind. She knew what Iggy was capable of. *I'm not hanging around the premises of a murderer.*

Heart thumping, she rammed the accounts book into the drawer and trotted back upstairs to grab her coat and bag. Almost light-hearted at the thoughts of escaping the place at last, she'd forgotten to blow out the candle on Iggy's desk.

TWENTY-NINE

Mary closed her carpetbag and was pulling on her coat when she heard a bang from somewhere downstairs. She froze. Was someone in the bar? Who could it be? Perhaps Lizzie was back to check on things. But no, that wasn't likely, not at this hour. What should she do? Lucy would be waiting for her down the street, and she needed to see that letter as a matter of urgency. And even more importantly, Mary wanted to leave this vile place once and for all. If there was someone downstairs, how would she get past them without them seeing her? She pressed her ear against the door, but there wasn't a sound. Perhaps it had been the wind catching a door or window and slamming it shut. Was fear of discovery and her imagination playing tricks?

And then she heard it. A creak followed by a thump, thump. It was getting louder. Someone was coming up the stairs. Someone heavy.

Mary panicked. There was no hiding place in the bare room. And she still had the letter in her pocket. If she were found with it, it would be bad. Very bad. She pulled her bag open and shoved the letter down inside with trembling hands.

The thump, thump was close now. Out on the landing. Then it came to a sudden stop.

'Jake!' a voice roared.

It was a man, no doubt about it. Was it Iggy Byrne? Mary's heart raced. It was too late to lock the door for he'd hear the key turning. However, she had no desire to meet *him*. Frantic now, she scanned the room for something, anything, to use as a weapon to defend herself.

The chamber pot.

Mary bent down and grabbed it from under the bed, then stood behind the door, the pot raised in readiness to bring it down on any head that came through that door.

'Jake! Wake up, you lazy bastard.' This time the voice was right outside her door. A rivulet of sweat trickled down Mary's back. Whoever it was, they were definitely in a very bad mood. With eyes firmly shut, she started a Hail Mary.

'Mr Byrne, is that you?' Mary heard Jake call out. His door opened with its distinctive whine of hinges.

'Who'd you think it is? Father bloody Christmas? Get out here, now.'

'Yes, sir,' Jake said, sounding very sleepy.

'What were you doing down in the office, boy?'

'Nothin', Mr Byrne. Don't go near it. Never do. Lizzie says not to.'

'Then how come there's a lighted candle down there, eh?'

Mary's heart dropped. *Feck!*

'Don't know,' Jake said. 'Maybe Lizzie left it.'

'Can't have been. Lizzie came home hours ago to tell me about that feckin' raid. That candle has only been lit for a short time.'

'Ah, I know, Mr Byrne. Must be Mary.'

Oh, thanks a lot, Jake. Mary clutched the chamber pot even tighter.

'Mary who?'

'The new barmaid, sir, who was asking all them questions about the other one... whatever her name was. I told Miss Lizzie about it. Bridget. Yeah, her. The pretty one that stole the takings from you, sir.'

'She in there?' Byrne demanded.

Bugger! was Mary's last thought before her door burst open.

Lucy stifled a yawn. This sitting and waiting in the carriage was getting on her nerves. Across from her, Phin had his eyes closed. She suspected he was asleep. But she would not wake him. When he had arrived home, he was grumpy, an unusual occurrence, and she reckoned his final meeting with DeWinter was the reason. Phin had presented his preliminary findings to him, which pronounced the security for the jewels was lax, and a new and more secure location within the castle was required. No doubt DeWinter took it as personal criticism, which indeed it was, though if she knew Phin at all, his presentation had been cloaked in diplomatic terms. Seeing how tired Phin was, she had said that she would take George along with her this evening to meet Mary, but Phin had insisted on coming.

But where *was* Mary? From George they knew about the police raid earlier in the evening. Perhaps that was the reason Mary was unable to get away. Lucy pulled back the curtain over the carriage window, pushing down the windowpane before popping her head out. The street was deserted, which was only to be expected at this hour, but there were no lights on in the pub. Had Mary forgotten and gone to bed?

'I don't think she's coming tonight, my dear,' Phin said with one eye open. 'We can send George around tomorrow afternoon.'

'I've a horrible feeling something is wrong.' Lucy sat back, chewing her lip. 'Could that blundering detective and his raid have upset the Byrnes? Is it possible they suspect Mary was responsible for it?'

'I doubt it. Why would they? It all amounted to nothing, in any event. From what George said, the DMP didn't find the men they were after. Don't worry. She'd have come if she were able. Mary is probably fast asleep and absolutely fine.' Phin tapped the roof with his cane. 'We will see her tomorrow night, I'm sure.'

THIRTY

Fergus was exhausted. Not only had the usual nightmares afflicted him, but when he lay awake in the small hours, all he could think about was Olivia and her situation. As he had predicted, late the previous afternoon, Malone had insisted on releasing Carver. Fergus had pleaded with him not to, based on Olivia's suspicions and finding the extra bottle of digitalis. But the chief inspector had been adamant; it was too circumstantial, and Carver was already making a lot of noise about an official complaint. Fergus, aware of the politics at play, had to back down as he suspected Malone had come under pressure from on high to release Carver. Perhaps his chief was right and there wasn't enough evidence to continue to hold him, but his gut was telling him otherwise. Having no choice, Fergus had sent a smirking Carver on his way and spent the remainder of the evening worrying about what might transpire when Carver arrived in Merrion Square.

What if Carver took out his anger on Olivia? Injured her or threw her out? Would she seek refuge with Lucy? Fergus couldn't be there to protect her. Hence the night of tossing and turning as each scenario, worse than the previous, played out in his mind, making his head pound.

Then, when he reached Dublin Castle this morning, he was met by Sergeant Hughes, who handed him a note from Chief Malone. With a groan, Fergus read it, then handed it to the sergeant.

'We are summoned to a murder scene at Great Brunswick Street.'

'Ah,' said Hughes. 'Isn't that where *she* lives, sir?'

His answer was a weary yes.

Dreading what they might face, he had jumped into a cab with Hughes. The situation couldn't be worse. If only he had set a watch on Carver, but there was no point in dwelling on that now. The man must have gone straight to Great Brunswick Street to mete out his revenge. After all, he had threatened the woman the previous day during his interview. If he were capable of that, what might he have done to Olivia? Fergus dreaded to think.

Ten minutes later, Fergus and Hughes slipped past the constable on the door of the house, and into the hallway. Fergus heard people upstairs and followed the voices. Constable Geraghty met him on the landing, holding up his hands.

'Sorry, sir, if you could hold on here for a moment. We've been asked to stay out of the room as the photographer is finishing up.'

Fergus gave in to his weary state, folded his arms and slumped against the banisters. After a sympathetic glance, Hughes stood by, his face inscrutable.

'Ah, Ryan, so good of you to join us,' Chief Inspector Malone drawled, a short time later.

Seamus stood to attention. 'Sir.'

'It's not pretty. I hope you haven't eaten,' Malone said. The photographer emerged from the bedroom, ashen-faced and shaking his head. He pushed past them without a word.

'Well, go on, man, get on with it. I want a report by five this evening,' Malone said to him, gesticulating towards the room. With a sour expression, he added, 'You should have expected something like this, detective. Despite who she is, we'll no doubt be pilloried for letting it happen.'

Fergus baulked at the comment and waited until Malone was out of earshot before he turned to his sergeant. 'Find out what you can, Hughes. I'd better take a look at her.'

'Will do, sir,' Hughes said.

Fergus walked into the bedroom braced for the worst. The room was stifling and in semi-darkness, the heavy velvet curtains almost closed. The stench of death and the buzz of many flies made him gag. He rushed to the window, dragged back the drapes and opened the sash. Leaning out, he took great gulps of air. Below him, Malone was about to step into a cab. He looked up and tut-tutted. But Fergus was impervious to his disdain, being too busy trying to control his heaving stomach. He stayed at the window and watched the chief's cab take off down Great Brunswick Street heading back towards the castle. *Amadán!* Stupid man, Fergus murmured. There were days he wondered how the man had ever reached the level of chief inspector.

Fergus turned away. He couldn't avoid the inevitable. There was a crime scene to inspect. After a deep lungful of air, he moved from the window. A huge ornate four-poster bed dominated the room, and sprawled in the middle of it was a very dead Celine Burton, whose eyes were fixed on the ceiling, frozen in horror. The bedclothes were almost entirely soaked in blood. Celine's clothes, which he assumed were nightclothes by their frilly and lacy nature, were also bloodstained. A knife lay on the bed beside her, smeared with blood. Fergus retreated, his handkerchief over his nose and mouth. There was so much blood it had to have been a stabbing frenzy. He retreated into the window embrasure for air once more and studied the scene. Her last moments must have been horrific.

After a few minutes, Hughes materialised in the doorway, and remained there, keeping his eyes averted from the corpse.

'When was she found?' Fergus asked, gesturing for the sergeant to precede him back out of the bedroom onto the landing.

'Early this morning, sir. About eight o'clock.'

'Who found her?'

'Her charwoman. She has a key. Comes in twice a week for a couple of hours.'

'Has someone interviewed the woman?' he asked.

'Yes, sir, eventually. She was very upset, but her statement has been taken.'

'Very good. You can let her go if you think she has given us as much information as she can. Has a doctor been called?'

'Yes. Doc Peters, as it happens. We just missed him. He wanted to take her away, but the chief said you had to see the scene first.'

That was exceedingly good of him, Fergus thought, with what he knew to be unreasonable irritation. No matter what Malone said or did, it made him vexed these days. 'Did Peters give any indication of a time of death?'

'He told Constable Geraghty he reckoned some time on Friday, but it's hard to pinpoint with this hot weather. He won't know for sure until he performs the postmortem.'

'Friday?' Fergus's mind spun between disbelief and disappointment. 'So, it couldn't have been Carver.'

'Not unless he has mastered the art of omnipresence, sir, no. You met him off the Cork train and brought him straight to the castle on Friday. *We* are his alibi.'

Fergus muttered a few curses under his breath, then asked, 'Did Burton live alone?'

'Yes, and there are no live-in servants.'

'Lodgers?' Fergus asked. The sergeant shook his head. 'How odd. A big house for someone on their own. I'd have thought she would have servants at least. She could well afford the luxury.'

Hughes sniffed. 'I reckon she had too many fingers in too many pies, sir. Didn't want anyone knowing what she was up to. Couldn't risk it. Servants see things. Servants talk.'

Fergus nodded. 'Aye. A cagey woman at the best of times, was our Celine. I assume the neighbours have been questioned. Did anyone see anything suspicious? Anyone entering or leaving the house since she was last seen?'

'A neighbour says he saw her being dropped off by her driver, who then left, at about eleven o'clock on Thursday night. The witness saw her enter the house. No one appears to have seen her after that time.'

'Alright, Hughes. You can send a message to Peters to have the body removed.' Looking very relieved, the sergeant headed back down the stairs and Fergus re-entered the bedroom. A few seconds later, Hughes showed his face at the door again. 'Sorry, I forgot, sir. Dr Peters did an initial examination when he was here earlier and has confirmed that the knife on the bed is the weapon. He said it matches the wounds.'

'Very kind of the killer to leave it for us,' Fergus said. 'But somehow, I doubt it will help us. It was probably taken from the kitchen.' Fergus pointed to the bed. 'That's a lot of blood, though. Our killer's clothes must have been covered in it.'

'Aye, sir. But if the attack happened during the night, it would be easy to slip away unseen.'

'Unless we are very, very lucky, Sergeant, and someone on the street saw something. Let's extend the door-to-door enquiries. It's a main thoroughfare. We can only hope.'

'Do you believe this is connected to Peggy O'Reilly's death?' Hughes asked.

Fergus shrugged. 'It might be. This attack was as violent. But until we find a connection, that can only be speculation. She had enough people wanting her despatched as it was.'

'True enough,' Hughes said.

Left alone in the room, Fergus made a cursory search, all the time conscious of the corpse on the bed and its staring eyes. Throughout her life those same eyes had beheld many dark deeds, many of which she had instigated or performed. Violence had defined her life, so it was almost inevitable that she would leave it in an equally violent manner. The thought made him shiver.

Fergus spotted a paisley shawl lying across a chair. He grabbed it and draped it over Celine's head. *Poor Lady Muck*, he mused, she hadn't been a pleasant woman, but even she deserved some dignity and respect in death.

As he found nothing of interest in the bedroom, he headed back downstairs. The front sitting room looked as though it was never used. Stuffed full of furniture and curios, it would be a nightmare to search. He would delegate the job to a constable. At the rear of the property was a small parlour. It was a cosy room with personal items scattered about. He reckoned this was where she spent most of her time. A desk stuffed with paper stood in the corner but yielded nothing of interest other than some bills.

Down the corridor towards the back of the house were a kitchen and scullery, which led out to a long and narrow garden. The back door lock had been jimmied, so there was no doubt that was how the murderer got in. It would have been a simple matter to lie in wait for Celine to come home and, when she was asleep, attack. She would have been defenceless.

Fergus wasn't surprised Celine had had enemies. But that attack had been vicious and very personal. Like Hughes, he suspected the violence was an echo of Peggy's murder. Might the same person be involved? But of the countless people Celine would have crossed, who'd need to silence her? Not threaten her, not rough her up, but kill her. Fergus reckoned only the threat to reveal a very big secret could have prompted this.

For instance, the person who had killed a sixteen-year-old girl forced into prostitution.

And Celine must have known who killed Peggy. The comings and goings of that brothel had been under her constant surveillance, with the help of Mulcahy. So, if she had protected the actual murderer by implicating Carver, it would explain a lot. Had she done a deal with the killer? But then foolishly threatened to reveal their identity when she tried a little blackmail. A dangerous game to play because whoever they were, they were unlikely to take the risk that Celine might blab to the police. That was the most likely connection between the two murders. But figuring out a motive for the killing didn't help him find the killer. They were back at the beginning now that Carver was cleared of both Peggy and Celine's murders.

This was all he needed. They'd have to start again because he must have missed something vital. It wasn't as if he hadn't suspected Celine was lying; it was second nature to her. And the brothel girls were too scared of Mulcahy to go against her. The fact was Celine had manipulated him, *and* he had let his infatuation with Olivia skew his judgement regarding Carver. He squirmed at the thought. What a mess. No one would talk, even though there was little honour amongst The Monto ne'er-do-wells. With Celine murdered, they would close ranks because what little trust he had built now lay in tatters.

Worse still, once the press got hold of the story, there would be lurid headlines declaring the city was in the grip of a serial killer. And Malone would enjoy making his life even more of a misery than usual. Feeling gloomier by the minute, Fergus pushed through the door and went down the overgrown pathway to the back gate. He looked out onto a dingy laneway, which ran behind the terrace of houses, giving access to those with stables or mews. It was the ideal escape route in the dead of night. Damn.

Perhaps he should have foreseen this; Malone was right. His foreboding that today would not be a good day increased.

THIRTY-ONE

It was after seven in the evening, and Fergus was still at his desk, head resting on his hand, reading over the statements from Great Brunswick Street. His frustration was escalating. The statements were of little use, as there wasn't even a hint of a clue to follow up. Celine, it would appear, had lived like a hermit. Most of her neighbours did not suspect her real identity. Some of their innocent descriptions of her almost made him laugh aloud. Except he knew the real story, and it would all come out in the newspapers, in due course. How shocked those neighbours would be to discover they had had a notorious brothel owner living in their midst.

Sergeant Hughes entered the office and cleared his throat. 'Inspector, Mrs Stone is downstairs at the desk, asking to see you, sir.'

Fergus was instantly alert and half rose from his seat. Was Olivia in trouble? With Burton's murder on his hands, he had not been able to visit Merrion Square to check on her as planned. 'Is it to do with Carver?'

'No, sir, I believe not. She didn't mention him.'

Somewhat relieved that it wasn't an Olivia-related emergency,

Fergus relaxed and sat back down. 'Can't you deal with it, Hughes? I'm very busy and I need to go through these statements before I leave this evening.'

'I would be happy to, sir, but she says it's urgent. Something to do with her maid.'

As much as Fergus admired Lucy, he was swamped. Malone was breathing fire and demanding results. How serious was Lucy's problem? However, she had been so eager to help it felt churlish to ignore her now. And the maid was trying to help him, too. 'Very well, show her up,' he said, shoving the statements back into a folder on his desk. It was sizing up to be a long and tiresome night.

An extremely pale Lucy Stone entered the office minutes later.

Fergus stood and came forward to greet her. 'Good evening, Mrs Stone. Whatever is the matter?'

'Hello, Inspector. I'm sorry to disturb you, but I'm convinced something has happened to Mary. We went to meet her last night as pre-arranged, but she never turned up. Phin assumed it just wasn't possible for some reason, but I've been anxious all day.'

Fergus showed her to a chair and leaned on the desk. 'I see. I can understand why you are worried, but I found Mary a sensible young woman. She wouldn't take any unnecessary risks. Please, share with me what you know.'

'We waited on Thomas Street until one in the morning.' She twisted her hands. 'She didn't show. Phin was convinced all was well, that it was probably because of the police raid earlier yesterday evening that she couldn't get away. But I know she would try to communicate with us, somehow. My instincts are usually sound. I think she may be in trouble. The Byrnes must have discovered the true reason she is there.'

Fergus felt the blood drain from his face. 'Hold on. What police raid?'

Lucy's face registered surprise. 'You didn't know about it? But it must have been one of your colleagues. He said he was looking for Fenians. Phineas said it related to the Crown Jewel plot. Wasn't it your cousin who told you of it in the first place?'

Confused, Fergus asked, 'Yes, it was. But how do you know about this raid?'

'Phin's valet, George, was in The Sleepy Druid at the time, incognito, keeping a watchful eye on Mary.'

Fergus glanced across the room and scowled at Detective Burke's empty desk. 'I didn't know about the raid, but I can guess who was behind it.'

'Does it matter in any event? Whoever they were looking for wasn't there. Then late this afternoon, at my behest, George went to the public house to see if he might get an opportunity to speak to Mary, to make sure she was alright. But the place was shut. He peered in the windows, but there was no sign of anyone, so he banged on the doors, front and back, but nobody answered. Then he hurried straight back to Merrion Square to tell us. Is there anything *you* can do? Lizzie Byrne is your cousin, is she not?'

'Yes, she is. I'm sure there's a simple explanation, but it might be best if we go there and see for ourselves. It will put your mind at rest.' Then he paused. 'But before we go, there is something you should know.' Lucy looked startled. 'It doesn't involve Mary, Mrs Stone. But there has been a development. Celine Burton has been murdered. Her body was found this morning at her home. Someone had stabbed her in a frenzied attack.'

Lucy's eyes widened as she gasped. 'It wasn't Carver, was it? Presumably he wanted revenge.'

He shook his head. 'That was my initial thought, too, but we only released Carver yesterday afternoon. The doctor who examined Burton is adamant she's been dead for several days.'

'Oh, dear. There's no room for doubt?'

'No. The condition of the body... The doctor is sure she died on Friday.'

'Ah, that's inconvenient.'

'Yes,' Fergus exclaimed, running a hand through his hair. 'Now, I am back at the beginning, for I have neither a killer for Peggy nor for Lady Muck. I do, however, feel there is a connection.'

'Are murders so rare?' she asked.

'Rare enough.'

'This is an unfortunate development for you, I can see that,' Lucy said. 'However, it would be worse to hang the wrong man.'

'There is that,' he conceded. 'Well, my mistakes are coming back to haunt me, Mrs Stone.'

'You're too hard on yourself. I was convinced he was guilty, too.'

'But don't you see, if Carver didn't commit either crime, I've lost valuable time to gather evidence against anyone else. Clues may have been lost and with time, witnesses' memories become more and more unreliable.'

'As a matter of interest, did Mrs Burton give you a full list of clients for the night of Peggy's murder?'

'Yes, eventually, but who can say it was the full list, plus she claimed some of her clients didn't use their real names and she couldn't help identify them. I have asked my sergeant to go back over the list and double-check, but it will take days to track them all down. And even then, there may be some clients from that night that slip through the net. The Monto is close to army barracks and the docks, so some of Burton's clients might have been in Dublin only briefly and are long gone. And if they gave a name, it's likely a false one.'

Lucy's brow furrowed. 'Yet, she was certain Carver was Carver. Isn't that somewhat convenient?'

'Exactly. She was determined to misdirect me, and if Olivia hadn't been so obviously under duress to provide that alibi, I should have been more objective. But Carver was jittery, which made him seem guilty. Now I realise it was because he knew he was being set up, not because he was responsible.'

'Inspector, anyone else in your shoes would have assumed the same,' Lucy said. 'And Olivia *was* under duress.'

'Oh, I don't blame her in the least,' he said. 'She was in an intolerable position. She still is. At least until Edith Carver dies. Even though she is living under such difficult circumstances, she won't abandon her, which is humbling, don't you think? We must be as stoic and keep going.' Fergus reached for his coat. 'Now, let us go to Thomas Street and clear up this mystery. Mary can't have disappeared off the face of the earth.'

Dublin City

A light drizzle was falling as Lucy, the sergeant, and the inspector made their way through the Dublin streets in a police carriage. After several attempts to start a conversation, Lucy was on the point of giving up. Ryan was the picture of gloom, lost in his thoughts. The poor man was under such a lot of pressure, Lucy thought with a pang of guilt, and the strain of the last week was showing; his face was drawn with fatigue. Perhaps she shouldn't have dragged him away from his desk. After all, between Phin, George and herself they could have launched this rescue mission without bothering Ryan. But she had considered it prudent because the Byrnes were related to him. Lucy hoped Fergus would have a better chance of reasoning with them if there was a problem.

In a last-ditch attempt to engage the inspector's interest, Lucy mentioned she had not seen anyone from No. 83 since Carver's release and wondered if all was well in the household. It worked.

The inspector leaned towards her, his features animated. 'I had intended to visit her today, but with Burton's murder investigation underway, I couldn't leave the castle. Do you have any reason to be concerned? Have you seen her or Carver?'

'No, neither of them. I'd guess she might be having an uncomfortable time of it, however. Carver may be in a foul mood, but at least we now know he isn't a violent man.'

'Perhaps not. Olivia once said to me he likes to use words as a weapon, and for someone as vulnerable as she is, that is almost as bad.'

'Very true,' Lucy said. 'She is too gentle for her own good.'

'Yes. She was most upset to hear that Carver was coming home, but I consoled her and reassured her as best I could.

Then, just as my anxiety for her safety abated, she shocked me with the revelation that she suspected Carver of poisoning his wife.'

'At last. Thank goodness. I'm relieved you know about the poisoning... possible poisoning.'

'*And* what shocked me even more was that she had told you about it,' he continued. 'Yet, no one thought to mention this matter to me... a police officer.' The inspector's gaze was icy.

'I'm sorry, but my hands were tied. She told me in confidence, and when we searched his room and found another bottle of digitalis, I begged her to go to you. But I could not convince her, so that was when I came up with the idea of switching the contents for something innocuous. I tipped out the medicine and swapped it for tea.'

'Thereby destroying evidence.'

'It was that or let him continue poisoning Edith,' Lucy snapped. 'Besides, Olivia was afraid she would be accusing him in the wrong. Mind you, I think that is unlikely. Who else would want to harm Edith? Who else would benefit from her death? It must be him. The servants are sure he has a mistress, which, you must admit, gives him a motive. So, if you knew about this yesterday, why was Carver still released?' Lucy asked, feeling puzzled.

'Because my superior didn't believe there was enough evidence. He said anyone in the house might have put the bottle there. A disgruntled servant or what have you.'

'I know the servants are poorly paid and generally unhappy, but would that not be an extreme reaction to a nasty comment or perceived injustice?'

'I should think it would be, and I said as much. Who would risk their life for that? However, Chief Inspector Malone was adamant that unless I had a witness who saw Carver administer the poison, he didn't want to know about it. And as well, we had arrested and detained the man for a murder he hadn't committed, putting the DMP in an embarrassing position.'

'Which is unfair. The evidence against him was strong, particularly the blood on his cane. It would have been remiss not to have arrested him in the circumstances.'

'My chief inspector doesn't see it that way,' he said.

'A political man?'

The inspector grunted. 'Yes.'

'Good grief, I imagine it must have been difficult for you to have to release Carver.'

'It certainly was, but I had to follow orders. I suspect someone is pulling strings for the man.'

'But if Olivia is right, then he is a *potential* murderer,' Lucy said. 'Are you absolutely sure he didn't kill Peggy?'

'At this stage, yes. The timing is off. Also, poisoning is such a slow, premeditated crime, whereas Peggy's death was so different. An explosion of anger, I would think, much like Mrs Burton's murder. I'm certain the killer is the same person in both cases. And Carver was either on the Cork train or sitting in a police cell at the castle when Burton was killed.'

'Then there is nothing you can do about Carver?'

'Cursory enquiries were the most my chief would allow. I have a constable looking into it.'

Lucy couldn't help herself. 'Perhaps tell him to speak to the doctor. Olivia says that he has expressed concern, too. And you might try to find the apothecary who sold him—'

'Are you considering joining the DMP, Mrs Stone?'

Beside him, Hughes stifled a snigger, and Ryan threw him a dirty look.

'Sorry,' she said with a sheepish smile. 'But I know you have two murders to solve and are probably short-staffed. Why don't we assist you in some way? I'll ask George to trace the apothecary. That would help, wouldn't it?'

'Yes, it would. However, if my chief got to hear about it, he'd have my head on a plate.'

'Oh, well then, we must ensure that he doesn't. And in the meantime, try not to worry about Olivia. I'll do my best to speak to her tomorrow, and if I do, I'll send you an update.'

'Thank you. If her situation becomes unbearable, I have encouraged her to go to you for protection.'

'Hopefully, she does, and I'm sure she appreciated your visit,' Lucy said, trying not to smile.

'I believe she was grateful for the warning, at least, but she would not consider leaving while her mother-in-law lives. You have to admire the lady's Christian values.'

Lucy responded with a smile. The man's infatuation was obvious. She was only sorry they would be back in England before any wedding was likely to take place.

THIRTY-TWO

Soon they were standing before Byrne's pub, which was shrouded in darkness. Tense with anxiety, Lucy stood by as Ryan looked in the windows before trying the front door. The door rattled but did not open. He banged on it several times, but no one answered.

'It's as George described it, Inspector. Your colleague closed the place down,' Lucy said, 'but where is everyone? They've hardly left the place unoccupied.'

'Try not to worry. There must be someone around. Hughes, stay here and keep trying this door. I'll try around the back.' He shifted his gaze to Lucy. 'Why not wait in the carriage out of the rain?'

Lucy answered with a dirty look. The inspector threw up his hands in defeat. 'Very well.'

Ryan grabbed a bullseye lantern from the carriage, and they hurried to the corner, before turning onto an adjoining street. A few yards down was an alleyway, which gave rear access to the Thomas Street premises. Ryan plunged ahead, and Lucy had no option other than to try to keep up.

However, it wasn't long before Inspector Ryan drew up before a wooden gate. A rough sign declared it was the goods entrance for The Sleepy Druid. After exchanging glances, Ryan pushed the door, stepped through, and Lucy followed. The yard they entered was full of crates and barrels, stacked against the high walls. Lucy stayed close to the inspector as he wound his way through to a back door.

However, yet again, his thumps on the door went unanswered. Ryan turned up the collar of his coat, squinting at Lucy through the rain, his lips pinched. Then his gaze slipped away, as if he were looking for something. Lucy was sorry for him. With two murders on his hands, the last thing he needed was a wild goose chase to find Mary.

Then, out of nowhere, he exclaimed, 'Aha', and stooped down between two barrels. When he straightened, he was holding a crowbar. 'Well, it's this or we stand out here in the rain,' he said to Lucy, before ramming the crowbar into the side of the door and heaving. There was a cracking sound as the lock gave way, and the door swung open. Lucy half expected someone to charge out and demand what they were doing. But the dark interior was silent as the grave. Lucy cringed. *Now that's an unfortunate turn of phrase.*

'Come on,' the inspector urged, sounding less than cheery. 'We'd best search the place now we have gained access.'

Lucy didn't hesitate to follow him inside.

They entered a musty-smelling, dark hallway. Lucy heard the striking of a match, and the inspector's lantern lit up the confined space. Ryan pushed open a door and looked inside. Peering over his shoulder, it was obvious to Lucy the room was used as an office, albeit one in disarray. However, as Ryan took a step inside, they were greeted by a loud hiss. With a yelp of fright, Ryan stepped back, almost knocking Lucy over. Heart pounding, Lucy watched as a large cat jumped down off the desk, rubbed against Lucy's skirts and sauntered away into the darkness.

'Bloody cat. I hate that thing,' Ryan exclaimed.

Slightly unnerved, Lucy followed it and saw the animal slip into another room. Lucy halted at the doorway from where she could make out a sink and a table. An empty kitchen. Frustrated, she turned back as Ryan emerged from the office. Other than their feline companion, they were alone in this part of the building.

The inspector continued through a door which led into the public bar. Ryan held up the lantern, sweeping it around in a slow arc. All was neat and tidy. Lucy saw the top of Hughes' helmet through the window where he stood outside on the pavement. He turned and waved to them. Ryan signalled for him to stay put.

'Isn't this odd?' Lucy whispered. 'Where is your cousin? And where is my Mary?'

Ryan's gaze was full of concern. 'Yes. Something isn't right. They'd never leave the place unattended. The locals would know it's been shut and would be up to all kinds of mischief. We'd better take a look upstairs.' Holding out the lantern, he walked past her, back into the hallway and made for the stairs.

Every step creaked as they climbed higher, ramping up Lucy's anxiety. She dreaded to think what they might find. If something had happened to Mary, something bad, she'd never forgive herself. She should have insisted she'd left when she had the chance.

There were two bedrooms on the first floor, both empty, with bare mattresses on the beds and no curtains on the windows. Everything was coated in dust.

'Do the family not live here?' she asked in a whisper.

'No. Not for years. Iggy owns many properties throughout the city, but they live in a house over on Gardiner Street,' he said.

As they traipsed up yet another flight of stairs, Lucy's hopes were fading. If Mary were here, she would have revealed herself by now. Ryan waited at the top of the stairs until Lucy drew level.

'Let's start with this one,' he said, pointing to a door that stood ajar. 'Hello?' he called out before pushing the door open. Silence.

Lucy gulped and pointed. 'That's her bag on the bed. This must be Mary's room.'

Ryan set the lantern down on a shelf. 'Strange that she would leave it behind if she has left.'

'She wouldn't.' Lucy wrung her hands as Ryan opened the bag and pulled out the meagre contents. Something white fluttered to the floor and under the bed. 'What's that?' she asked.

The inspector bent down and picked it up. 'It appears to be a letter.'

Lucy grabbed the lantern, and stepped closer, holding it up so they could both read it.

It began: *Iggy, you've put me in an awful position...* and was signed off by CB.

Lucy was stunned and could not believe what was in black and white in front of her. 'CB? Celine?' Lucy asked in a strangled voice.

Ryan was breathing hard, his gaze when it met hers intense. 'Yes, it must be. I can only assume—'

'Your cousin Iggy killed Peggy.' She gulped. 'And then he must have murdered Burton to keep her quiet.'

The inspector sank down onto the bed, the letter in his hand. He was nodding slowly. 'Yes. That's the only explanation that fits.' He glanced at the note. 'What possessed her to write such a letter? She must have known how he'd react. She left him no choice but to silence her. My God, I knew he was violent at times—I was on the receiving end only recently,' he said, touching his cheek. 'And my cousin Lizzie had hinted at it, too, but murder? I can't believe it.' His mouth turned down. 'It sounds as though he had free run of Burton's place because of this loan he gave her. It makes me sick to my stomach.'

'That I can understand, but what she says in the letter must be true. It all makes sense. Your cousin is the murderer, and Burton helped him cover it up by implicating Carver.'

Ryan waved the letter. 'And then she got greedy and tried to blackmail Iggy.'

'Which is all well and good and I'm glad we are finally getting to the truth, however, I'm more concerned about where

Mary has disappeared to. And why did she have that letter in her bag? I would have thought she'd have come straight to you or me with it.'

'Yes, that is odd. I had asked her to do a little investigating when the coast was clear. She must have found this letter somewhere in the building. You see, I'd asked her to find evidence of illegal alcohol sales between Iggy and Burton. I never imagined she'd find something even worse. Trust me, if I'd known how dangerous Iggy was, I'd never have asked it of her. He must have caught her snooping. Luckily, she had the foresight to hide the letter. If he'd found that in her possession, God only knows what he'd have done.'

Lucy's blood ran cold at the thought. 'But he must have taken her somewhere. Otherwise, she'd be here or back in Merrion Square. She must be in trouble. We must keep looking for her. Come on!'

Ryan stuffed the letter into his pocket with a grunt of agreement. Lucy headed out onto the landing and pushed the adjacent door open, aware of Ryan right behind her. With a roar, a huge shape came charging towards her from inside the room. She sidestepped in time but ended up pinned to the banisters on the landing. Ryan wasn't as lucky. He took the full impact of the charge. Lucy stared, petrified, as an enormous man wrestled the inspector to the ground.

'Stop!' she cried, terrified that Ryan would be killed. Was this brute Iggy Byrne who had killed the women? Would she be next?

'Jake, Jake! It's me, Fergus. Iggy's cousin,' Ryan managed to shout, even though he had taken a few nasty punches to the abdomen and chest.

Ryan's words must have penetrated, for suddenly, the man stopped hitting him and peered down into the inspector's face. With a grunt, he got to his feet. Lucy took a few steps back, wary that he might turn on her. But to her astonishment, the man held out his hand and helped Ryan to stand.

'Sorry, Inspector,' he said. 'Thought ye were thieves.'

Coughing, Ryan's eyes were watering as he dusted himself down. 'It's alright, Jake. Sorry if we scared you.'

Lucy, confused, almost laughed. This was bizarre. Why did Ryan treat the man like a frightened child and not the thug he appeared to be?

The inspector turned to her. 'Mrs Stone, this is Jake. He works here as a potman.'

Something in the way Ryan introduced him, told her the man was harmless. At least if you weren't a thief. Relieved, Lucy's fear evaporated.

'Mary, the barmaid, Jake. Where is she? We need to find her,' Ryan said.

Jake scratched his temple; his massive brows pulled into a line. 'She was naughty, and Iggy was angry. She left with him, 'bout an hour ago,' he said. 'He wouldn't let me go with them in the gig, and I wanted to go. Don't like it here on my own.'

Lucy and Ryan exchanged worried glances. 'What about Lizzie?' the inspector asked.

'Don't know. She didn't come in today. I've been on me own. No Mary, no Lizzie,' Jake said. 'I don't like it. Very quiet.'

The inspector smiled gently at the giant. 'I understand, Jake. There's no need to be scared. But we need your help. We need to find Mary. Have you any idea where Iggy was taking her?'

Jake shifted on his feet, not meeting Ryan's eye. 'It's Sunday, ain't it?'

'Yes,' the inspector said.

'He always goes to the grave on a Sunday. They'll have gone to visit old Mrs Byrne.'

THIRTY-THREE

Fergus's nerves were on edge. What had been a frustrating case from the beginning, was now a complete disaster. And this trip to Glasnevin might be a futile endeavour, but what else could they do? It was the only clue they had, even if the source was as unreliable as Jake. Iggy had always been unpredictable, but Fergus feared he was dealing with a man who had lost his sanity and not just his temper. A murderer. He still couldn't believe it. Worse still, it was down to him to find him, arrest him and eventually see him hang. His own flesh and blood. He shivered, hoping Lucy Stone wouldn't notice. He doubted she realised what they were up against. Through his pocket he felt his pistol, but it gave him little comfort. A madman was capable of anything, and Iggy bore a grudge against him. Any confrontation they were going to have was bound to end badly.

For most of the journey from Thomas Street across the city to the suburb of Glasnevin, he and Lucy had argued. She insisted she was coming into the cemetery with him to help find Mary. In the end, he threatened her with arrest if she tried to intervene. It was the only way he could try to keep her safe. Even Hughes had been shocked when he said it, his brows shooting up, but there was no way he was putting himself in the position of having to explain to Phineas Stone why his wife was injured or, worse, dead. He had dealt with some strong-minded women before, but how Lucy's husband put up with her, he had no idea. If pushed, he would have to admit he admired her tenacity and bravery; however, if she could be tenacious and brave somewhere else tonight, that would suit him much better.

As the police carriage pulled up at the front gates, Fergus saw an empty gig at the side of the road. 'That must be Iggy's,' he said, pointing it out. 'At least we know they are here.'

Leaving a sulking Lucy in the carriage, Fergus spoke to Hughes by the cemetery wall. 'Don't let her out of your sight.'

'No, sir... but I can hardly restrain her if—'

'Sergeant, if that woman comes into the cemetery, I'll have you back on the beat.'

'Sir,' Hughes answered, but Fergus knew the sergeant, no more than himself, doubted anyone could keep Lucy Stone in check. 'It's imperative we keep her safe. We are dealing with a man on the verge of insanity. You've read the letter, Hughes, so you cannot doubt it.'

'I have indeed, sir. Most shocking. And can I just say how sorry I am.' This was accompanied by a meaningful glance.

'You guessed I'm related?' Fergus asked, his heart dropping.

'Yes, although I don't see a need for anyone else to know, sir. But...'

'Yes?'

'You don't need to do this alone. Perhaps we should bring in some back-up,' the sergeant said. 'This place is vast. He could easily elude you.'

'I have considered it, Hughes, but this is my mess, and I want to bring him in, even if it risks my relationship to him being revealed. I must do the right thing.'

'Sir, I understand why, but I'm not happy about you going in alone.'

'Thanks, but I'm ordering you not to. I'm hoping Miss O'Reilly is alive, and that I can reason with him to release her so that this doesn't have to turn into more of a disaster than it already is. Right. If the potman is correct, Iggy has taken Miss O'Reilly to his wife's vault. I want you to stay here at the entrance gate in case he attempts to make his escape. This is the closest exit to his wife's crypt and his most likely escape route. Take the bolt cutters, cut the padlock as quietly as you can and leave the gate unlocked and ajar. Hopefully, he'll take the bait if he's making a run for it. But for now, stay hidden and don't come in unless I shout for you.'

With one last pleading-for-patience glance at Lucy, who was glaring at him from the carriage, Fergus walked along the boundary wall of the cemetery, every sense on high alert. He didn't want to go in the main gate as it was close to the vaults and he might be spotted. With the cemetery locked up for the night, he needed to find an isolated spot where he might get over the wall without alerting Iggy, or a local resident who might raise a hue and cry, thinking he was a resurrectionist. The thing he most wanted to avoid was half of Dublin's DMP officers making a noisy arrival and Iggy bolting. All he had in his favour was the element of surprise. With this in mind, he hurried away from the main entrance.

He was soon on a stretch of pavement which wasn't overlooked by houses, and the solitary streetlight was half masked by a horse chestnut tree. As luck would have it, there was a doorway cut into the wall. The door was locked but after a quick scan of the road, he scaled the wall using the metal handle as a foothold and swung himself over the capping stone. He dropped to the ground on the other side of the six-foot wall and crouched down behind a head-stone, breathing hard. It was dark inside the cemetery, and to add to his woes, the intensity of the rain had increased.

All was silent, bar the pitter-patter of the rain as it bounced off the surrounding headstones. Soon, he was soaked through, and his hands were cold and stiff. He ripped off his sodden gloves and shoved them into a pocket. It was preferable not to wear them anyway if he needed to use his pistol.

Hoping it would distract from the knot of dread in his stomach, he tried to visualise the cemetery in his head. Prospect Cemetery was one of the largest in Dublin, and Iggy's wife's vault was in an underground circle near the main carriageway, close to the main gates. Fergus needed to visualise a route that would take him directly to the vaults. If he were fumbling about lost, he would either alert Iggy to his presence or miss him entirely. He couldn't afford to make a mistake by heading in the wrong direction.

As his eyes became accustomed to the darkness, Fergus made out the rows of headstones that led down towards the main path. If he slipped between the rows that ran parallel to the path, it would give him cover. He set off, keeping low and moving slowly, trying to avoid the patches of noisy gravel or tripping over the kerbing which surrounded some graves. Every so often, a twig would snap beneath his feet, or he would lose his footing on the damp leaves. However, it was almost impossible to move without making some noise. He only hoped that the noise of the rain would cover his movements.

Soon he slipped past the chapel, its spire inky black against the sky. Ahead was a copse of yew trees. As he sought shelter beneath their ancient boughs, he almost died of fright when a bird, disturbed from its roost, swooped past his head. He paused to slow his racing heart, leaning against a tree trunk, grateful for a moment of shelter under the trees. But he was spooked, and not just because he was alone in a cemetery at night. It didn't help that the ancient trees lent the carriageway and surrounding area an unsettling and eerie atmosphere.

Fergus glanced towards the gate. No sign of his officers or the police carriage. Good. Hughes was keeping out of sight as instructed, and he hoped Lucy was behaving and still in the carriage. He turned his gaze in the other direction, to where Iggy might be: Glasnevin's famous underground vaults. Soaring above them was the iconic round tower, the resting place of Daniel O'Connell. For anyone with Republican leanings, the cemetery was especially sacred. For someone like Iggy, it was almost a place of pilgrimage.

Fergus drew out his pistol and moved forward again as noiselessly as possible. But he soon ran out of cover and had to stop. It was decision time. There was open space between where he stood and the steps down into the vaults. If Iggy were lying in wait, Fergus would be an easy target as soon as he stepped away from the headstones. There was no alternative, however. Taking a deep breath, he crossed the bridge over the sunken path, which ran around the vaults, almost at a run. Then, panting heavily but thankful to still be alive, he paused at the top of the steps. He was aware he was still vulnerable, but he needed to get his bearings. Damnation! Martha had died almost ten years ago. Although he had attended the funeral, for the life of him, Fergus couldn't remember exactly which vault she was in. The path curved away to the right and left under the bridge. As he squinted into the darkness, he realised there were plaques above some doors, inscribed with family names. He prayed Iggy had followed suit.

Most of the vaults were the resting places of the well-to-do, MPs and government officials. They cost a fortune. But Iggy had insisted only the best would do for his beloved Martha. At the time, the remaining members of the family had been shocked at the extravagance of it all. Fergus's mother had reckoned the cost had almost bankrupted the man. And every Sunday since, Lizzie had informed Fergus, Iggy visited the cemetery. Fergus considered this beyond morbid, but in this instance, it was fortunate if it meant he might find Mary quickly. After all, a vault was the perfect hiding place... or the perfect place to leave a corpse. He shuddered at the thought not only because he liked Mary but because he knew the Stone family would blame him.

Was Mary still alive? he wondered. Why had Iggy taken her? Had she been caught investigating on his behalf? Her finding the letter was a stroke of luck, for now he knew the truth. But did Iggy know she had discovered it? He cringed at the thought, although the fact it had been in her bag suggested Iggy was unaware that she *had* found it. The only problem was that Iggy's temper was notorious. If he had found her in a compromising position, such as rifling through his office, what would he have done? He had killed twice already. Madness was driving him, Fergus was certain.

Hardening his resolve, Fergus made his way down the steps and stood uncertain at the bottom. He had no choice but to pick a direction and be methodical. The rain was heavier now, drowning out most sound, but not all. He stood, stock-still, straining to hear. That was a low whimper, like a small animal in pain, and it was coming from his right. He had to investigate. Pulse racing, he felt along the wall with his left hand, gun ready in the right, walking with deliberate slowness to avoid making noise on the gravel path.

At each vault's metal door, he stopped and pressed his ear to it. Nothing but silence each time, and suddenly he was dogged by doubt. Perhaps it was only an injured animal he had heard. But three more doors down, he heard something else. A faint scratching noise, then a whimper. Fergus knew he had to act fast and take a chance. He glanced up.

The inscription on the lintel above the door read 'Byrne'.

This had to be Martha's resting place. Fergus's heart pounded. If Iggy was inside with Mary, Fergus was done for, but if he wasn't, it was a chance to get Mary away to safety. Saying a silent prayer, he pushed down on the door handle. The metal door grated against the stone step as he slid it back. He jumped away, waiting for a reaction. There was none. Bolstered by the fact that he hadn't been met by a bullet or an enraged Iggy, he peered into the gloomy interior. A strange smell emanated from inside, and he tried not to think what it might be. Now he could hear whimpering, and it sounded like it originated in the vault's rear. But it was almost pitch-black inside, so he followed the sound with his hands outstretched, waving them back and forth. Then, his fingers touched cold stone, and he stopped. He guessed it was the altar where families left flowers and offerings. The whimpering was very close now. Fergus shoved the pistol back in his pocket.

He reached out and felt a slender arm. Relief flooded through him. It had to be Mary, not Iggy luring him in, as he had suspected. 'Mary? Don't be afraid. It's Inspector Ryan,' he whispered. However, the arm tried to jerk away, so he held firm. The unfortunate woman couldn't stop shaking. He felt for her face, and it was wet with tears. 'Don't cry.' Her response was muffled, and he realised she had been gagged. 'You must be very brave, Mary, and not make a sound when I take this off.' He loosened the gag and threw it to the floor. 'We must leave quickly and as quietly as possible,' he said. 'Have you any idea if Iggy is still here?'

'No idea,' she managed between sobs.

Fergus lifted her down from the altar, and she clung to him. When she let go, she almost fell over. She could not stand up by herself, which was unfortunate. Half carrying her, he moved towards the door, where he paused to make sure the way was clear. There was no trace of Iggy, so he took off as fast as he dared, half dragging Mary with him until he got her to the bottom of the steps.

'I'm sorry,' she whispered, her voice trembling. 'My legs are like jelly.' She started to cry again.

'Hush, you must be quiet until we get out of here,' he urged.

'I want to go home,' she cried. 'I'm not going back to that awful pub.'

'You won't have to. Now hush, Mary,' he pleaded in a whisper, all too aware that Iggy could be anywhere, lying in wait, and might hear them. In the darkness, his cousin had the advantage. Should he try to bait him to get him out in the open? But it struck him that he might not even be there. Perhaps Iggy had left Mary there to die, hoping she would not be found until it was too late. But Fergus had no way of knowing for sure. Just as easily, Iggy might be waiting for them to climb the steps, so he could ambush them. He'd have to be cautious.

'Mary, come and sit down under the bridge here while I check it's safe. Don't worry. Mrs Stone is waiting for you out in the carriage.' *Or at least I hope she is.*

Mary clutched his arm. 'Please don't leave me alone,' she said. 'He wants to hurt me.'

'Why?'

'I'm not sure,' she said, her voice trembling. 'I'd found this awful letter and wanted to give it to the mistress, but just as I was about to leave, he entered the building. I panicked when I guessed who he was, but it was too late and there was nowhere to hide. Jake gave me away.'

'You hadn't met Iggy before?'

'No. I had just enough time to stash the letter in my bag before he came crashing in the door. Stupidly, I'd left a candle burning in his office when I was searching the desk, so he knew I'd been nosing around. I denied it, but he flew into a rage. For hours he made me sit in the kitchen while he ranted and raved at me. I thought I was a goner, I did. He'd killed my cousin. Then he went awful quiet like. I didn't like that either. He made Jake watch me while he went off. Then he came back with a gig and made me come here with him. He scared me.' She burst into tears once more.

'I'm sorry, Mary. I should never have let you go in there.' Cold anger gripped Fergus, fuelled by his own guilt. He pulled out his pistol once more. 'Stay here. I'm going to find him. Not a sound.' Mary slid to the ground, hugging her knees. 'Good girl.' She was in such a dreadful state, he doubted she even heard him.

Fergus wiped the rain from his eyes as he climbed the steps. Visibility was decreasing by the minute. About halfway up, he stalled. To his horror as he looked up, he realised there was a large shape above him, leaning on a walking cane, standing on the platform. Iggy. It had to be.

THIRTY-FOUR

It had been a long time since Lucy had met such an intransigent character as Fergus Ryan. In fact, he reminded her a little of Phin when they had first met. However, as much as she admired Ryan and understood his concerns, Mary was *her* maid and therefore her responsibility. Deeply frustrated, she watched Inspector Ryan walk off down the road. It took considerable constraint for her not to jump down from the carriage once he was out of sight. Instead, she watched the sergeant disappear behind the carriage, to reappear only moments later with a huge bolt cutter in his hand. The carriage driver, when bid, jumped down, and the two men set to work on the front gate. Lucy heard the crack as the padlock broke in two and fell to the ground. Both men froze for a moment before jumping back to stand behind the pillars. However, no one came out of the cemetery to challenge them. The driver climbed back up onto the driver's seat of the carriage while Hughes retrieved the pieces of the padlock, then withdrew to stand behind a pillar at the entrance once more.

'This is intolerable. I can't just sit here. He'll never find her on his own,' Lucy muttered. As she opened the carriage door, Hughes swung around and gestured for her to get back. Ignoring him, Lucy stepped down, pulling the collar of her coat up against the driving rain.

'Sergeant,' she said as she drew level, 'we can't leave the inspector on his own to deal with this. What if Byrne has accomplices or is armed?'

Hughes stiffened as this idea struck home, but to her disappointment, he said, 'Ma'am, I have my orders. Please return to the carriage.'

'Nonsense.' Lucy dipped into her bag and withdrew her pistol to show him. 'You see, I'm not without the means of defending myself. Let's face it, if I weren't here, he would have taken you in with him. Admit it.'

'Ma'am—'

'Come along. We've no time to waste,' she said, heading for the gate. She slipped through the opening before Hughes could stop her. Lucy took up a position behind a large tree near the entrance. She heard the sergeant curse under his breath as he followed her in.

'Good man. You know it's the right thing to do. Now, do you have any idea where this vault might be located?' she asked as he drew alongside.

He pointed straight ahead. 'Down that path, ma'am, beneath the round tower.' As she moved forward, the sergeant grabbed her arm, pulling her to a stop. 'I'll go first,' he said.

'Oh, very well.'

Lucy kept close to Hughes as they ran from tree to tall headstone in an effort to stay undetected. However, as they approached the tower, they had to cross a path in the open. Hughes hesitated and threw Lucy a quizzical glance.

With rain running down her face, Lucy shrugged. They had no way of knowing whether Ryan was down below in the vaults yet. If they went charging in, it might put him and Mary in danger. Lucy was about to voice the thought when Hughes grabbed her arm and pulled her down behind the headstone.

'There's someone there,' he whispered.

Lucy chanced a peek around the side of the monument. The bulky outline of an individual was visible, standing stock-still at the edge of the curved platform above the vaults. They were staring downwards.

'Is it Byrne?' she asked. 'Have you any idea what he looks like?'

'I do, but I'm not sure,' the sergeant whispered, squinting. 'It's too dark to be positive.'

'What should we do?'

'I'll circle around and come up behind him and try to grab him. If you stay here, you can block his exit if he tries to make a run for it.'

Aggrieved she couldn't think of a better alternative, Lucy muttered, 'Agreed.'

Hughes hesitated. 'Are you sure you're happy to use that pistol?'

Admittedly, her track record wasn't great, but Lucy almost screamed in frustration. Instead, she took a deep breath and shooed him off. 'Perfectly happy.'

'Please be careful.' After one last lingering glance, Hughes slipped away, off to the left. Lucy watched him scramble from headstone to headstone until he disappeared from view. Suddenly, she was alone and not feeling so brave. Hopefully, with the rain so heavy, Byrne wouldn't hear Hughes creep up on him until it was too late. Now, all she could do was cross her fingers and wait with her pistol at the ready. Minutes passed with agonising slowness. Every so often, she peeked out. The man was still there and still looking down. Was he speaking to someone? It was so frustrating. She couldn't hear anything but the thumping rain. She willed the sergeant to hurry up.

Cold and miserable, but determined to stick it out, Lucy hunkered down to wait.

. . .

'Iggy?' Fergus shouted, his pistol trained on his cousin. He couldn't see if Iggy had a weapon, but he took his time climbing the steps. No sudden movements was key; he had no wish to startle the man. 'It's over, Iggy. You'd best come with me, back to the castle.'

Iggy laughed, turning his head to stare right at him. 'Well, polis, I'd love to oblige, but I'd sooner not, thanks. I've heard how you lot treat your *visitors*. So, here you are. I had a feeling you might turn up. What's that young chit to you, anyway? Sweetheart? Oh no, sure you're too busy betraying your next of kin to be in the petticoat line.'

Fergus gritted his teeth, determined not to rise to it. Instead, he said as smoothly as he could manage, 'You can't go around kidnapping young women, Iggy. It's not nice.' He halted on the last step but kept his gun aimed at his cousin.

'Is she one of your narks, then? Hmm, that makes more sense, I suppose. And I caught her red-handed, I did. Nosing around in me office. Up to mischief. But no one betrays me and Lizzie.'

'No, Iggy. She's just a barmaid,' Fergus said, but Iggy laughed. 'There was no need for this. If you come along quietly, we can sort all of this out.'

Iggy huffed and moved closer to him. 'Why are you meddling in my business, boy? If you weren't prepared to help the family and come work for me, you should stay away. Look the other way.'

Fergus's anger swelled. 'I would gladly stay away, Iggy, but when you go around killing prostitutes and madams, you leave me little choice.'

Iggy spat on the ground. 'Oh-ho! You know about that, do you? Well, I did the world a favour, getting rid of those two. Neither deserved to live. Tarts, the pair of 'em.'

A roar of rage ripped through the air, and before he could react, Mary flew past Fergus towards Iggy. Fergus made to grab her as Iggy raised his cane to strike her down. Fergus had to hold on for dear life as Mary tried to wriggle out of his grasp. All the while, Iggy was charging at them. Fergus had seconds to react but couldn't do it. He couldn't shoot his cousin in cold blood. He twisted, trying to remove Mary from danger. The cane came down on his shoulder, knocking the gun from his hand and loosening his grip on Mary.

And then, time slowed.

Mary fell to the ground as Iggy made a grab for her. Propelled by his own momentum, Iggy tripped over her and fell headfirst over the parapet and down onto the vault path. He landed with a sickening thud.

Fergus was vaguely aware of Sergeant Hughes appearing out of the gloom and helping Mary to her feet. But he could not move, transfixed by the sight of his cousin's twisted body on the ground below. A dark pool was forming beneath Iggy's head. Next thing Fergus knew, Lucy Stone was there, too, hugging her maid.

'I'd better check, sir,' Hughes said to him before descending the steps. He knelt beside the body and felt for a pulse. When he looked back up at Fergus, he shook his head.

THIRTY-FIVE

The rain had ceased, and it was close to midnight when Fergus arrived at the Byrne house on Gardiner Street. There was a light on downstairs, so he hoped Lizzie hadn't retired for the night. Dragging her from her bed to tell her the awful news would be the last straw in a night he would never forget. However, Lizzie answered his knock almost immediately.

'Evening, Lizzie. Sorry to call so late,' he said, taking off his sodden hat and holding it in his hands.

'Fergus, how bedraggled you are, but what a nice surprise.' She stood back with a smile. 'No bother. Come on in. Now, don't worry. Himself is out, so you won't get any grief. Rough night? You look like you could do with a drink.'

Fergus followed her into the front parlour, struggling to find the words to tell her. He still couldn't believe it himself. Iggy dead. Deep in gloom, he slumped down into an armchair and placed his hat on the floor. What made it worse was that Lizzie was in a cheery mood, and now he was going to destroy it.

'Come on. I was about to have a nightcap. Won't you join me?'

Lizzie asked, going to the sideboard and reaching for a bottle of whiskey.

'Maybe in a minute, Lizzie. I'm sorry. Could we sit and talk first? I have something to tell you,' he said. He did not know how she'd take the news. He'd always suspected Lizzie's relationship with her father was fraught. But now she'd be on her own. How would she cope? She'd need his support for sure.

Lizzie sat down and then leaned forward, her eyes narrowed. 'My God, you're soaking wet. You'll catch your death, you will. Have you been out all night in that rain?' She crossed the room to stand before him. 'You should take better care of yourself. Time you got yourself a wife.' Then she laughed and held out her hand. 'Come on, take off that wet coat at least. I can put it in front of the range in the kitchen.'

'Thanks.' Fergus shrugged out of his coat, then sat waiting for her return, rehearsing in his head what he was going to say.

As Lizzie walked past him, she touched his shoulder. 'What's up, Fergus? You're as white as a sheet. Have you seen a ghost?'

He waited for her to sit. 'That's not too far from the truth. I'm sorry, Lizzie. I've come with bad news.'

Lizzie inhaled and sat back. 'It's me Da, isn't it? I reckoned something was up. He hasn't been home since Saturday evening. When I told him about that raid... well, let's say he didn't take it very well. Blamed you, in fact, even though I told him it was some other officer leading it. So, I've stayed away from the pub, hoping to avoid him until things calm down.'

'I'm sure he was livid about the raid, but I knew nothing about it. Couldn't warn you.'

'It doesn't matter, Fergus. It amounted to nothing. What's he done, then?' she asked with a quirk of her mouth. 'Have you finally locked him up for something?'

'There's no easy way to say this. He's dead, Lizzie. Tonight, in fact.'

Lizzie gazed at him, her expression blank. Was it shock? Did she not understand what he had said?

'Well, it was only a matter of time, I suppose,' she said at last with a shrug. She rose and headed for the sideboard while he reeled at her words. 'I think we'll have that drink, now, cousin.'

'Lizzie! You do realise what I've said. Iggy died this evening.'

'Oh yes. I heard you.' She handed him a glass of whiskey and clinked his glass. 'Might I ask what the circumstances were? I'm curious. I mean, I know he had plenty of enemies. People he has crossed, stolen from and bullied. Or was it one of those poor souls he'd charged exorbitant interest to over the years who finally cracked? You knew about the moneylending, I assume?'

'Yes,' he managed, his mind whirling. If he didn't know better, the news of Iggy's passing pleased his cousin. Their relationship must have been worse than he had realised. 'Iggy's death was an accident. It happened at Glasnevin Cemetery. He tripped and fell... Look, Lizzie, I was there and witnessed it. In fact, we were after him because evidence emerged that implicated your father in the murder of that young prostitute in The Monto, and Celine Burton as well.'

'Because of Celine's blackmail attempt?'

He stiffened. 'You knew about that?'

'I... well, I came across a letter from Burton, you see.'

Fergus rooted in his pocket and held up Celine's letter. 'This one?'

Lizzie took it from him and handed it back after a mere glance. 'Yes. It's good you have it now. Mind you, I'd suspected him for The Monto murder. He'd been going there a lot of late. And then I found his overcoat in the bin out the back here on Friday evening. I know blood when I see it, so I reckoned he'd harmed someone. When I saw the newspapers, I realised *who*. Not that Celine Burton is any great loss to the world.'

'Lizzie, why are you so calm about all of this?'

'Dearest Fergus, you are so naïve, aren't you? I've wanted rid of him for years. I even contemplated taking the boat. If you only knew what I've had to put up with since Ma died. It really stuck in my craw that he wanted you to come into the business, for you to take over, when all the while I was there, keeping everything going. Did he ever thank me? No. He laughed at me when I suggested I could manage it all, because I was a mere girl. The truth is I hated him. Why do you think I came to you about those Fenians? I wanted Da locked up. Put away.'

Fergus sat forward to ask, 'Was that even true?'

'No, of course not, Murphy and O'Neill talk a load of codswallop with a few pints in them, but they're harmless. I was sure your lot would believe it, though, and if you arrested Da for treason or whatever, he'd lose his pub licences.'

His blood turned to ice. 'And you'd just take them over?'

'Exactly. And why not? I'm clean. I've had no part in Da's mischief. But that stupid Inspector Burke couldn't pin a tail on a donkey, never mind make an arrest as I'd hoped.'

Fergus chuckled, despite his despair. 'Oh, Liz. You should have come to me.'

'You're too honest for your own good.' She sipped her whiskey, regarding him with amusement above the rim of the glass. 'Now, tell me. That Mary Cahill, if that's even her real name. You're responsible for hoisting her onto me, aren't you? Oh, don't look so surprised. I figured out she was working for you. Jake told me she was asking a lot of questions. She wasn't subtle about it.'

'Yes. Mary had her own reasons for wanting to insinuate herself into The Sleepy Druid, so I helped her. In return, she agreed to be my eyes and ears. I was looking for evidence. I suspected Iggy was supplying Celine Burton with alcohol for her brothels.'

'Yes, Celine and a few of the other madams as well. Very lucrative business, but it was stupid to risk our licences like that. I was livid when I found out. But Da always did love to take risks. Then, about three months ago, Celine came to Da looking for money cos she wanted to buy another property. Once she'd taken the loan, he had her over a barrel, if you'll forgive the pun.' She flashed him a smile. 'Part of the deal was that she'd only get her booze from him. What Celine didn't realise was that Da had his eye on her business. He kept upping the interest rate on her loan.'

'Hoping she'd be forced to hand her business over as payment?'

'Correct. A controlling interest, at least. He already had Mary Hawkins under his thumb.'

'Burton's chief competition. I didn't know that.'

'Yeah, well, Da never missed an opportunity to grow the business. He'd started to turn the screws on Burton in the last few weeks.'

'But then he murdered that girl, and after that, Celine had the upper hand.'

Lizzie chuckled. 'She thought she had.'

'Hence the letter she sent Iggy. Why didn't he destroy it?'

'He thought he had done just that, but I regularly go through his office and I found it scrunched up in a ball in the corner. I guess he threw it there in a fit of rage. I couldn't believe my luck; I had leverage at last. After The Monto murder, Da was acting strange. Hardly left the house and was drinking like a fish. When I realised what your Mary was up to, I ensured that letter was in a place where it would be found by anyone rummaging around.'

'Why didn't you send it to me? You must have known those were my cases? After all, you wanted Iggy out of the way.'

Lizzie gave a shrug. 'It was more fun that way. I suppose if Mary hadn't found it, I would have made sure it got to the castle, somehow.'

'Fun, Lizzie? The poor woman might have ended up dead. Your father caught her snooping and dragged her off to Glasnevin tonight. Left her tied up in your mother's vault, of all places. God knows what he intended to do to her. We might not have found her either if Jake hadn't reminded me about the place and your father's weekly visits.'

'Well, I'm sorry to hear that. But you know as well as I do how obsessed Da is... was, about the cemetery. He hasn't been right in the head since Ma died... Is Mary alright?'

'A little shaken by her ordeal, obviously, but she'll be fine.'

'Who is she?'

'A lady's maid. The young woman your father murdered, and her sister, Bridget O'Reilly, were her cousins.'

'Ah, that explains all the questions about that Bridget article. Why Da offloaded her on me, I'll never know. Bridget was useless —and the backchat out of her! Turned out she was a thieving little culchie—'

'Lizzie! Burton enslaved that young woman and then your father did the same. She's a child.' Fergus glared at her, his patience now well and truly exhausted. 'You cannot condone that?'

Lizzie went to refill her glass. 'Da was always up to something. Business is business, cousin. What more can I say?'

Disgusted, Fergus grabbed his hat and stood. 'We will need you at the morgue tomorrow morning to make a formal identification of your father.'

Lizzie twirled her glass, looking up at him with amusement. 'Well now, could *you* not do it, being as you're family... and being his favourite? Don't scowl at me so, Fergus. You must understand, I'll be fierce busy setting the business to rights with Da gone. I've no doubt there's rent and loan repayments to be collected, not to mention hirin' and firin'.'

'God almighty!' he exclaimed.

Lizzie smirked. 'Calm down, cousin.' She waved at the chair he had just vacated. 'Have another drink.' He glared back at her. 'Oh, very well. I'll see if I can spare the time sometime next week.'

'Tomorrow.'

But she cocked a brow and laughed.

Too angry to speak, Fergus stormed down the stairs to the kitchen, grabbed his still-damp coat, and flew from the house, swearing he'd never return.

THIRTY-SIX

Merrion Square, Dublin, Monday, 30th July

Lucy left Mary's room to find George hovering on the landing. 'How is she, ma'am?' he asked, his brow puckered with concern. 'Will she be all right? Is there anything she needs?'

'She's still distressed, I'm afraid, but that is only understandable after such an ordeal. I've urged her to get some sleep, but she can't seem to stop crying, poor thing. Even the little bunch of flowers from the garden which Ellie picked didn't cheer her up.'

'Would it help if I talked to her, ma'am?'

'You can try, George. She sets a lot of store by your wisdom.'

'You're too kind, ma'am.' After a pause, he asked, 'Perhaps I should fetch a doctor?'

'That might not be a bad idea, George. It so happens I saw the doctor go into the Carver house about ten minutes ago. You might catch him when he is leaving.'

'I'll do my best,' he said, before heading down the stairs. Lucy followed, lost in thought.

Her sleep had been fitful, for she had relived Iggy Byrne's fall over and over again for hours. The sound of him hitting the ground had been stomach-churning, and she deeply regretted the impulse to peer over the parapet. What had possessed her? But at least Mary was safe and physically unharmed.

Phineas was already at the breakfast table when she entered the dining room. When he saw her, he jumped up. 'My dear, I'd hoped you'd stay in bed for a little while. You had quite an adventure yesterday evening. I hope you didn't catch a chill.'

'No, just a murderer.' To her disbelief, her chin wobbled, and she wanted to cry.

He hugged her close, and she wrapped her arms around him, feeling some of the tension leave her body at last.

After a moment or two, she gazed up at him. 'It was awful, Phin. I'd forgotten how ghastly it is to witness a death. He was a horrible man, but it was terrible to be a bystander. And poor Fergus. The man was his cousin, after all.'

'Yes, very distressing for him. But it means Iggy has escaped the noose,' Phin remarked.

'Well, you know my views on the death penalty,' she said with a shiver. 'It's inhumane.'

'Yes, but if it acts as a deterrent, even to some, it has its uses.'

'We will have to agree to disagree on that, Phin. Anyway, I hope I didn't keep you awake. I know I was tossing and turning most of the night.'

'No more than usual,' he said, trying not to laugh.

Lucy tapped him on the arm. 'Be nice. You'd have been the same if you'd witnessed it all.'

He took her by the hand and drew her to the table before pulling out a chair. 'Sit and eat. You'll feel all the better for it.' Then he poured her some coffee. 'By the way,' he said, holding up a letter when seated again, 'this arrived from the PM this morning, thanking me for my report.'

'That's a relief. He's happy with it?'

'Very, thankfully, and I quote, "a thorough investigation, Mr Stone, which the cabinet and I will find most useful". I imagine DeWinter will be summoned to Number Ten to account for himself.'

'And will they implement your suggestions?' she asked, buttering some toast.

'I hope they execute at least some of my ideas. What a disaster it would be if those jewels were ever stolen. It would be an enormous embarrassment for the government in London and Her Majesty's representatives here.'

George put his head round the door. 'Ma'am, the doctor was available and has gone up to see Mary now.'

'Excellent, thanks, George. I'll speak to him when he's finished with her.' George nodded but didn't leave. Something about his expression prompted Lucy to ask, 'Was there something else, George?'

'While I was waiting for the doctor, I spoke to Sally, Mrs Carver's maid. I believe there have been developments in the Carver household, ma'am. From what I gather, the mistress of the house passed away about an hour and a half ago. That is why the doctor was called.'

Lucy jumped to her feet, all thought of breakfast forgotten. 'Should I go? Poor Olivia, she must be distressed.'

Phin reached out and gently tugged her back down onto her chair. 'My dear, I doubt Carver would admit you. Finish your breakfast. We can talk to the doctor when he comes down. He will confirm or deny the report.'

They didn't have to wait long before they heard voices out in the hallway. George entered, the doctor right behind him. Introductions were made, and Lucy offered Dr Grainger some coffee, which he refused.

'There is no great cause for concern, Mrs Stone,' the doctor said as he sat down. 'I suspect your maid is remarkably resilient in general, and although she is naturally distressed at the moment, some rest should restore her spirits.'

'I do hope so. But what she went through yesterday was dreadful. She was in a shocking state by the time we got her home. I assume she explained the circumstances?'

'A few details, yes. A most unfortunate incident. I hope the criminal in question was detained.'

Phin flicked Lucy a glance before saying, 'In a manner of speaking, yes. It is certain he will no longer be a menace to Dublin's young women.'

'Excellent. I am glad to hear it. Well, as I said to your butler, she should be fit as a fiddle and able to resume her duties in a couple of days. I have left a draught to help her sleep if she needs it.' Dr Grainger rose from the table. 'You must forgive me. I have to finish my rounds. I'll bid you good day.'

Lucy rose to escort him to the door. 'Dr Grainger, we understand that poor Edith Carver has passed away this morning. So very sad. How is the family bearing up?'

'Yes, poor dear lady. A very tragic case,' he said. 'Her daughter-in-law has been nursing her and is, understandably, most upset. Mr Carver, as always, is stoic at this most distressing time, though I fear it is only a matter of time before grief brings him down. He was devoted to her, you know.' The doctor leaned closer. 'As the lady has passed, I can tell you that her condition was always volatile. I held little hope for a recovery. The family knew this, but it has still been a nasty shock. However, she might have died at any time as her heart was very weak. Now, I must go, I have another patient to call upon. I have left my direction with your butler if you should need me again. Good day.'

Lucy shut the door after him and spun around to Phineas. 'Volatile, indeed. What nonsense. Carver didn't care for her one iota. Poor Edith. And how Olivia must be suffering. I must speak to her and give her what comfort I can.'

'You can't, Lucy, unless she comes to us.'

'Phin, don't you realise? We must act without delay. That house must be searched. Edith was fine on Thursday and Friday. Her condition deteriorated again upon Carver's return on Saturday. He must have decided to finish her off. What a dreadful and callous man he is.'

'I thought you had neutralised the digitalis in his second bottle,' Phin said, draining his coffee cup.

'I did. So, he must have had another one hidden somewhere, and we must find it before he disposes of it.'

'And how do you propose we do that, my dear? He's hardly going to let us do it with his blessing.'

'Why, we must alert Inspector Ryan immediately. He can insist on a search.' Lucy pulled the bell. When George appeared a minute later, she gave him the instruction.

THIRTY-SEVEN

Lucy had been pacing the drawing room, waiting for the inspector to arrive, and was relieved when Ryan rushed in ahead of George. He went straight up to her. 'What's happened? Is Olivia in danger?'

'No, no, I'm sure she's perfectly fine. But you need to search that house right now. Mrs Carver died this morning.'

'But is Olivia safe?' he asked.

'Yes, yes, as far as I know. I haven't seen her today, but the doctor who attended Mary this morning did. She is upset, naturally. But, Ryan, we must go now.' Lucy looked past him into the hall. 'How many officers did you bring?'

'Only my sergeant is with me,' Ryan said, greeting Phineas with a nod.

'Inspector,' Phineas said, putting down his newspaper.

'Then you will need our help,' Lucy said. 'Edith Carver died about two hours ago. Her condition worsened suddenly... after Carver came home. He must have overdosed her again.'

'Lucy, we don't know that for sure,' Phin said with a warning glance.

'Well, let us not waste time arguing about it. We should get started,' she said. 'If we find the poison, the inspector can arrest him.'

Ryan ran a hand over his chin. 'Yes, perhaps you are right, and I am anxious that Olivia does not come to any harm. It would be best if she left that house immediately.'

'You're absolutely right. In fact, I shall help her pack,' Lucy said. 'Phin?'

The inspector also turned to Phineas. 'Would you come with us, sir? Olivia's accusations regarding her father-in-law give me enough reason to enter the house and check out what has happened. But if we are to search the place thoroughly, I will need more help.'

'Exactly. Do come, my dear. You can read your paper later,' Lucy said to Phin, before clutching Ryan's arm and dragging him out the door. 'George?' she called out.

'Yes, ma'am?' George appeared from the nether regions.

'We may be out for a while... oh, you know very well what we're about.'

'I do indeed, ma'am,' George said, sanguine as always as he helped Phin into his coat. 'I'm available if you should need me. May I wish you luck in your endeavour?'

'You may.'

As they approached No. 83, they passed the police carriage. Lucy nodded to Hughes, who was standing on the pavement, gazing expectantly at his inspector as he approached.

'Wait here, Hughes, until I call for you,' Ryan said. 'I need to be careful with Carver. Everything must be done above board and according to regulations.'

'Yes, sir.'

As they got closer to the Carver house, Lucy spotted Olivia through the library window, seated at the desk. Her head was bent, and she was writing. She must have heard them for Olivia looked up, her eyes widening. She gave Lucy a wobbly smile before she turned away, shoving her letter to the side. Lucy wondered who she could be writing to.

Inspector Ryan leaped up the steps, but the bellpull was already disconnected, and a black bow of crepe was attached to the door. This didn't deter him, however. He knocked twice and stood back. Olivia's maid opened the door, and he stepped forward.

'Good morning, Sally. We are sorry to intrude at this sad time, but I'd like to speak to your master, please.'

Sally's eyes flicked towards the library. 'Well, sir, the house is in mourning. I don't think the family is receiving visitors.'

The inspector stiffened. 'Please convey my compliments to Mr Carver and tell him that I wish to speak to him. It's official police business.'

Sally glanced at Lucy, who raised her brows. Sally was usually most cooperative, so why was she being obstructive? She must know why they were here.

'Best you come in, so,' Sally said with a disapproving quirk of her lips, stepping back and opening the door fully. 'If you could wait here in the hall, please.'

A stranger appeared at the top of the stairs. 'I'm done now, Sally. That poor cratur. Sure, she was as light as a feather, skin and bone she was. Mr Carver has gone back in to sit with her. Bless him, but he looks wretched.'

It took a lot of effort for Lucy not to make a disparaging remark.

'Thank you, Aggie. We're most grateful,' Sally said. The woman came down into the hall, nodded to Lucy, Phin and Ryan and was ushered out the door by Sally.

'Widow Kelly was here to lay out the mistress. Mrs Carver was too upset to do it,' Sally explained before disappearing up the stairs.

All three stood in uncomfortable silence. Suddenly, Lucy regretted her haste. It didn't help that Phin was giving her 'what now?' looks. It was bad form to impose themselves on the family at such a time, even in the circumstances. Carver might have helped his wife die, but perhaps he was genuinely mourning her. Yet no, that wasn't possible. The man was a cad. His treatment of Olivia was proof of that.

The library door opened, and Olivia came out, a handkerchief clutched in her hand. 'How good of you to come. I was just writing a note to you, Lucy, to inform you...' She trailed off on a sob.

Ryan caught her hands in his. 'Olivia, I'm so sorry. I know how fond you were of her.' He glanced up the stairs. 'But do not worry. I've come to confront him. This will all be over soon, and you will be free of him.'

Chin trembling, Olivia's gaze swept over them all. 'Please be careful. I think he is unhinged.' Then she whispered, 'He's acting as if he is grieving her, but don't be taken in, Fergus. She was doing so much better when he was away...' Her voice broke. 'But since Saturday evening, she... it's all too dreadful.'

'Was he with her this morning, before she died?' the inspector asked.

Olivia nodded, dabbing at her eyes. 'Before I even had a chance to check on her. And last night, too. He normally doesn't do that.'

'Was her medicine tampered with?' he asked.

'No, certainly not the bottle I use, but as I told you before, he has his own supply.'

'Do you think he realised the other bottle had been tampered with?' Lucy asked.

Olivia gave another little sob, holding the handkerchief up to her cheek. 'He must have had more than one, Lucy. Wicked man.'

Lucy turned to Ryan. 'Then we must search now, before he can hide or dispose of the evidence.'

Ryan opened the front door and called Hughes in. Olivia moved beside Lucy and tucked her arm through hers. Lucy patted her hand. 'Don't worry. This will be over soon, my dear,' Lucy said. Then she happened to glance at Phineas. He was watching Olivia with a frown.

'Please stay here,' Ryan said. 'Hughes and I will go up and speak to him now.'

'Inspector?' They all turned around. Carver was standing at the top of the stairs, glaring down at them. Olivia gave a little gasp and stepped away from Lucy. Carver's pallor and red-rimmed eyes were obvious to Lucy even from down in the hallway. *My goodness, the man should be on the stage,* she thought. All for show—grieving indeed.

'What is the meaning of this intrusion? My wife passed away this morning. This is police harassment, and I won't stand for it. Get out of my house at once!'

'Come down, please, Mr Carver,' Ryan said, folding his arms. Lucy had to admire his sangfroid. Hughes moved up to stand beside the inspector. 'We need to speak to you about your wife's death. We can discuss it at the castle if you prefer.'

'What are you implying? This is outrageous. I'll be making a formal complaint to your chief inspector.'

'That is your right, sir.' Ryan glared up at him. 'Now, please.' He beckoned to Carver, whose colour was now extremely high. Carver slowly came down the steps, his gaze never leaving the inspector. Ryan gestured for him to enter the library ahead of him. Hughes brought up the rear and closed the door.

'Well, that would appear to be that,' Lucy said.

'We'll see,' replied Phin. Olivia glanced at him from under her lashes, then stared at the floor.

Lucy was full of sympathy and put her arm around Olivia's shoulders. The woman's future happiness depended on what would transpire in the library.

A few minutes later, the door opened. Ryan came out, his expression bleak, followed by Hughes, who was leading a hand-cuffed Carver by the arm. The man was deadly pale, as if in shock. Lucy supposed he never thought he'd be caught. Ryan stood aside, and Hughes marched his prisoner out the door. But Lucy saw the venomous glance Carver cast Olivia as he passed her.

Olivia stood gnawing her lip, tears streaming down her face, as she watched them go down the steps. 'Oh dear. I can't believe it's all over.'

Lucy hugged her. 'It is. Now, don't cry again, my dear. You must be strong.'

Olivia breathed shakily. 'I... I should be with Edith. I can't leave her on her own—someone must wake her until the funeral. It's too cruel.'

'Are you sure, Olivia? You can move in with us if you wish,' Lucy said.

'No, no, it wouldn't be right to leave the house now. I'll be fine now *he's* gone.' Olivia walked up to Ryan. 'Thank you, Fergus. You have no idea what a relief it is. If it's alright, I'm going to sit with Edith for a while.'

His gaze was full of concern and, if Lucy wasn't mistaken, love. 'Certainly,' he said. 'You must do what you think is right.'

They watched her climb the stairs. Lucy felt so sorry for her. What would the future hold for her? Seeing the expression on Ryan's face, however, she surmised there was a good chance it might include the police inspector. Lucy glanced outside and saw the police carriage pass by on its way to the castle.

'We'd better carry out the search. I'll need the evidence for my chief inspector,' Ryan said, clearing his throat. 'We should probably start in Carver's suite.'

THIRTY-EIGHT

Lucy and Phineas carried out a methodical search of Carver's bedroom, while the inspector investigated the bathroom. They checked every drawer, and Phineas even pulled out all of Carver's clothes from the wardrobe and searched the pockets.

'It's well hidden, Lucy,' he said as he put the clothes back. 'And it doesn't help that those bottles are so small. It might be a good idea to search the bed.'

'Ahem.' It was Ryan, standing in the doorway holding up a small blue bottle.

'It was where Olivia showed me the other day.' He held it up to the light. 'I'd say the level has gone down.'

Lucy took it from him and uncorked it. She recognised the same smell as before; it had held digitalis at some point. 'I'd say this is the bottle I emptied. Most of this should be tea and probably harmless.'

Phineas joined them. 'That's not enough to convict him. Olivia is right. There must be another bottle stashed somewhere.'

'Why don't I try the library? Olivia said that he spends a good deal of time in there on his own. There must be countless hiding places in there.'

'That's an excellent idea, Lucy,' Phin said. 'We'll continue looking upstairs then join you.'

Lucy sat at Carver's desk, her gaze roaming around the room. This might take forever. Every wall was lined with bookcases. She groaned, for that meant she'd have to pull out every single book to check behind it. And what if the bottle were secreted inside a book? It would be easy enough to cut out a hollow section to hide one of the tiny bottles.

But then a sudden flashback made her smile. She recalled that night at Somerville Hall in her father's library as she and Mary had searched for the sapphires her husband, Charlie, had hidden. But that memory did not help her, for there was no horrible stag's head in this library.

Gosh, she hadn't thought about Charlie in ages. Her marriage to him was a lifetime ago now. Was it shameful that she didn't miss him, even a little? It hadn't been a perfect marriage, and his lies and risky business affairs led to his death, plunging her into considerable danger. It was as if during those ten years with him, her life had been in a state of suspension. And yet, his death had released her, and on the very day of his supposed accidental death, she had met the mysterious and slightly scary Phineas Stone. It was all ancient history now. Everything had changed. As she had fallen in love with Phin, everything in her world had shifted, not just because he loved her in return, but because he let her be the woman she was meant to be.

With a wee shake of her head, Lucy brought her focus back into the room. She wasn't sorry all this business was wrapped up, and with Phin's report with the PM they could plan their return home to London. That thought cheered her up. But first, they had to find evidence strong enough to convict Carver. A little blue bottle, so seemingly innocent, held the key.

Concentrate, Lucy.

She'd start with the desk. A photograph of Edith and what must have been his son, James, had pride of place. Edith was sitting and James stood behind her, his hand on her shoulder—a typical studio portrait. Lucy picked up a second photograph, this time of James and Olivia's wedding. Lucy could discern a strong likeness to his father in James, but what surprised her was the expression on Olivia's face, as if she were fed-up. Of course, people didn't bother to smile in photographs. Studio sessions were so tedious. The process took too long, and you'd end up with a sore jaw and a terrible picture if you attempted to maintain a smile. She placed it back down.

There was a pile of books on the edge of the desk. Lucy scanned the titles. All of them were banking related. Lucy flicked through the pages and shook out the books to no avail. There was nothing for it but to search through the desk drawers. Maybe there was a secret compartment in the desk. There always was in those mystery novels she loved to read. With renewed enthusiasm, Lucy set to work and as luck would have it, the desk wasn't locked, but there was no evidence of a secret cubby-hole or a small blue bottle.

Lucy sat back, scowling at the bookshelves. Maybe the others would be successful upstairs, and she wouldn't have to haul out dusty books for the entire morning. Above her head, she could hear noises. Carver's bedroom must be right above the library, for someone was moving about and making a racket. Then a door slammed shut. Suddenly, all was silent once more. With a groan, Lucy turned her attention back to the other side of the room. Time to tackle those pesky bookcases.

As she was about to stand, the door opened, and Phin and Ryan walked in. Ryan was grinning. 'We found them.' From his pocket he pulled out two digitalis tincture bottles. Identical to the official bottle on Edith's bedside table.

'Where were they?' Lucy asked, skirting around the desk.

'Hidden in a leather pouch under the mattress,' Ryan said.

'So, do you have enough to charge him now?' Lucy asked.

'Not exactly. There must be a postmortem to determine if she was overdosed, but with Olivia's statement and yours, we should have a solid case. Unfortunately, Hughes hasn't been able to find a local chemist that recalls selling digitalis tincture to Carver, but he may have been clever enough to go to a remote part of the city to purchase it.'

'Yes, I'd imagine he'd be wise enough to do that,' Phin said. 'My man George has also been visiting local apothecaries, and so far, he hasn't had any success either.'

'Thank you for that. My chief wasn't taking Olivia's claims seriously and had refused to release more officers to help us check out our theory.'

'Not at all, we are glad to help, aren't we, Lucy?' Phin asked, smiling across at her.

'Always,' she said.

Phin turned back to the inspector. 'Well done, Ryan, you got your man. However, your enquiries will take time. I'd advise you to stick with it though and get as much evidence as you can; otherwise, a defence team would destroy your case in court. Juries dislike loose ends. What you really need is a witness who saw him give her the digitalis.'

'I'd guess he was putting it in her morning tea,' Lucy piped up. 'That was why he always insisted on being alone with her.'

'Yes, perhaps one of the servants will speak up now he's gone from the house. Thank you both for your help. I'd better get back to the castle before my chief goes on the rampage when he discovers Carver is back in custody. Mrs Stone?'

'Yes, Inspector?'

'Please tell Olivia that I will call back later today,' he said.

She grinned back. 'I will. She will need plenty of support in the weeks ahead.'

'Y-yes, I suppose she will.' With a nod and his colour rising, Ryan strode out the door.

Phineas joined her at the desk. 'Well, that all appears to have turned out well. Shall we go?'

'You go ahead. I want to pop my head in and tell Olivia we found those bottles and that all's well. And, most importantly, I will pass on the inspector's message.'

'Lucy, let them be,' he said, half laughing.

'Sometimes love needs a little help.'

'Speaking of which... I'll see you later.' Phin kissed her cheek, and there was a glint in his eye. 'Don't be long. I've seen so little of you lately.' Lucy tucked her arm through his and walked him out into the hall to the front door.

A quick kiss, and Lucy waved him off. As she closed the door, it struck her how eerily quiet the house was, bar the ticking of the grandfather clock coming from the library. It wasn't that surprising. With the house in mourning, even the servants would tiptoe around, trying not to disturb the grieving family. Well, not exactly a family now with Carver under arrest. Just Olivia. Lucy gave herself a little shake. In all the fuss, it was easy to forget that poor Edith was laid out in the bedroom on the floor above. She'd better go up and see how Olivia was coping. Perhaps she'd be able to persuade her to join them for dinner later that evening.

Lucy tapped on Edith's door, but there was no response. She tapped again. Silence. Lucy squeezed the handle down and eased the door open enough to see inside. The curtains were pulled, so the room was dim, but she saw Edith laid out on the bed. Otherwise, however, the bedroom was empty. Lucy moved to the bedside and looked down at Edith. Even in the dim light, the poor woman's face was colourless and waxen. Lucy hoped she had found peace at last. But where was Olivia? Perhaps it was all too much, and she had gone to lie down.

Lucy crossed the landing to Olivia's room. 'Olivia? May I come in?' she asked, but nobody answered. She was hardly asleep, was she? When there was no reply to her knock, Lucy opened the door and peeped in, then stood rooted to the spot. The room was empty, but it was in total disarray. There were clothes scattered across the bed and the chairs, some even on the floor. Female attire... As if someone had packed in a hurry. Why? Where on earth was Olivia?

But as she stared at the chaos, a horrible heaviness in the pit of her stomach grew. And then she caught that very distinctive whiff. Digitalis. She scanned the room, her heart thumping. Olivia's lilac half-mourning dress was on the floor and there was a dark brown stain around the pocket of the skirt. Lucy picked up the dress and carefully prised open the pocket. Inside was a small broken blue bottle.

Lucy dashed from the room and hurried down the flights of stairs until she reached the basement kitchen. Two servants, a young maid who was coming in the door carrying a basket of laundry, and the cook who was preparing vegetables at the table, looked at her in astonishment as she entered.

'Can we help you, ma'am?' the maid asked.

'Hello, I hope so. I wonder if you know where Mrs Carver and Sally, her maid, are. I can't find them upstairs.'

The maid shared a glance with the cook, pursed her lips, then said, 'Why, they left, ma'am,' she said, indicating the back door. 'About ten minutes ago.'

Lucy's heart pounded. 'Left? Out the back door?'

'Aye, out to the laneway at the back where the cab was waiting.'

This didn't sound right; it didn't make sense. 'Did they say when they'd return?'

Again, a look passed between the servants. 'They both had bags and their hats and coats on. Don't think that pair are planning on comin' back,' the cook said with a huff. 'Bad suss to the pair of 'em, I say.'

Totally confused, Lucy asked, 'Where have they gone? Do you know?'

'I can tell you that, ma'am. Sure, Sally asked me to hail the cab for 'em, like, and me trying to take in the washin'. Off to Kingstown they are.'

Kingstown. Lucy grappled with this. That was the ferry port. Why would Olivia be going there? She had no reason to leave now that Carver had been arrested.

'Nothing's been right since that madam arrived,' the cook

announced with a pointed look at Lucy. 'Nothin' but death.' She crossed herself.

'Oh, aye. A bad egg, as me Ma would say,' added the maid. 'Poor Master James had a terrible time with her and him the loveliest human being you'd ever meet. Tantrums and the like. He was a saint to put up with her.'

'They all were,' the cook said, scraping some carrot peelings into a bucket. 'The poor mistress. She was always so good to that thankless madam. I reckon that's what made her ill.'

'Oh, aye. I remember the rows, spectacular they were and all,' the maid jumped in with enthusiasm. 'And then the carry on when the poor man died. Outrageous, it was. Why she wasn't sent on her way, I'll never know.'

'You are talking about *Olivia* Carver?' Lucy asked, her heart thumping in her chest.

'The very one, ma'am. A wee devil, and no mistake,' the cook pronounced as she chopped up another carrot.

'And always snooping around. Why, only the other day I saw her going into the master's room when he was out,' the maid said. 'What business had she going in there? And that Sally one, with her airs and graces, looking down on us cos she's English.' The maid tossed her head. 'Always running secret little errands. I've seen her go out with letters; ones her nibs didn't want the master to know about, I reckon.'

'Oh, my good God!' Lucy exclaimed, clutching the back of a chair. This couldn't be true.

'I reckon she's off to meet up with her fancy man,' the maid continued.

'What? Who?'

'Well, I don't know his name, like, but I saw them together in the Phoenix Park about a month ago. I was with me friend and I couldn't believe it. Strolling along they were and she gazin' up at him like he was a prince. Mind you, he did look well in his uniform. Proper smart he was.'

The cook sniffed. 'Shameless behaviour and her not out of

mourning. I remember you tellin' me about it,' she said, laying down her knife. 'And then all the trouble began with the mistress getting ill. I can tell you, that woman would be the last person I'd want nursing me. Cold as stone, ma'am, and I don't mind telling you that policeman has it all wrong. And that's a fact. If there was anyone poisoning the mistress, it was Olivia Carver, and no mistake.'

Lucy was momentarily lost for words. Her grip on the chair back tightened. 'Why? Why would she?'

'That's easy to answer. Sure, she gets half of the mistress's estate because poor Master James died, God rest his soul. A pretty penny it is, too,' the cook answered.

Stunned, all Lucy could do was stare at the servants. This didn't sound like the Olivia she knew. Could they be describing the timid creature she had come to know? Lucy inhaled deeply. So, the vulnerability had been an act. All the while Olivia had been planning to despatch her mother-in-law and implicate Carver. She had manipulated all of them for her own ghastly ends. If the cook was right, it would explain why Olivia had fled the house.

Yes, it was making horrible sense. The digitalis! She had encouraged them to find it, led them to it, in fact, so they'd believe it was Carver administering those extra doses. Olivia had found that first bottle very quickly... probably because she had planted it in the first place. And all the ones found under Carver's bed, most likely. Most telling of all, why was there a broken bottle of it in Olivia's dress?

Half in a daze, Lucy left the kitchen and climbed back up to the hallway as her thoughts tumbled through various scenarios and some frightful conclusions.

How stupid and blind you have been, Lucy Stone.

The more she thought about it, the cook's awful suspicion was making more and more sense. It had all been a web of lies.

No wonder Olivia had bolted.

THIRTY-NINE

Merrion Square

Soon Lucy's distress was overtaken by the need for action and she raced out of the house. As she approached No. 81, she spotted George crossing the road from the park and she rushed up to him.

'Is everything alright, ma'am?' he asked.

'No, George, it's not. Where's Phin?'

He glanced back across the road. 'He has just taken the children into the park for a walk.'

Lucy quickly explained what she had discovered. 'I must get to the castle as quickly as possible. Inspector Ryan has arrested the wrong person, and Olivia Carver must be tracked down.'

'You fear she is going to Kingstown to catch the boat?'

'Absolutely. What other reason could there be for her to go there?'

At that moment, a cab came into view. George flagged it down. 'Dublin Castle, as quick as you can,' he shouted up to the cabbie. As he helped Lucy into it, he said, 'Don't worry, ma'am, I'll let the master know what has happened. Godspeed.' With that he banged on the side, and the cab took off.

To Lucy the journey was endless, a constant stop-start and

darting around trams, carriages, gigs and carts. However, the cabbie appeared to be enjoying it, if his shouts, taunts and teasing of other road users was anything to go by. Eventually, the cab swung onto Exchange Court and pulled up outside the DMP offices.

Lucy jumped down. 'Wait here, please,' she said to the cabbie before taking off at a run towards the main door. The constable standing outside made to stop her, but Lucy cried, 'This is extremely urgent. I must see Inspector Ryan immediately.'

For a few seconds the man looked at her in indecision. Perhaps he thought she was deranged.

'Please, constable,' she managed in a calmer tone. 'A murder suspect is fleeing to Kingstown. The inspector must be told. At once.'

Despite his sceptical expression, the constable stepped back and waved her through.

'Thank you, and don't let that cabbie leave,' Lucy instructed as she dashed inside. Hitching up her skirts, she scooted up the stairs. As she gained the first landing, she spotted Ryan and his sergeant coming out of the inspectors' office.

'Inspector!' Lucy called out.

Ryan swivelled round, his brows shooting up. He broke into a smile. 'Why Lu... Mrs Stone, what on earth are you doing here? I'm afraid I can't talk to you now, for we're about to interview Mr Carver.'

'No, you mustn't,' she cried, rushing up to them. 'He didn't do it. The man is innocent. *Olivia* is the murderer.' She quickly recounted finding the digitalis in Olivia's dress pocket and all that the Carver servants had revealed. Last of all, she told him Olivia had bolted.

Ryan stared at her as if she were mad. 'Olivia? No. You must be mistaken.'

'I wish I were. She fled the house along with her maid. What the Carver servants had to say about Olivia was truly shocking. Both of us misread her true character, but that is irrelevant now.' She paused to catch her breath. 'They have taken a cab to

Kingstown. The Carvers' maid hailed it for her and that's how I know. I think they plan to leave the country, so you must hurry. They have half an hour on you as it is, but there's a cab waiting outside for you.'

With a bewildered expression, Ryan said, 'My God, I can't believe it.'

Lucy tugged his sleeve. 'Neither can I, but there's no time to discuss it. You must go after them. Quickly.'

'Yes, yes...' He turned to Hughes. 'Sergeant, best you come with me.' Then he faced Lucy, his expression desolate. 'No, don't even ask. You must go home, Mrs Stone. Let us deal with this.'

The two men dashed for the stairs. Lucy stood looking after them, her overriding emotion pity for the young man whose heart she had just helped break.

Kingstown, Co. Dublin

Fergus stared unseeing out of the cab window during the forty-minute journey. Shock and anger kept him silent, brooding, and poor Hughes had given up trying to engage him in conversation as they had passed through Irishtown. This Carver affair had been nothing but a disaster. Error had compounded error and if Carver had been sent to trial and hanged, it would have been a fatal one. He dared not contemplate what Chief Malone's reaction would be when he learned of yet another fiasco related to this case. His career could well be over, but at this moment he was too numb to care.

And now he had to arrest a woman he had fallen for so deeply. Perhaps, therein, lay the problem. She had sensed his attraction and used it against him. How could he have been so blind? His only consolation was that she had fooled everyone else just as thoroughly.

The cab turned onto the main road into Kingstown that skirted along the railway line running parallel to the sea. In the distance, he could make out Howth Hill, glowing green in the early afternoon sunshine, on the far side of the bay. How he wished he was there, not in this miserable cab on such an undertaking.

'We're almost there, sir,' Hughes said. 'Hopefully, the steamer hasn't left port yet.'

Fergus pointed to Carlisle Pier. 'It hasn't, but the tide is high. They'll depart shortly.'

'They'll have had time to buy their tickets, sir. I reckon our best chance of finding them will be the waiting room.'

'I hope so, because finding them on the ship will be challenging.'

'You could always demand the sailing is delayed until we find 'em,' Hughes said.

'And you can imagine Malone's reaction to that if she turns out not to be on it,' Fergus replied.

The cab dropped them on the pier and Hughes followed Fergus into the main building. They ran straight to the waiting room, but the area was almost empty. There was no trace of either Olivia or her maid.

'What time does the steamer depart?' Hughes asked a porter.

'In about forty minutes, constable.'

'Have the passengers boarded?'

'Oh, aye. Most of 'em.'

'Thanks. Sir? What do you want to do?' Hughes asked. 'There's time, so I could run up to the station and bring back more constables. It's just up on Upper George's Street. We'll never find 'em on that boat with just the two of us.'

'Yes, yes, that's a good idea, Sergeant. I'll stay here in case they try to leave the ship.' Fergus watched him sprint off. He felt numb. No matter how much he grappled with this truth, Olivia's betrayal was difficult to accept.

Fergus paced the pier, every so often glancing up at the ship's deck, half dreading that he might see her. A tiny part of him hoped it had been a ruse, and that she wasn't on that blasted ship, that she had made good her escape. The thought of her facing the gallows made his guts twist.

Shortly after, Fergus spotted Hughes and three other constables striding towards him. A police Black Maria followed, pulling up close to the gangway. Fergus gave the Kingstown officers descriptions of the two women as Hughes stood by, impassive. Fergus sent two of the constables onto the ship, keeping one standing guard at the bottom of the gangway.

'Sir? A word,' Hughes said.

'What?' Fergus snapped. The sergeant's eyes held nothing but sympathy. 'Sorry, Hughes... I—'

Hughes walked a few yards away from the ship, out of earshot of the constable. 'I understand, truly I do. Sir...' He reached out and patted his upper arm. 'Fergus, I think it best you stay here on the pier. Let me do this... as your friend.'

Fergus stared at him, his throat tightening. He should have known Hughes had figured out his emotional state. Overwhelmed, he could only nod his assent. Hughes briefly placed a hand on his shoulder before he strode off. Fergus turned and walked down the pier, fighting to control his breathing, conscious of the quizzical looks of passersby.

The first scream Fergus heard, ten minutes later, ripped through him. His gaze was drawn to the ship where the passengers on deck had turned from the railings, some craning to see what was happening on the far side. He could guess only too well; they had found her. He moved closer to the gangway, bracing himself for what was to come.

The first constable to appear had Sally in handcuffs. She threw Fergus a wry glance, her lips puckered into an ugly grin. The officer marched her down onto the pier and straight to the door of the waiting Black Maria, before pushing her up the steps and inside.

Fergus's mouth was dry, his heart pounding in his chest, but he stood his ground.

He saw Hughes first and was shocked to see his face was bleeding from scratches on his cheek. Next came a constable holding on to what could only be described as a wild woman who was kicking out and screaming obscenities.

Olivia?

Fergus took a step forward, horrified. Could this be the same woman to whom he had offered his protection?

When she spotted him, Olivia stopped struggling and stared before a cunning expression crossed her beautiful face. Suddenly she broke into a smile, so normal, it sent ice through his veins. She held up her handcuffed hands. 'Fergus, there's been some terrible mistake. You must believe me. I've done nothing wrong.'

'Olivia, Carver's servants give a very different account of you,' he replied, doing his best to keep his features impassive.

Olivia's eyes darted about and then she drooped against the constable as if in a faint. Fergus waved towards the Black Maria. 'Get her out of my sight.'

Hughes and the constable had to half carry her, but at the top of the steps of the police van she looked at Fergus and shouted, 'I hope you rot in hell!'

FORTY

Bash was reading aloud to Lucy, sitting on her lap, when a grey-faced Inspector Ryan was announced. 'We will finish this later, sweetheart,' she said to the little boy. 'I wish to speak to the inspector.'

'Yes, Mama.' Bash clambered down, clutching his book. Then he strode right up to the policeman and looked up into his face. 'You look sad, sir. Are you really a police inspector?'

Colour rushed into Ryan's cheeks. 'I am, son. Inspector Ryan of the DMP.'

'D-M-P—what does that stand for?' Bash asked.

'The Dublin Metropolitan Police.'

Bash stood absorbing this. 'Then you must know Chief Inspector McQuillan. I like him because he often brings me sweets. Sherbet lemons are my favourite'—Bash lowered his voice to a whisper—'and his, too, and I always have to share with him. Thankfully, my sister doesn't like 'em, otherwise I'd only get a few. But he's nice, and he helps my father with his cases, you know.'

'Unfortunately, I haven't had the pleasure of meeting the

gentleman. I believe he is with the *London* Metropolitan Police. A different force from mine.'

'And what—'

'Bash,' Lucy admonished him with a chuckle. 'That's enough now, off you go and find Jenny. Your father and Ellie will be back from their walk soon.' Once the door had closed, she beckoned Ryan over to sit beside her. 'I'm sorry about that. He's awfully inquisitive.'

The inspector smiled. 'I wonder where he gets that from.'

Lucy smiled at the compliment and patted his arm. 'His sister is as bad; in fact, between us, I think she is worse. Phin despairs, but I'm rather proud of them. They have so much more freedom to explore the world than I had at their age. Now, are you here to see Phin?'

'I had hoped you were both here.'

'Oh dear, he will be sorry to have missed you.'

'And I, him.'

'Won't you take tea? I'm sure he won't be long. He's taken Ellie to the park. Or perhaps you could stay for dinner? You'd be most welcome.'

'Thank you, but no. I must return to Dublin Castle immediately. There is a mountain of paperwork on my desk. But I was passing and knew you would be eager for an update.'

Lucy sat forward, impatient to hear the latest news. 'Yes, indeed. That's most kind of you.'

'I almost forgot, you must forgive me. How is Mary?'

'She is getting better. We were a little concerned at first, but she has rallied. I've sent her home to her mother for a while so that she can fully recuperate in peace and quiet, which, if you haven't guessed, means away from my twins with their high energy and constant questions.'

'I'm relieved to hear she is on the mend. That day she had to spend with my cousin can't have been pleasant for her. It is my belief he was close to madness. He could have killed her.'

'She won't forget it easily. Terrifying is how she described the incident to me, but she will be fine. Now, tell me. How are you bearing up? I know we are still in shock. In fact, I still can't believe it. Olivia, a consummate liar and a cold-hearted murderer.'

Ryan swallowed hard. 'Yes. I'd never have thought it possible. The irony is, if she hadn't panicked and run, we might never have found out.'

'Lord, yes. Thank heavens I went looking for her. If she hadn't bolted like that, I might not have found the digitalis or spoken to the maid and the cook, and poor Carver would have been hanged based on the evidence she planted.' Lucy gave him a quizzical look. 'Have you found her? I've been scanning the newspapers this morning in the hope of news.'

'Yes, we caught up with her and Sally at Kingstown on the steamer. Half an hour later, and we might have missed them.'

'And? Did you arrest her?'

'No. I couldn't bring myself... Hughes offered to do it. Just as well for she reacted badly. She has a very ugly side which she showed when she realised she could not manipulate me anymore.'

'I'm so sorry, Fergus. Has she admitted to the poisoning?'

'Eventually, she admitted it, as cool as you please. She claims— and this is awful—that the Carvers had treated her so badly that she was owed a financial reward. She also blames her brother for agreeing to a marriage settlement that left her at the mercy of the Carver family. Can you believe it?'

'Now I can, yes,' Lucy said. 'I totally misread her character.'

'We all did. She didn't realise until she was married how financially insecure her husband was. They had to exist on a small allowance from Myles Carver once her dowry was spent. When Olivia complained to James about their lack of funds, he mentioned his mother's will, probably hoping to appease her. Upon Edith's death, he would inherit a vast sum of money. Unfortunately for Edith, James told Olivia that if he pre-deceased his mother, the money would come to her. It turns out that Edith Carver was the only child of Nicholas Perdue and had a substantial trust fund.'

'That name sounds familiar,' Lucy said.

'The newspaper empire Perdue, from Manchester,' Ryan explained.

'So, Edith's estate was worth a small fortune, and Olivia wanted to get her hands on it. But first, of course, she had to ensure that Carver was no longer in the picture. How wicked she is. And Mr Carver. How is he holding up?'

'As one might guess, he was upset at being arrested and his wife barely cold. I'll not live that down for some time.' Ryan shuddered. 'Then yesterday evening, we had to tell him about Olivia. He lost control completely, and we had to call a doctor for him. The latest I heard is that, after his wife's funeral, he will go to the south of France to stay with friends.'

'The poor man. A dreadful business, and who would not feel sorry for him? I do feel guilty. Olivia painted him as a villain, and we all believed it. And what is worse is that it was such a close-run thing. But you had to arrest him yesterday morning, it would have been negligent not to. The evidence was so strong, and Olivia was so convincing.'

'Utterly convincing, I'm sad to say. But you're too kind. I should have questioned everything, as my chief inspector went to great pains to point out. Anyway, when Mr Carver eventually calmed down, he told us he had suspected something wasn't right. Edith's illness and her decline were too rapid. Dr Grainger confirmed to us that Carver had tackled him about it on several occasions. Carver admitted that his wife's will was easily accessible as there was a copy in his safe, and it was entirely possible that Olivia had seen it, which would have confirmed what her husband had told her.'

'And she hatched her wicked plan, no doubt encouraged by her lover.'

'I believe so. Carver didn't know that his son had already told her about the inheritance. The sad thing is that Edith treated Olivia as if she were a daughter and loved her dearly. But at some stage before his death, his son had confided in Carver that Olivia was difficult. Carver's relationship with her was always strained as a result. I think he may have blamed her for his son's premature demise.' Ryan shrugged. 'That's debatable. James Carver's death certificate states he died of sclerosis of the liver, and we know for a fact he was a heavy drinker. Anyway, Carver was on the point of sending Olivia back to England to her brother when Edith fell ill. To his astonishment, Olivia declared she would nurse Edith.'

'Not out of filial duty, I dare say, but so she would have access to the unfortunate woman and despatch her. How heartless she was.'

'Unfortunately, yes. We tracked down Carver's old valet, and he confirmed much of what Carver said.'

'And yesterday the kitchen servants said as much to me about Olivia, including that there had been tantrums while James was alive.' Lucy clutched his sleeve as a horrible thought occurred to her. 'You don't think she might have killed her husband as well?'

Ryan twisted his mouth. 'God only knows. The thought crossed my mind. We could exhume James Carver, but I have no evidence of foul play, so I doubt I'd get permission. Anyway, she will hang for murdering Edith.' His voice broke, and Lucy patted his hand.

'How were we taken in, Fergus? She fooled all of us. By rights, she should have been a performer at the Gaiety Theatre.'

'Yes, well, I've learned a valuable lesson. Don't get emotionally involved with witnesses or suspects.'

'You, my friend, will find a woman who is far worthier of your affection. One lapse, Fergus, that's all it was. If it's any consolation, I was convinced she liked you. Have you been able to trace her lover?'

'No. She refuses to name him, as does that maid of hers. Such loyalty.' He shook his head. 'Such a joke. She manipulated and did her best to kill the people who gave her shelter and welcomed her into their home like a daughter, and yet she protects a virtual stranger.' He gulped. 'She must love him very much. The thing is, I saw him with her.'

'What?'

'I was on Grafton Street one day and saw her meet a couple on the street. He's an army man and his wife is an invalid. At the time, I assumed they were merely acquaintances. We will try to find him, but once Olivia's arrest is in the public domain, I'm sure he will do his best to disappear.'

Sensing his underlying distress, Lucy changed the subject. 'And your cousin, Lizzie Byrne, how is she managing? She must be very upset.'

'On the contrary.' The inspector gave a dry laugh and regaled Lucy with the conversation he had with Lizzie on Sunday night.

'Good gracious. Another scheming female,' Lucy said. 'I trust you will not judge my entire sex by those two women. Will you charge her in relation to Bridget's treatment?'

'It's all hearsay. Without Bridget's testimony, there is little I can do.'

'Ah, but I have news for you. Chief Inspector McQuillan's men found Bridget, and she is safe and well.'

'That's excellent news.'

'Yes. It turns out we were right, and she did flee to England, using the money she stole from the pub. About two weeks ago, she made the crossing on the mail boat to Holyhead. From there she travelled to London but under her sister's name because she was afraid that the DMP were after her for stealing. Thankfully, she reverted to her own name once she arrived. And then the most extraordinary thing, and Mary will be delighted to hear this. Bridget's conscience was plaguing her, and she went to a police station to hand herself in. That's how she was found.'

'Good grief,' Fergus exclaimed. 'She was admitting she'd taken the money from Lizzie's pub?'

'Yes. Luckily, they spotted the name and that Vine Street police were looking for her. McQuillan was notified, and he has taken her under his wing.'

'Did she know about Peggy's murder?'

'It would appear not, poor child. McQuillan told her that

under the circumstances, she won't be charged... unless you think your cousin will press charges?'

'Well, she won't because then she would be obliged to explain how Bridget ended up in her pub in the first place.'

'Yes, I can see how that would be awkward for her. Anyway, McQuillan has persuaded Bridget to return to Dublin, and he will let you know when. I'm sure you will wish to question her.'

'Yes, I do. If she names Mulcahy as the person who tricked the girls into going to Burton's house, we can put him away at last. Just a shame we didn't get to talk to Bridget before Burton was killed. My problem was that Burton claimed Peggy had come to her and asked for a job, and she denied all knowledge of Bridget.'

'Which is absolute nonsense.'

'Yes, it is, but with Peggy dead and Bridget missing, what could I do? None of the other women in the house would gainsay Burton. Too afraid. It's an endless cycle of poverty and violence. My great hope is that someday we will rid the city of the blemish of The Monto. Sadly, there is no political will to do it at present.'

Lucy couldn't resist. 'And we know why—too many influential and powerful men are the clients. It will take the likes of Father McGuinness to make a stand, I fear.'

'Perhaps, but I'm not sure he would be brave enough to stand up to the madams and the gangs. He'd be risking his life.'

'I will give him every encouragement. But what about the girls at Celine's brothel? What will happen to them?'

He wagged a finger at her. 'Ah, Mrs Stone, I know what you have been up to. Father McGuinness has informed me about the charity you have asked him to set up and have funded. A few of the girls have already come to him for help. Thank you. In particular, my childhood friend, Ginny O'Mara, could not have benefitted more from your intervention. She left for England on Sunday. Though I fear it may be too late for her to start over, for I suspect she is ill.'

'Consumption?' He nodded. 'I thought so, too,' Lucy said.

'Yes. It's rife in the tenements around The Monto and the rest of the city. She sent me a note before she left which I only received this morning. In it she named Iggy Byrne as the distressed client she heard that night in Burton's house. If only she'd told us on Saturday when we spoke to her. I think she always knew it was him, but until she was safely out of the country, she didn't want to name him for fear of reprisal.'

'That's understandable. Those women live in fear. I hope she is well enough to make a new life for herself. Everyone deserves a second chance... and a little sprinkling of luck.'

'Indeed, they do. So, do you and Mr Stone plan to stay in Dublin for the entire summer?'

'I would like to, but unfortunately a tricky case has come up back home, and although Phin's brother, Sebastian, is a capable young man, he is struggling with this one. We sail home on Saturday.'

'I'm sorry to hear it,' the inspector said. He rose and extended his hand. 'It was a very great pleasure to make your acquaintance, Lucy. I will notify you when a date is set for Olivia's trial. You will come back to give evidence for me, won't you?'

'I will.' Lucy returned his firm grasp. 'It's been a pleasure for us also, Fergus, and please remember if you ever find yourself in London, I insist you call on us.'

Not long after, Phin and Ellie joined her. Ellie ran up to her, clutching several bedraggled flowers in her hand. 'For you, Mother. Look, these are so pretty. Father says they are the same colour blue as your eyes.'

'And yours, pet.' Lucy sniffed the flowers, smiling up at Phin and then Ellie. 'Thank you, darling, you are very kind. Run along now, Bash is waiting for you up in the nursery. I believe there are plans for a cricket match this afternoon. George is setting it all up for you.'

'Father, will you play, too?' the little girl asked, clutching at Phin's hand. 'Please.'

'Wouldn't miss it for the world, princess. You'd best get changed.'

'I will.'

Ellie clambered up onto the sofa, slapping a kiss on Lucy's cheek before running from the room.

Phineas sat down, scooping up Lucy's hand. 'I'm exhausted. That child has so much energy.'

'Just be thankful you didn't have Bash with you as well. You'd better lie down and rest before the match.'

Phin brought her hand to his lips. 'Yes, my dear. If you insist... and only if I have you for company.'

Lucy grinned. 'Behave! Anyway...'

'Anyway?'

'While you were out, I had a caller. Inspector Ryan.'

'Oh, I'm sorry to have missed him.'

'The poor man, Phin. I could murder that woman, I really could. She has broken his heart, and he doesn't deserve it. Such a scheming madam.'

'What did he have to report? I take it she has been caught?'

'Yes, on board the steamer bound for Liverpool, no less. They were lucky to catch her, for it was about to depart.'

'Then all's well that ends well,' Phineas said.

'I suppose so, but I can't believe I didn't realise what she was up to. It would appear that she found out that Edith was going to leave her a small fortune. That was her motivation. And not content to let the poor woman pass away naturally, she decided to speed things up *and* implicate Carver. What's that awful expression? Kill two birds with one stone.' Lucy shook her head. 'So evil. Did you ever suspect her?'

'Only on Monday. All that crying and handwringing she did in the entrance hall didn't ring true, but no, I didn't suspect her of *murder*. I believed she was playing the victim to manipulate Ryan into falling in love with her. Needless to say, I didn't know she was in line to inherit from Edith. If we'd known about that, we would have suspected her much earlier instead of taking what she said about Carver at face value.'

'You're right.' Lucy gritted her teeth. 'I could kick myself for being so obtuse. But she was so clever and manipulating. And it's not the first time I've been taken in by a clever murderer.'

'If it's any comfort, it happens to us all. So, madam, now you have your sleuthing hat back on, so to speak, does this mean we will be working together again?'

'Well, it is necessary that I give it some consideration, Phin.'

'Is that so?' he asked, brow raised.

'Yes, you see, I was thinking of setting up my own agency. I believe some competition might do you good.'

Dear reader,

Huge thanks for reading *The Carver Affair*, I hope you enjoyed Lucy's latest sleuthing adventure in Dublin. If you want to join other readers in hearing all about my new releases and bonus content, you can sign up here:

www.stormpublishing.co/pam-lecky

If you enjoyed this book and could spare the time to leave a review that would be hugely appreciated. Even a short review can make all the difference in encouraging a reader to discover my books for the first time. Thank you so much!

It was always my intention to bring Lucy and her entourage to Dublin, my native city. What I hadn't realised was how much fun it would be. Research is always enjoyable and when the locations to be explored are a short distance away, it is even better. Dublin, in the late 19th century, was no different to any other large city in Europe, with its share of poverty and crime, and having grown up not far from the notorious Monto area which features in the book, the history of which has always fascinated me, it was a no-brainer to feature it in the story. Many of the Monto characters were inspired by the real-life inhabitants.

It may be of interest to note that the Irish Crown Jewels were actually stolen from Dublin Castle in June 1907. They were never recovered, and no one was ever charged.

Luckily, most of my working life was spent close to the beautiful Georgian quarter centred around Merrion Square, which back in Victorian times was as far removed, socially and economically, from The Monto as it was possible to get. I often walked through the square, which is now a public park, and reflected on the history of its inhabitants. As soon as I had decided on Dublin as my setting for this novel, I thought it would be an interesting location for Lucy and Phin and the Carver family to live.

I hope you enjoy this brief journey through Victorian Dublin. I know Lucy has, and you never know, she may wish to return someday...

Thanks again for being part of this amazing journey with me and I hope you'll stay in touch—I have so many more stories I'd love to share with you.

Pam Lecky

<www.pamlecky.com>

instagram.com/pamleckybooks

linkedin.com/in/pam-lecky-b0b646109

bookbub.com/profile/pam-lecky

ACKNOWLEDGEMENTS

Without the support of family and friends, this book, and indeed my entire writing journey, would not have been possible. My heartfelt thanks to you all, especially my husband, Conor, and my children, Stephen, Hazel and Adam. I am very grateful to my chief beta readers, Lorna and Terry O'Callaghan, who have read every draft and given me invaluable feedback.

Special gratitude is owed to my agent, Thérèse Coen, at Susanna Lea & Associates, London, whose belief in me, along with her sage advice, helped to bring Lucy Lawrence to life.

Producing a novel is a collaborative process, and I have been fortunate to have wonderful editors, copyeditors, proofreaders, and graphic designers working with me. To Kathryn Taussig, my editor, and all the team at Storm Publishing, thanks for believing in this series. A massive thank you to Bernadette Kearns, my original editor. All the books in the Lucy Lawrence series benefited hugely from your input.

I am extremely grateful to have such loyal readers. For those of you who take the time to leave reviews, please know that I appreciate them beyond words. To the amazing book bloggers, book tour hosts and reviewers who have hosted me and my books over the years—thank you.

Special thanks are owed to ESB Archives for invaluable information on the electrification of Dublin city, retired Garda Jim Herlihy for sharing his extensive knowledge of the history of the DMP and RIC, and Terry Fagan, a fount of knowledge on all historical details relating to The Monto area.

Last, but certainly not least, I am incredibly lucky to have a network of writer friends who keep me motivated (and sane), especially Valerie Keogh, Derville Murphy, Catherine Kullmann, Jenny O'Brien, Brook Allen and Tonya Murphy Mitchell. Special thanks to the members of the Crime Writers' Association, the Historical Novel Society Irish Chapter, and all the gang at the Coffee Pot Book Club.

Go raibh míle maith agat!

Pam Lecky
    January 2026

9 781837 001828